THE HOOKUP EXPERIMENT

CRYSTAL KASWELL

Copyright

This is a work of fiction. Similarities to real people, places, or events are entirely coincidental.

Also by Crystal Kaswell

Inked Love

The Best Friend Bargain - Forest

The First Taste - Holden

The Roomie Rulebook - Oliver

The Hookup Experiment - Patrick

Inked Hearts

Tempting - Brendon

Hooking Up - Walker

Pretend You're Mine - Ryan

Hating You, Loving You - Dean

Breaking the Rules - Hunter

Losing It - Wes

Accidental Husband - Griffin

The Baby Bargain - Chase

Dirty Rich

Dirty Deal - Blake

Dirty Boss - Nick

Dirty Husband - Shep

Dirty Desires - Ian

Dirty Wedding - Ty

Dirty Secret - Cam

Pierce Family

Broken Beast - Adam

Playboy Prince - Liam

Ruthless Rival - Simon

Tempting Teacher - Max

Sinful Serenade

Sing Your Heart Out - Miles

Strum Your Heart Out - Drew

Rock Your Heart Out - Tom

Play Your Heart Out - Pete

Sinful Ever After – series sequel

Just a Taste - Miles's POV

Dangerous Noise

Dangerous Kiss - Ethan

Dangerous Crush – Kit

Dangerous Rock – Joel

Dangerous Fling – Mal

Dangerous Encore - series sequel

Standalones

Broken - Trent & Delilah

Come Undone Trilogy

Come Undone

Come Apart

Come To Me

Chapter One

"The Hookup Experiment"
Posted by Hearts and Thorns
Thursday June 16, 9 P.M.

I'm horny.

There's really no other way to say it.

Sure, there are other terms (I'm fond of randy), but they all make the same point: I desire sexual satisfaction.

My hand isn't enough. My vibrator isn't enough. My fantasies of Chris Evans—

Not enough.

I know. It's beyond strange, diving into my carnal needs here. This is usually a space for messy things. But this is messy.

Sex without love?

That's a first for me.

And this is all medication induced.

My new prescription didn't *just* lift my depression. It left me craving contact too.

I feel my body again.

I feel awake again.

I want again.
Not love or affection.
Sex.
And I know exactly where I can find it.

Chapter Two

IMOGEN

Okay, I don't know *exactly* where to find satisfaction. That's a slight exaggeration. Otherwise, my online-journal entry is accurate.

It's a strange hobby, offering my secrets to strangers, but I'm completely addicted to the feeling of throwing my thoughts into the universe. It helps me let my guard down, find clarity, and keep a sense of humor.

Yes, I'm a mess, but I'm here. I'm alive. I'm ready to booty call an available man.

How exactly does that go?

It's been a long, long time since I've craved sex this way. Since I've craved sex at all. My last prescription killed my O.

This one might be worse. I'm way too aware of my need for satisfaction.

My ex-boyfriend is off the table.

An App isn't inviting.

Which leaves one excellent option: Patrick Murphy.

The very cute tattoo artist who a) put the hearts and thorns on my ribs, b) left his card with a casual "call me anytime" and c) put his hands on my skin in a way that felt both safe and sexy as sin.

Maybe it's the rush of neurotransmitters from my new tattoo. It's been eight hours and I'm still buzzing. But, for once, I don't want to question my desires.

Patrick has already seen me topless. He knows I'm flat, and he wants to sleep with me anyway. I might as well call.

I channel my roommate's confidence, find my cell, and get straight to the point.

Imogen: Hey, Patrick. This is Imogen. The rib tattoo.

He answers quickly.

Patrick: The gorgeous woman who insisted she didn't need someone to hold her hand?

Imogen: I didn't.

Patrick: I know. How's the piece holding up?

Imogen: Beautiful. Do you want to see?

Patrick: Sure.

Imogen: Here.

No. This is too coy. Men don't understand hints. I need to be more explicit.

Imogen: I need a little help with after-care. In person.

Patrick: Oh?

Imogen: If you're free.

Patrick: Now?

Imogen: Now.

Patrick: You're direct.

Imogen: Why mince words?

Patrick: It's easier, for some people.

Imogen: For you?

Patrick: Not exactly. You said you go to UCLA, right?

Imogen: I live in Brentwood.

I send the cross-streets.

Patrick: Twenty minutes.

Twenty minutes to prepare for my first tryst in over a year.

No problem.

Chapter Three

IMOGEN

Major problems.

What the hell do I wear to host a booty call? My pajamas aren't sexy. I don't own any worthy lingerie. Maybe a trench coach, with nothing under it?

But where would I get a trench coat? This is Southern California. The only people who wear trench coats here play detectives on TV.

No. This isn't for him. It's for me. What makes me feel sexy?

Dark lipstick. Winged liner. Black panties.

There. My skin flushes as I stare at my reflection. It's not that I get off on myself. More the thought of a near-stranger seeing me in only my underwear.

He knocks.

I grab the Fiona Apple shirt I wear to sleep and pull it over my head. I don't feel nearly as sexy in the baggy tee, but I'm not in danger of flashing the neighbors.

The dozen footsteps to the front door feel like a million. My heart thuds against my chest. My stomach flutters. My sex clenches.

Then I open the door and I see him and lust washes my nerves away.

Patrick Murphy is standing on my doorstep in snug jeans, a plain white t-shirt, and a leather jacket.

He's even more handsome than he was this afternoon.

He's super fucking hot.

Sandy hair, freckles, green eyes.

He's tall, but not too tall. Muscular, but not too built. Adorned in ink, but not too—

Well, how could a tattoo artist have too much ink? Really?

"Come in." I pull the door open.

"Thanks." He gives me a long, slow once-over, focusing on my bare legs and the hem of my t-shirt. "Nice place."

"Have you looked at it?"

"No." His eyes meet mine. "Do you want a drink?"

"I'm supposed to offer."

"Might as well mix things up." He smiles.

My heart thuds. He's cute. Way too cute. Cute and sexy is a dangerous combination. A feelings-inspiring combination. And I'm not interested in feelings. Only satisfaction. "Water for me. You?"

"Where are the cups?"

"You're going to serve me a drink in my apartment?" I ask.

"I'm a gentleman."

"Are you?"

"Cups?" he asks.

Okay, sure, why not? I lead him to the kitchen side of the main room then I open the top drawer. (Our place is big, by Brentwood standards, but it's not exactly huge. The kitchen and two-person dining table are on one side. The couch and TV are on the other).

He pulls two glasses from the top shelf and fills both from the tap. "Unless you prefer bottled?"

"This is perfect."

His fingers brush mine as he hands me the glass. "I'm not a gentleman."

"But you make sure a lady comes first?"

"You've heard that one?"

"Hasn't everyone?" I ask.

"Probably." He takes a long sip. "What do you like?"

What do I like? I don't even know. Not anymore. "Not talking."

"No? No dirty talk?"

My cheeks flush. "I haven't tried it."

He smiles. "This should be fun then."

"Do you have condoms or should I grab mine?"

"Latex. Do you have an allergy?"

"No. Latex is good. Thanks."

Again, he smiles.

"What?"

"This isn't usually how this goes."

"How does it go?" I ask.

"A lot more pretense."

"I'm not big on pretense," I say. "Besides. You've already seen me topless."

"I barely saw anything."

"You did too."

"I did too." He takes another sip and sets the glass down. "But I *am* a gentleman at work."

"You don't stare at client's breasts?"

"Unless the piece requires it." He crosses the space to me. "How does it feel?"

"Huh?"

"You need help with after-care?"

"Right."

"Did you wash with soap?"

I nod.

"A&D ointment?"

"Not yet."

"Allow me." He pulls a small tube from his pocket, places it on the kitchen table, washes his hands in the sink, and turns to me.

His hands brush the hem of my t-shirt. His fingers skim the bare skin on my stomach.

Fuck, he's close to where I need him. No one has been this close in a long, long time. The soft touch is enough to set me on fire.

He moves to my left side as he rolls my t-shirt up my stomach. He only lifts enough to expose the new ink, not enough to expose my breasts.

I hold the extra fabric.

He squeezes ointment on his finger and applies with a gentle touch.

It's strange—not at all what I expect from a booty call—but it's only sexier for its oddness. He's tending to my body, my skin, the work he put on my skin.

We collaborated on this. Maybe that's why I feel so comfortable with him. Because I shared a vague idea and he turned it into something beautiful.

I want to celebrate being alive but acknowledge how hard it is too. Is a heart covered in thorns too cliché?

Maybe it is. But he made it into something unique and beautiful.

"There." He holds the t-shirt above my new tattoo. "Perfect. You want to see?"

"There's a mirror in the bedroom."

"That wasn't a come-on," he says.

"That either. It's that or the bathroom."

"Do you have a bathroom kink?"

"Not that I know about."

He smiles that same *you're interesting and I like it* smile. "Can you hold this?" He drops the fabric.

I don't reply. I let the fabric fall and I lead him into the bedroom. My bedroom.

When was the last time I invited a man into this space? Anyone into this space? The marvel of a main room is I don't have to share my bedroom with anyone.

The last time I slept with someone… my ex, his place. It wasn't great. It was never great, but it wasn't his fault. It was the combination of my meds and my inability to let go.

Patrick is a near stranger. I don't need to worry about what he thinks of me tomorrow. I don't need to consider our future or whether or not I love him (or if I'm even capable of the kind of love he expects).

No, this is crystal clear—sex.

Only sex.

The end.

I toss my t-shirt over my head and turn to the standing mirror. "It looks perfect."

"It does." He pulls a condom from his pocket and tosses it on the bed. Then he closes the distance between us. He places his body behind mine, wraps his arm around my waist. "Anything you don't like?"

"Having to issue verbal responses." I can't form thoughts and stay in my body at the same time. Not usually.

He laughs. "Then show me."

I can do that. I turn so my neck is to him.

He understands my request. He presses his lips to my neck as he pulls my body against his.

My eyes flutter closed. It's almost too much, already. I want him too badly, already.

Is this how normal people feel? No wonder they make terrible sexual decisions all the time. This is fucking amazing.

A moan falls from my lips as he pulls me against his hard-on.

He kisses a line down my neck, brings his hands to my hips, turns me around, so we're eye to eye.

For a split second, I look up at him. I try to find intention in his green eyes, but I only find desire.

It's intoxicating.

I bring my lips to his.

He kisses back with the perfect mix of need and patience. He meets me halfway, soft where I need that, hard where I need that.

I fall into the back and forth, my tongue playing with his, my hands curling into his skin. I'm a horny teenager, lost in the bliss of making out, happy to kiss and touch for hours without any expectation of more.

Only I want more. I want everything.

I pull back with a sigh. He does away with his t-shirt and lowers me onto the bed.

My body responds before my brain has a chance. My brain is already slowing down, letting my thoughts dissolve. The same zen state I reach when I race.

There's only me and my body.

Only here, there's me and my body and his body and an intense desire to enjoy his body.

I turn onto my side and tangle my legs in his.

He toys with me as he kisses me, his palm on my breast, his thumb against my nipple.

He's good at this. Way too good at this.

It's intense, almost too intense, but that feels good in its own way.

Only, I have no idea how to respond. I feel too good to respond. I can't stop to consider what he wants, how to give as much as I take. I'm too wracked with bliss.

Sensation overwhelms me as he toys with me again and again.

I surrender to the feeling for minutes. Hours maybe. I'm not sure. Finally, my anticipation slows, and I find my footing enough to push him onto his back and climb on top of him.

I kiss him here. I roll my hips against his.

"Slow down." He lets out a low groan and digs his fingers into my thighs. "Or I'll come too fast."

My entire body buzzes. Yes. I want that. I want to make him come. It sounds so obvious like this, but I've never felt the desire before. I've never craved a man's orgasm.

It was… obvious. Expected. Of course, he'd come. That's how it always goes.

But right now?

I need it. I need it so fucking badly.

"Fuck me." The words fall off my lips. It's easy. Too easy, but I don't care about that either. I only care about finding satisfaction. "Please."

He responds by flipping me onto my back.

I do away with my panties.

He slides his hand between my legs.

I nearly come from the contact of his thumb against my clit. I have to kiss him harder. I have to dig my hands into his hair.

Even then, it's not enough. Every brush of his thumb winds me tighter. Tighter. So tight I can barely take it.

Then I'm there, groaning against his lips as I come, pleasure rocking through my pelvis, spilling all the way to my fingers and toes.

It's almost too much to take.

He rubs me through my orgasm, then he slips two fingers inside me. He warms me up, slowly at first, then faster.

"You're wet." He groans into my neck.

I nod. Then I let my head fall back. This is good. Too good.

He stretches me again. Again.

And, again, I'm too overwhelmed to respond.

Again.

I reach for his button. His zipper.

I rub him over the fabric of his boxers.

"Fuck." He groans into my neck as he reaches for the condom. Then it's his jeans, his boxers.

And he's there, naked in my bed.

We're naked in my bed.

He rolls the rubber over his cock; he spreads my legs' he brings our bodies together.

He fills me with one slow, steady stroke.

I'm ready. I take him with ease, even as he stretches me wider, drives deeper.

I wrap my legs around his hips, and I kiss him hard.

We stay locked like that, moving together, bodies a tangled mess as he pumps into me again and again.

I don't think. I raise my hips to meet him; I kiss him hard; I rake my nails over his back.

Every thrust winds me tighter and tighter, but it's not enough. The angle isn't there.

Then I shift my hips and it is.

An internal clitoral orgasm.

Fuck. I know too much. But I don't care about that either. Only about finding another round of satisfaction.

I dig my nails into his back and I raise my hips to meet him. Again and again, the two of us winding me tighter and tighter.

Then I'm there, my sex pulsing around him, pulling him closer.

He keeps that perfect speed until I release his back, then he moves a little faster, a little harder, the rhythm he needs.

There's something sexy about knowing he's close, feeling the change in his breath, the shudder of his thighs.

Then he's there, groaning against my neck, pulsing inside me.

He works through his orgasm, shifts off me, takes care of the condom, dons his boxers.

"Thanks." I don't move. I don't want to move. I want to lie here and absorb this.

"Thanks?" He laughs again. "You're different."

"What do people usually say?"

"Thanks is good." He takes a long look at me.

"You, uh, you can stay if you want," I say. "But I have an early class and my roomie will freak if you're here alone, so…"

"Do you want me to stay?"

No, but—"I won't kick you out of bed."

"Until tomorrow?"

"Basically."

He smiles. "Next time, we can do this when you don't have class. Go for round two in the morning."

Hmm. Is that why people spend the night after a booty call? "I've never had morning sex."

"I'll pop your cherry sometime."

Sometime. In the future. He wants to do this again.

"If you want." He pulls on his jeans and his t-shirt. "If this was a one-time-thing, I'm happy to be used."

"Is it that untoward?"

"I like thinking of it that way. It's sexy." He finds his socks and shoes and sits on the bed to don them. "But I'm happy to be used again. If you're game."

"If I'm what?"

He smiles, proud he wore me out. "Exactly."

He is handsome. And this was amazing. But it's overwhelming too. And seeing him again… that sounds like a relationship. The start of a relationship. And that's messy. Too messy.

"Are you going to be okay?" he asks.

"I'm just going to sleep here."

"In that case—" He gathers my sheets and drapes them over my body. "Good night, Imogen." Patrick leans down and presses his lips to mine. "Call me if you want to go again."

"Just sex?"

"Just sex." He says it casually, as if he's said it a million times before.

Maybe it's casual for him.

But for me?

A second session of just sex? A third? An entire no-strings-attached arrangement?

Is that actually possible?

Chapter Four

IMOGEN

For a few minutes, I lie in bed, soaking in the satisfaction coursing through my body.

Bit by bit, my blood returns to my brain. My senses shift to their usual *I'm thinking about everything, all the time* mode.

My sheets smell like Patrick. The pine scent of his soap and something all him.

Hell, I smell like him. The sweat and saliva and other recently utilized bodily fluids.

I find enough energy to move into the shower. I soap, shampoo, condition, try to straighten my thoughts.

Maybe it doesn't have to be complicated.

I want to see him again.

He wants round two. Three. Infinity.

But then he's not in his shower, wondering where I stand. I know I shouldn't stereotype, but he's a man, and he's smooth enough he must be experienced.

My thoughts swirl. Orange-scented soap. The taste of his lips. The feel of his hands on my skin. The way his smile sent my stomach into free-fall.

There's only one thing to do when I'm in this state: write.

I turn off the shower, dry, admire my tattoo one more time (it's seriously amazing), and slip into my pajamas.

Then I set up on the couch with my laptop, and I shift into the zone. It's hard to explain. I'm not a writer, really. I don't have dreams of poetry books, fiction novels, memoirs on Oprah (does Oprah still have a show?).

But, here, with my hands on my keyboard (or around a pen), I'm in the zone. Writing is the only way I can really under-stand what I'm feeling. And I'm not good with feelings. That's why my life is such a mess. These things don't come naturally to me.

Maybe it's my parents (they barely acknowledge emotions). Maybe it's genetics. Maybe it's the result of the wrong friends, wrong schools, wrong TV shows. I don't know, but I know I'm not like my sister.

She leans on people, works as a team, talks when she's over-whelmed.

I'm only capable of sharing my feelings with anonymous strangers. But, hey, I'm sharing them. That's progress.

How do other people find the energy for relationships, anyway? Even if I wanted something serious (and I don't) and Patrick wanted the same (and he doesn't), I don't have the space.

Between class, swim-practice, and my once-a-week job giving lessons (not to mention Sunday dinners with my parents), I don't have the room for anything else. Even now, during summer session, with a lighter workload and a lack of swim meets, I use my extra time to stay functional.

But maybe this is a part of that goal.

Sex is a part of life. And it's a very relaxing, fulfilling activity. Maybe it's a part of my self-care.

I just need to put it in terms I understand. Scientific terms.

Psychology and economics (I'm double majoring) explain people as well as anything does.

Psychology: Human beings need connections with other human beings. Human beings need to satisfy their carnal urges.

Economics: Random hookups have low opportunity cost, but they present a lot of risks, especially for women.

Question: How can Imogen Nguyen best fill her needs?

Hypothesis: Patrick Murphy is a talented potential friend with benefits. But the relationship part? That's destined to end in misery.

Evidence: Imogen's past relationships (see the ex-boyfriend who called me "heartless"), Patrick's ease of coming and going (or is that a positive? It means he gets it), Imogen's complicated, messy history. Does a guy like Patrick want messy?

Or…

Are all those things reasons why I should try this?

Sure, I'm no good at love.

But sex?

Well, I may or may not be talented there, but Patrick enjoyed himself enough to request a second round. So I'm 1 for 1, so far.

Sex: 1 for 1.

Relationships: 0 for 1 (four, if you count high school boyfriends).

The sound of the door breaks my concentration.

Jade steps inside with a yawn. She hangs her coat on the hook by the door and places her purse over it.

"You're up?" She eyes my spot on the couch curiously.

"Can't sleep," I say.

"You had sex."

How the hell can she tell that?

"You did! Details."

"Why are you so interested in sex?" I ask.

"It's all biology, baby. I thought you'd understand."

If she's referring to me as a fellow scientist, well, that's a first. People in the so-called hard sciences usually dismiss the so-called soft sciences. "We had a nice time."

"And…"

"What else is there to say?"

"Who? When? Where? How? Why?"

"A guy I met recently. An hour or two ago. Here. I texted him. And... do I really need to explain why?"

"What guy?"

"A friend of a friend." That's true enough.

"So, it was a booty call?"

"Basically."

"Strictly sexual. That is how I like it. But you... I don't know."

I raise a brow.

"You're a nice girl."

"No one has ever called me nice."

She laughs. "You can hide behind the combat boots if you want, but we both know the truth, you're a good girl deep down."

"I am?"

"When's the last time you went to a party?"

"I don't like parties."

"Or drank until you threw up?" she asks.

"How is this the definition of bad girl?"

"You're the future shrink," she says.

Not exactly, but, hey, she's trying. "And you're the bad girl?"

"You said it."

I can't help but laugh. Jade is ridiculous. And she's proud to be that way.

"This is a step in the right direction," she says. "If you want the label."

"What else do I need?"

"A lingerie collection bigger than your book collection."

"How is that even possible?"

"Exactly."

Damn, that's a good trick.

"A taste for something weird. It's fine if you're vanilla. But vanilla is vanilla."

"I appreciate the support," I say.

"Is this the first guy you've brought home?"

"I had a boyfriend last year."

"Here."

"I guess."

She nods. "You have seemed… different the last few weeks."

"Different?"

"When we walked to class together, you were checking out every hot guy."

Was I?

"Usually, you're in your head. You barely notice guys. I thought maybe you liked women, but you don't notice them either."

Honestly, I'm floored Jade pays this much attention to me. We're not the type of roomies who sit and talk about boys over ice cream. We occasionally eat together or walk to campus together, but that's the extent of our interactions.

We both enjoy our apartment as a quiet place to host a guest or two, max. And for all her interest in sex, she rarely invites anyone to spend the night.

"Yeah, you just seem… horny, I guess," she says.

"I was focused on finals."

She nods, accepting my answer, but not completely buying it. "Was it good?"

"It was." I didn't know sex could be that good.

"But…"

"But?" I ask.

"You don't look happy about this turn of events."

"He asked if I wanted to see him again."

She stares blankly.

I stare back.

"He was fantastic?"

"Yes."

"And you enjoyed his personality well enough?"

"He's sweet, yeah."

"So where's the problem?" When I don't respond, she moves forward with her assessment. "Oh, I get it. The good-girl thing.

After casual sex, you can't face him again. You're embarrassed by your lust."

"I am not embarrassed by my lust."

"By the whole one-night thing. I get it. I had to get over it too."

Really? Jade was once embarrassed by her sexual appetites? That's hard to believe. "It's not that."

"Uh-huh."

"I'm not looking for a boyfriend."

"It doesn't sound like he's looking for a girlfriend."

"What if he is?"

"Did you tell him you want to keep it casual?"

"Yes."

"Then you've done your part."

Maybe.

"You don't have to admit it, but we both know you're horny now. And you love a regular thing."

"I do not."

"You eat the same breakfast every day."

"Lots of people do that."

"And swim laps after class, every day."

When did she notice that?

"If you really do have more *energy* now that you're past finals, this is the best way for you to do it."

"Maybe."

"Oh, I can use it for my project on human sexuality! We need to find a subject and run an experiment. The professor suggested a self-experiment. But this is better."

"No."

"Okay, fine, but you might as well make it an experiment."

"It was."

"Officially?" she asks.

"Unofficially."

"So make it official."

"I was considering that."

"Great minds."

Jade and I thinking alike? That's scary.

"Really, Imogen. You have time. You have needs to fill. Why not a hookup experiment? That way, it's a success, no matter the outcome."

From a scientific standpoint, sure, but she's not the one risking her heart.

Chapter Five

PATRICK

I wake sore, satisfied, and wanting all at once.

There's a new entry of my favorite online journal.

Hearts and Thorns

The sharp-tongued, witty, vulnerable woman who offers me her heart and soul. She offers it to anyone who stumbles on her site, but when I read her words, they exist for me and me alone.

It's a little odd, following a stranger, but we all do it. We listen to podcasts or buy celebrity gossip magazines or follow influencers on social media.

Sure, most people aren't invested the way I'm invested in her life.

But, hey, I have my reasons.

My fingers itch to unlock my cell. I want to read every word, to sop up every drop of her thoughts. This is my favorite part of the day, week, month; my little slice of her.

But I don't have time to get lost in her. I don't even have time to shower. Not that I want to wash the smell of Imogen from my skin.

I shift from affection for a stranger to lust with ease. Maybe that's ridiculous. Maybe I'm a hypocrite, wanting a woman I don't know after screwing another woman I barely know, but, hey—

We're all hypocrites somewhere.

And Imogen practically kicked me out of her apartment. It's not as if she wants to spill her guts.

She called. I answered. We both had fun.

Win-win.

Fuck, I can't keep thinking about this or I'm going to be late *and* hard.

I pull on the first clean outfit I find and I race to work.

When I arrive at the shop, my ten o'clock client is waiting. He's not in a rush—he's shooting the shit with Dare—but I can't exactly excuse myself to read my online crush's latest post.

Besides, that's not how this works. She stays in my cell, on my computer, in my bedroom.

Work now. Words later.

I meet my client at the counter, finalize the mockup, move him to my suite.

One line at a time, I fall into the familiar routine. The smell of sweat and A&D ointment, the feel of skin against my gloved hands, the hum of the tattoo gun, the mumbling pop-punk emanating from the speakers.

For some reason, our manager loves the genre. I don't mind the riffs, but the lyrics? Why are these suburban guys so angry at women for screwing someone else?

Move the hell on.

Not that I'm a bastion of letting go. Sure, I'm not screwed up over an ex—I don't have any exes of note—but I'm still obsessed with the woman I lost.

And I do love the arc of this album (our manager has an old school devotion to albums). The lyricist starts out cheeky, pushing people away with his wit. Song by song, he drops his defenses, admits hurt, pulls people closer.

In the end, he's still a mess, but he's not afraid to face it.

I always think of *Hearts and Thorns*, though I'm sure she'd hate the comparison. She loves women who pour their hearts out. Sometimes, I listen to her favorite artists, to get a feel for what she went through, to find a deeper level of understanding.

But there's no way I'm going there right now.

I shake off my thoughts and slip back into my work. The sleeve is epic. A massive octopus sinking a ship in stormy seas. I draw the last line of black ink. That's it.

My client rouses as I turn off the gun.

"That's it?" he asks.

My eyes flit to the clock. "Two hours."

"I can take more." He's in the zone, buzzing from adrenaline and dopamine, ready to face a mountain of pain.

"I know you can." He'll come down soon, but I might as well stroke his ego. "I'm wiped." I wrap his arm in plastic. "Take it off when you shower. Then breathable clothing."

"We can't finish today?"

"We'll be done soon. I promise."

I walk him to the counter and shake his hand.

Luna flirts all through checkout. Sweet smile, hair twirl, giggle, the works.

She's not really the sweet smile type. More the *I know what I want and I ask for it* type. The same as Imogen.

They're friends, actually—Luna recommended me. And they're both sexy in a take-no-shit way.

Not that I want Luna. She's a knock-out, no question, but I've never felt an interest.

Now, she's my friend, and fellow Inked Love tattoo artist, Oliver's girlfriend. And that's simply out of the question.

Luna switches the music to one of the mumbling teen girls she adores. Would Imogen like the artist? She was wearing a band shirt, but, for some reason, I keep picturing her in nothing but the combat boots she wore to her appointment.

The ring of the bell distracts me from my dirty thoughts.

Luna waits until the client leaves, and the door swings shut, then she clears her throat. "Earth to Patrick."

"You're Earth?" I ask.

"Mars to Patrick?" she offers.

"Venus."

"You think I'm the goddess of beauty? That's sweet."

"But you prefer the god of war?" I ask.

"Why not both?" She smiles and her grey-green eyes light up. She's not sunshine, exactly, but she's pretty damn joyful.

She's good for Oliver, the world's grumpiest tattoo artist (and trust me, that is some stiff competition).

Speaking of the recently sober artist—"Is Oliver in?"

"Luna, it's great to see you today. I love your outfit. Very chic." She motions to her snug black dress.

"You look hot."

"Okay, that's boy for chic."

"Is he in?"

She clears her throat. "Let's try again."

"You are working the counter?" I ask.

"I'm not trolling for johns."

"You're filling in as our assistant manager over the summer?" I ask.

"Yes," she says.

"Does that not leave you in charge of scheduling?"

She makes a *hmm* noise. "Even so." She motions to me. "One more shot, Tricky. 'Luna, you look great today.'"

"Does it need to be about how you look?"

"Anything. As long as it's not a question about my boyfriend."

I'm tempted to fuck with her. She hates when I refer to her as Oliver's girlfriend.

In theory, I get it. She wants to be her own person. She doesn't want a qualifier. But there's something about the idea of belonging to someone—

It's kinda nice.

Luna clears her throat.

"You look great today, Luna. Is that a new dress?" I try.

"It is. Thanks for noticing." She smiles. "No, Oliver isn't working today. He's off this week."

"Trouble in paradise?"

"He's at Berkeley, visiting Daisy." His kid sister. Luna's best friend. Complicated shit.

"It's June."

"She's taking a summer course."

Is that why Imogen is in Brentwood? Or was she born and raised in Los Angeles? "Is Holden miserable?" Holden is Daisy's boyfriend.

Once upon a time, Oliver and Holden were best friends. Until the whole 'I slept with your sister thing' (Holden slept with Daisy, Ollie's sister). And then the whole 'I slept with your best friend thing.' (Ollie and Luna hooked up. And Luna is Daisy's best friend).

I swear, I need a diagram to follow the gossip here.

"He's there too," she says.

"Weird."

"Kinda," she says.

"Why aren't you there?"

"Are you kidding? I'm not getting in the middle of that catfight."

"You must miss her?"

"Like crazy," she says. "But we talk three times a week. And I'll be up there in a few weeks."

"Once the dick-measuring contest ends?"

"It's almost sweet," she says, "like they're competing for who loves her the most."

"Does that bother you?"

"Not the way you mean," she says.

"How do I mean?"

"Because Oliver is my boyfriend and I want all his love?"

Guilty.

"I'm an only child."

She's lucky that way. She can't lose a sibling. But, hey, I know better than to say that. "Siblings are annoying."

"Yeah, but they know what it's like to grow up in your house, with your family. I wish I had that."

Dare crashes the almost intimate moment. "You look hot today, Luna." He winks and runs his fingers through his dark hair in a total *you know you want me* move.

"Is that what you wanted?" I ask.

"I prefer words like 'sophisticated' and 'gorgeous' but I know they're a little long for you two," she says.

"Sophis-ta-what?" Dare plays dumb.

"You look nice too," she says. "The iconic Inked Love uniform."

He is wearing standard-issue hipster tattoo artist gear. White v-neck (it doesn't compete with the colorful ink and it shows off the tattooed biceps). Jeans (his are dark. Some are light. Holden is the only one who dares to wear shorts). Trendy kicks. (Checkered Vans for Dare today. Grey eco-friendly sneakers for me).

"Aren't you hot in jeans?" she asks.

"I hope so." He turns to show off his ass. "Tell me I look good."

She motions *so-so*.

"Brutal," I say.

"You can deny it if you want, but I know you see it," Dare says.

"Your motorcycle jacket?" she asks.

"No. That's Tricky's thing," he says. "He's the brooding one. Well, when your boyfriend isn't here. Or maybe when he is. Love and all that."

"Yes, love and all that is how I think of my relationship." Luna laughs. "How do either of you get laid? You have no charm."

"Charm has nothing to do with it." Dare flexes a bicep.

"That tracks," she says.

"Ah, you don't mean that." Dare smiles.

"Really, I do. The personality… not good," she says.

"That's why he only sticks around for a night. It's not long enough for someone to get to know his personality," I say.

Dare nods *it's true*.

She laughs. "You two are just like Ollie and Holden. Well…" Like they were, before the whole *I'm screwing your sister* thing put a wedge between them.

"Only more beautiful." Dare avoids the messy stuff, the same way I do.

Everyone in my life avoids the messy shit. Everyone except my secret online exhibitionist.

"Exactly what I was thinking," Luna says.

"Is this guy giving you trouble?" Dare motions to me.

"I'm used to it," she says.

"What is up with him?" Dare asks.

"Isn't he your best friend?" she asks.

Dare motions *sorta*. "He's all right."

"Too good-looking, huh?" I try to jump into the banter, but I don't deliver the enthusiasm. "Ruining your game."

"You are a shit wingman, yeah," Dare says. "But it's not looks. Come on." He motions to his face. Turns to Luna for backup. "Be honest. I'm better looking than Tricky."

"You're both so annoying, it's really hard to not bring that into the rating," she says.

"Who's more annoying?" Dare asks.

"That's like comparing bad coffee with… equally bad coffee," she says.

"Not your best metaphor," he says.

"No." She laughs. "It's not."

He chuckles. "You don't want to hurt Patrick's feelings. I get it. He does have a fragile ego."

"You've found me out," she says.

"It wouldn't matter either way," Dare says. "Patrick is never interested in women."

"Oh? Really? You like guys? How did I not know that? Can I set you up?" Luna asks.

"I don't like guys," I say.

"Asexual?" Luna asks.

"Look at him," Dare says. "No. Smell him."

"Pass," Luna says.

"He smells like oranges," Dare says.

"I love citrus," I say.

"Orange soap. A girl's orange soap," he says.

"Why can't a man use orange soap?" Luna asks.

"A man, sure? Tricky, no way," Dare says.

"Maybe he's evolving," Luna says.

Dare shakes his head *I don't think so.* "You have that look too. Satisfied."

Luna nods *kinda.*

"But oddly unsatisfied," Dare says. "What happened? Too fast?"

"Why do you care about my sex life?" I ask.

"So you have a sex life." Dare taps his chin. "Interesting."

"Get a hobby," I say.

"This is my hobby," he says. "Who's the girl?"

"A girl who requested my company," I say.

"Now, I know that's bullshit. Who would request your company?" he asks.

Luna laughs. "That's harsh. Even for me."

"Truth hurts sometimes," Dare says.

"Takes one to know one," I say.

He laughs.

This is our routine. This has been our routine since we were kids. We've been friends forever. We've kept it light forever.

But, today, it feels wrong.

I don't want light bullshit.

I want something real.

"Something new?" Luna asks.

Maybe. If she's game. Imogen is interesting. Different from

other people I know. Very different from other woman who invite me to their apartments. But I'm not in the mood to discuss it with them. "I need coffee." I check the clock. Thirty minutes until my next appointment. It's not enough time, but I can't wait another second.

"I can put on a pot." Luna motions to the coffee machine on the counter. The drip isn't up to her standards, but there's "*No way she's drinking coffee from a pod*."

"Nah. I'll pick up something," I say. "You want anything?"

"Blue Bottle?" she asks.

"Yeah." It's two doors down.

She bites her lip, no doubt weighing her desire for an excellent iced coffee against the ridiculous prices at the San Francisco chain. "If you don't mind."

"Black or NOLA style?" I ask.

"Ooh, tough call. Black," she says.

"Got it," I say.

"Thanks, Tricky. I owe you." She blows me a kiss.

Dare says something to her, something about his jealousy. He flirts. Or teases. I can't always tell with him.

I don't enjoy it the way I normally do. I don't feel the warmth of the shop. Or enjoy the pink string lights. They make me think of Thorn.

They make me think of Imogen—

The color of her sheets—

The tattoo on her ribs.

The tattoo I put on her ribs.

Even when I step outside, into the warm June afternoon, I don't feel the warmth of the sun or the cool of the breeze.

Only the intense need for every one of my Hearts and Thorns's thoughts.

I make it all the way to the coffee shop, into line, then I read.

Chapter Six

The Hookup Experiment (Part Two)
Posted by Hearts and Thorns
Friday June 17th, 2 A.M.

I should be asleep.

But I can't find slumber in my room. My sheets smell like satisfaction.

I know, I know. Satisfaction is a feeling, not a smell. But it's all over the room. The lingering presence of another person in my space. Another person, reading my body, finding what I want, touching me, making me come.

And let me tell you…

I came.

I came like I've never come before.

It turns out I'm not frigid. Well, not physically anyway. My ex might be right. After all, I did end things because it made sense. I was ruthless about it.

He was studying abroad; I didn't want to do long-distance —the end.

But maybe it was more than the practicalities.

Maybe that was an excuse.

Am I about to compare myself to a fictional serial killer? I am. On *Dexter*, the TV show, the main character can't stay in relationships for long, or have sex with his girlfriends, because they start to see he's missing something. (Don't worry. I only watched the pilot because he insisted. I didn't hate it as much as I expected. It's pretty funny, actually).

It was like that. I knew he'd see I was missing something. Not a secret hobby as a vigilante murderer. But some ability to connect that other, normal people have.

Maybe I wasn't fair to him. Maybe he would have tried and understood. It doesn't matter. I didn't want to try.

This is a long way of saying—

I'm in the same place.

I still don't want love.

But I do want sex. And not the way I wanted it with him. Or even in high school, with the perfect mix of hormones and self-destructive tendencies and a belief sex made me cool and interesting racing through my veins.

There's nothing self-destructive about this impulse.

(Is there? Is the impulse evolving like a virus outsmarting me?)

I want to want because I feel awake and alive.

And I want to see this guy again.

Because I like the way his hands feel on my skin. And I like the way his groans sound in my ears.

And I even like the smell of him in my bed.

But is that really just sex?

Or is it more?

I am a woman of science. I can experiment. And most scientists, the pioneers anyway, use themselves as subjects at some point.

But what's the hypothesis?

What outcome do I really want?

To fall in love?
Or avoid it at all costs?
Maybe that's the experiment.
Maybe I can see if I'm as heartless as my ex suggested.

Chapter Seven

PATRICK

S he's hilarious.

Funny and vulnerable and sexy at once.

I read the post again. I drink every drop. I'm greedy that way. Too greedy.

But, hey, isn't this why people read? They want the insight into someone else's thoughts and feelings. The only difference is *Hearts and Thorns* is a real person and I've spent months following her journey.

Maybe I'm a little too invested, but I see the way readers talk about books. They're just as obsessed.

I read the post again. I'm happy for her. Really.

But I'm also jealous.

It's bizarre. I've never seen her. I have no idea if she's tall or short, thin or curvy or athletic, blonde or brunette or pink-haired. There's no way for me to want her, physically.

But I do.

Even though I slept with another woman last night.

Even though I'm going to ask the other woman to sleep with me again.

A voice interrupts me. A familiar one.

Luna.

She slides into the seat across from me and picks up the plain iced coffee on the table. "I assume this is mine."

"Yeah."

"Thank you." She takes a long sip and stares at my cell, waiting for me to give in to temptation.

Or maybe that's me.

"Don't stop on my account," she says.

"It's nothing."

"Uh-huh. You forget to come back to Inked Love over nothing."

Shit. It's time for my next appointment. I'm too distracted.

"Don't worry. Your client called. She's running late. Lucky break."

"Yeah."

"You okay?" she asks.

"Yeah."

"You don't look okay," she says.

"It's…"

"You don't have to tell me. I get it. You're like Ollie."

"How am I like your boyfriend?" I ask.

"Well, you're not as handsome."

I almost laugh, but I don't. This is too weird. I can't explain it to her.

"He doesn't let on when he cares."

"I don't—"

"You're not going to convince me, so don't bother," she says.

I set my cell on the table face-down. "It's nothing."

"Your fuck buddy?"

"We're not buddies. It was one time."

"But you want to be buddies?" she asks.

"I made the offer."

"Oh. I'm sorry, Tricky. I am exaggerating about your personality. It's not totally horrible," she says.

"It was last night."

My phone buzzes on the table.

"Is that her?" she asks.

"How would I know?"

"You weren't talking to her?" she asks. "Getting a text that says 'sorry, but you didn't meet my criteria'?"

"Do women do that?"

"I've heard stories," she says.

"The six-six-six rule?" I ask.

"What?"

"Six feet, six inches, six-figure salary."

"That isn't a real thing," she says.

"My sister told me. Molly." The one who's still here, not that Luna knows the full story.

"And she knows this how?"

"A client, I guess. A writer."

"Writers do know a lot of strange things."

"Yeah." And they're smart and sexy and witty. Or maybe that's just Hearts and Thorns.

"You don't make six-figures, do you?"

"Rude," I say.

"And you're, what, five eleven? Five ten?"

"I don't think it's my height," I say.

"Only fifteen percent of men are six feet or taller," she says.

I raise a brow.

"You don't look up the percentiles you fall into?"

No. Who does? "I always forget you're a nerd."

"I'm smart, not a nerd."

"Aren't you studying chemistry?"

"With a minor is statistics," she says. "You really need data fluency these days. Everyone does."

Okay…

"I'm in the ninety-fifth percentile," she says. "Women's height."

"Congratulations," I say.

"Are you going to look?" She motions to my cell.

"In front of you?"

"Yeah, why not?" she says.

"Maybe I want some privacy."

"You really shouldn't work at Inked Love."

"Isn't this sexual harassment?" I ask.

"Probably. Do you want to report it to HR?"

"Who's HR?"

"Chase?"

"Chase is scary calm now that he's a dad."

"Yeah, he has a real daddy vibe, for sure," she says. "Kidding."

"Are you?"

She motions *sorta*. "Okay, I can go back to work, but you have to go back with me."

That's fair. I am late, and she is the assistant manager for the moment. "It might be SPAM."

"Just look."

I do.

And it's not SPAM or a new entry from *Hearts and Thorns*.

It's Imogen.

Imogen: This might be a little forward, but I would like a round two. Actually, I'd like to try to make this a regular thing. I had fun last night. I'd like to have fun all summer.

Luna squeals. "Good news?"

"Yeah," I say.

"Why do you look so glum?"

"I don't," I say.

"You don't look excited," she says.

"I am." I think. I want to see Imogen again. Badly. But there's something a little cold about the text.

She's laying down the law, yeah.

And it's a law I should like.

A beautiful woman wants sex without strings because she wants me.

That's the ideal arrangement.

"Can I see?" Luna asks.

I show her the phone.

"Oh, I get it. You like her."

"I wouldn't sleep with her if I didn't like her."

"No, you *like* her."

Shit, I do.

"Aw, I've never seen you like anyone. This is cute. Can I take a picture?"

I flip her off.

"Do you need some pointers? First relationships are hard."

"I've had relationships."

"Who?"

I name a few exes.

"Those weren't relationships, Tricky. Can you name a single thing about any of them?"

"Yeah. Orange was Andrea's favorite color."

"A meaningful thing?"

"Orange isn't a popular color." And what does that matter? Sure, my romantic relationships have been a little surface level. I was surface level. That was what I wanted. It was all I could do. Besides—"Imogen isn't looking for a relationship."

"She made an offer. You can counter."

"She was clear," I say.

"Even so."

Maybe. Or maybe this is perfect. "She wants no-strings attached sex. Why would I turn that down?"

She smiles *do you really expect me to buy that?* "Is that all it is?"

"What do you mean?"

"There's nothing else going on?" she asks.

"Just thinking about someone."

"Another woman?"

"Not exactly."

She raises a brow.

"You'll think it's stupid."

"I already think it's stupid."

"You're easy to talk to. Anyone ever tell you that?"

She laughs. "Everyone, yeah." She takes a long sip. "The truth feels better than a lie, doesn't it?"

"You're like her that way," I say. "Brave."

She actually blushes. "Thank you. But flattery won't help you. Wait? Who's brave?"

"I follow her online diary," I say. "It's a one-sided thing. We don't talk one-on-one. But I feel... I don't know. I guess I want that with someone. The intimacy."

"That's not the same thing as a relationship, Tricky."

"I know."

"She shares and you do, what... phone sex?"

"No. I don't know her."

"It's all her, revealing herself to you. Relationships go two ways."

"Yeah." I know that. I just love this. "But I—"

"Don't know if you want to have a just-sex relationship or try to find something real?"

"I can finish my own sentences."

Luna softens. "Come over tonight. We can talk, watch trashy reality TV, drink Bud Light."

"Am I ever going to live that down?"

"Don't drink the Bud if you don't want the rep."

"You wouldn't be caught dead drinking a light beer."

"True. But you can bring some for yourself."

"I'm okay," I say.

"We'll drink too much coffee then."

"Oliver won't mind?"

She clears her throat.

"Not 'cause I need his permission to hang with his girlfriend."

She shoots me a *this better get good, fast* look.

"Because I don't want you to screw with your relationship to help with mine."

"Ollie respects my friendships with men. Besides, you're obviously into Imogen. You're welcome, by the way."

"I am?"

42

"Who sent her to you?"

That's true.

"I could see you two together," she says. "She's like you in certain ways. Withdrawn and serious, but with a lighter side too."

"That sounds more like Oliver."

"Oh no, we have the same type." She laughs. "Good thing we're both straight."

"Yes, that's the only thing stopping us from dating the same people."

"I know." She laughs and lets the mood shift back to lightness.

I go with it. I meet her for takeout and reality TV. We don't talk about much, really, but the next morning, the situation is clear: I want to see Imogen again, whatever that means.

Patrick: I like fun. How do you want to start?

———

A FEW HOURS LATER, MY PHONE BUZZES AGAINST MY JEANS. My fingers itch to read, but this time my temptation is physical.

Imogen.

I'm home, working on a mockup for a client. Plenty of time to talk. Or invite her here to not talk.

Imogen: Tea and cookies. What do you think?

Patrick: Romance a guy.

She sends a picture of her legs stretched over her dark-pink sheets. The color is perfect against her tan skin. Gorgeous and sexy and erotic as hell.

I'm already picturing her naked in those sheets.

And I'm picturing myself waking up next to her in those sheets. Luna was right. I like her. I really like her.

Patrick: Should I come over?

Imogen: I have homework.

Patrick: Should I stop distracting you then?

Imogen: I could use a break.

Patrick: But not that much of a break?

Imogen: That will put me out of commission for too long.

Patrick: I wore you out?

Imogen: Don't let it go to your head.

Patrick: Too late.

Imogen: Do you do this a lot?

Patrick: Text friends?

Imogen: Casual sex?

Patrick: Sometimes.

Not often, since Deidre died. But sometimes.

Patrick: I have girlfriends, sometimes, but not usually anything serious.

Imogen: I'm not looking for serious.

Patrick: I know.

Imogen: I haven't done the casual sex thing before.

Patrick: You fooled me.

Imogen: Really?

Patrick: Mostly. You're different from the women who invite me to their place.

Imogen: What did I miss?

Patrick: Nothing. You were perfect. Just different.

Imogen: Different how?

Patrick: More direct.

Imogen: Women aren't ordering you onto your knees?

Patrick: Is that a request?

Imogen: It's usually safe.

Patrick: Kneeling?

Imogen: Cunnilingus. There's a low risk of STD transmission.

Patrick: That. That's how you're different.

Imogen: Because I bring up STD rates?

Patrick: The way you do it.

Imogen: I'm a scientist.

Patrick: You study STDs?

Imogen: Behavioral economics. The nexus of economics and psychology. And I'm undergrad. I'll be a senior next year. But still. Why beat around the bush?

Patrick: I like that.

Imogen: Thanks. I think.

Patrick: Don't think. It's a compliment.

Imogen: I'll take the compliment, but I'll definitely think.

Patrick: Right. You are a scientist. I like Jurassic Park. Where's that leave me?

Imogen: Who doesn't like Jurassic Park?

Patrick: It's not painting scientists in the best light.

Imogen: Sure it is. People do good for science. People do bad for science. It's like anything. You should read some of the old psychology studies before there were serious ethics. They were messed up.

Patrick: Anything interesting?

Imogen: A lot interesting, but nothing sexy.

Patrick: I like interesting too.

Imogen: I'm sure you've heard of the Milligram experiments? Testing people's obedience by asking subjects to shock an unseen patient, even as they scream or beg for mercy.

Patrick: It sounds familiar. What's the verdict?

Imogen: Most people follow orders. Those who don't tend to be less agreeable in general. That's another personality metric, one of the "Big Five." (Mine is low. Which means I don't compromise as easily, but the flip side is I don't compromise my integrity as easily either). Or they don't see the experimenter as a person in an elevated position. Other scientists, doctors, professionals.

Patrick: I can see that.

Imogen: It has a certain common sense to it when you look at the history of the world. Or when you reflect on your own experience. We all feel the weight of what other people expect us to do.

Patrick: Is that an issue you've had with men?

Imogen: I don't like being expected to perform certain acts.

Patrick: Anything in particular?

Imogen: Really?

Patrick: I can guess, yeah, but I prefer not to make assumptions.

Imogen: Or… you want me to say something else.

She's so sure of herself. I love it.

Patrick: I want you to tell me what you like and what you don't like, so we both enjoy ourselves.

Imogen: Even if I don't like your favorite things?

Patrick: You don't know my favorite things.

Imogen: What are they?

Patrick: I asked first.

Imogen: I don't like being expected to do anything, period. Men usually expect one thing: head, even in situations where they'd never expect sex. It's not that I don't like it. Well, I don't really know if I like it, honestly. It was just okay with my ex. I didn't hate it, but I didn't love it either.

Patrick: That's fine.

Imogen: Really?

Patrick: Why wouldn't it be?

Imogen: Because men like blow jobs.

Patrick: So?

Imogen: So? Isn't it… disappointing?

I really like her.

Patrick: I enjoy receiving, yes, but I prefer to give. And there's plenty of other things I enjoy.

Imogen: It's not off the table. It's just it feels more personal to me. I'm not sure if I'll want to do it in a casual relationship. Maybe. But if I do, only if we're exclusive and we're both safe. I know the STD transmission risk with oral sex is low, but I'd rather not worry.

Patrick: I'll get tested this week.

Imogen: Has it been long enough you're sure?

Patrick: Yeah. But we can take it at whatever pace you want.

Imogen: Is this how these conversations normally go?

Patrick: No. Most people leave all this unsaid. But this is smarter. No crossed wires.

Imogen: People don't think it's sexy.

Patrick: Maybe it's not as sexy as reading someone's body. But it's way hotter than realizing you overstepped because someone didn't want to say no. Or letting someone overstep because you don't want to correct them.

Imogen: Has that happened to you?

Patrick: I hope not. But when I was younger, I was dumber too. I didn't see things as clearly.

Imogen: That's true. I agreed to things I wasn't comfortable with because I thought I should.

Patrick: Did someone push you?

I already want to deck the asshole. And I'm not a violent person.

Imogen: No. Not the way you mean. Only the expectations. The social pressure. Women are as bad as men. There's this sort of "Oh, you don't do that?" vibe. "Are you not cool? Are you a prude?"

Patrick: Men are like that too.

Imogen: Right. And men don't always want sex, all the time, any way, anyone, just because they're men.

Patrick: Don't spread that too widely.

Imogen: Our secret.

Fuck, I really, really like her.

Patrick: What are you into?

Imogen: I'm not sure, actually. It's been a while.

Patrick: Happy to help you find out.

Beyond happy.

Patrick: We can experiment as much as you want.

Imogen: I was actually thinking that. It probably sounds ridiculous, but it helps me to put things in scientific terms.

Patrick: A hookup experiment?

Imogen: Exactly. We try new things. I find what I like. If it's not too imposing on you.

Helping her figure out what she's into?

What a gift.

Patrick: Hell yeah. What should we do first?

Imogen: I still like the idea of morning sex.

Patrick: That's perfect. But if you spend the night, I'm not going to be able to wait until the morning.

Imogen: Even if that's what I want to try?

Patrick: Is it?

That's kind of hot, actually. Waiting for her. Making her wait.

Imogen: I don't know. I never have.

Patrick: How about next time?

Imogen: Okay. Next time. This time… I could use a distraction after dinner with my parents Sunday. If you don't mind being used.

Patrick: Being used for sex by a gorgeous woman? No, I don't mind.

Imogen: Your place?

Patrick: Eight?

She's direct. I like that.

I really like it.

Imogen: Nine.

Patrick: Do you want to spend the night?

Imogen: As long as we're clear it doesn't mean anything.

Patrick: We're clear. Anything you want between now and Sunday.

Imogen: Anything how?

Patrick: Pictures. Texts. Calls.

Imogen: Sexual ones?

Patrick: Or other ones.

Imogen: No. I'm okay. Actually, could you pick up some stuff for break-fast and chai? I'm no fun before my morning tea. And I want the morning sex to go well.

Patrick: Sure, but I'll need a list. I don't know tea.

Imogen: You drink Bud Light, right? That's what Luna said.

Patrick: How the hell did that come up?

Imogen: She really judged you for it.

Patrick: She's a snob.

Imogen: Probably, but I am too. I'm from Newport Beach.

Patrick: Really? You don't seem like the type.

Imogen: I'll take that as a compliment.

Patrick: Fancy breakfast. Got it.

Imogen: I'll teach you how to make chai.

Patrick: I'll teach you anything you want to know.

Chapter Eight

IMOGEN

Sunday dinners are a family tradition. Even when my parents are at their busiest, even when my sister's softball schedule means she's hundreds of miles away, we connect Sunday night for dinner.

Usually, it's here, in their Newport Beach house. I guess it's still my house too. We moved here when I was in middle school, after my parents' business really took off.

We went from living in a tiny apartment to living in a three-bedroom house on the beach.

It's not huge, but it's big enough (and expensive enough). I have my own room.

I linger there, in my space, before dinner. I sit on my twin bed, soak in the dark pink sheets and comforter, the white desk covered in colorful lyrics, the bare walls. No more band posters or photographs or moody poems.

Only pure, clean white.

That's the way they like things—clean.

I don't want to sit through another awkward dinner. Even if it comes with the comfort of Mom's cooking.

Right on cue, the scent of lemongrass fills my nostrils. But that can't be possible. It's my imagination.

Mmm. Beef, coconut, fish sauce, rice.

Maybe it is my imagination, but my imagination is making me hungry. Why is her food so comforting when her presence isn't? It's this blank wall that screams *we can't talk about this*.

Worse, Julie doesn't know.

My kid sister has no idea what happened last year and I have to keep things that way.

Awesome.

I try to ignore the scent of lemongrass, but it's too strong. Opening a window doesn't help. The ocean breeze is familiar in its own way.

It's too much, being here. My head is too full. I need to channel my thoughts into words, but my notebook and my laptop are in the car, and I don't have time. I just need a few deep breaths.

There. I find a sense of calm. I meet my sister downstairs; I help Mom set the table.

And I disappear. I stay here, yes. But I don't taste the food (the biggest loss, really). I don't smell the breeze. I don't feel the shifts in the air.

I retreat behind my walls, far from the sharp corners that might hurt me.

It's routine. The same habit I adopted as a kid, when I realized things went more smoothly when I kept my feelings to myself, only stronger. Infinitely more powerful.

I autopilot the conversation with expertise. Wow, is Julie really being scouted by Stanford and Harvard? The winters on the East Coast are harsh. And the bay area is still too cold for her.

It's wonderful I'm devoted to my studies—summer school and a double major—but have I thought about grad schools yet? Am I studying for the GRE? What about letters of recommendation?

Eventually, Julie shifts the conversations to the business, and Mom goes into great detail on a supplier issues. They sent the wrong kind of flour. Can you imagine? And the beans aren't up to snuff! (They run a ridiculously successful bakery and coffee chain).

After Mom finishes, she asks Dad about the movies he's been watching recently—he loves aging American action stars—and he goes off on that.

And, pretty soon, I'm washing dishes while Julie dries, returning to the moment one scrub at a time.

"Are you okay?" She rubs an already dry plate with the blue-and-white checkered towel in her hand.

"Busy," I say.

"You don't have to BS me," she says. "I'm not stupid."

"Are you sure? All that softball might be melting your brain."

She laughs. "In your dreams."

"And it must be hard, being the beautiful one."

She hip-checks me. "You tell me."

"I'm okay," I say.

"Sure, Immy. That's why you're spending the entire summer at UCLA. 'Cause you don't want to avoid being here."

"Maybe I'm devoted to my studies. Like Mom said."

"Yeah, you're a nerd, for sure," she says. "But we both know it's more than that."

It is. But I can't tell her. Mom and I agree here, terrifyingly enough.

"You're weird with Mom now."

"We always fight."

"No, it's different. Cold."

"It's nothing you need to worry about," I say.

"Very reassuring."

"I promise."

"If it's no big deal, tell me," she says.

"I love you." I finish the last dish and give her a hug. "But I have a hot date tonight."

"Really?" Her dark eyes light up. She looks a lot like me, only more compact. A little shorter, a little curvier, a little more muscular. "You're seeing someone?"

"It's more of a fling," I say.

She squeals. "Is he cute? Do you have a picture?"

"I don't want to announce it."

"They know you date."

"They know, maybe, but they like to pretend otherwise," I say.

"I took a guy to prom."

"That's different. You're the golden child."

"Please. They love how much you love school."

They do. Julie shines in social situations, but she's not as book smart. She has her own problems. Which is why I need to take control of mine.

And I don't even have a problem. I'm good. I'm great.

I'm better than great. I'm horny.

I check the coast is clear—Mom and Dad are talking business on the porch—and I show my sister Patrick's Instagram.

She scrolls until she finds a picture of him. "He's adorable. Tall?"

"Tall enough," I say. "Not that you'd ever be able to tell." I take my cell and hold it over her head.

"Hey! I can jump." She does, in fact, jump.

I lift the phone higher.

She laughs as she leaps for it.

"You're going to break something."

"So show me more of him," she says.

I hand her the phone.

She takes it to the table and studies the images. "Oh my god. This is you." She finds a recent shot of his work. The tattoo Patrick put on my ribs. "You talked about this design for three weeks straight."

I did.

"You didn't tell me! Can I see! Please. I won't tell."

"Okay, but fast."

She nods *of course* and watches with wide eyes as I peel my shirt and my bra up my stomach.

It's extremely weird, but it's sweet too.

"Wow." She just stops herself from tracing the lines. "That's beautiful. Can I get one too?"

"You're not eighteen."

"But he's your boyfriend, right? He'll break rules."

"He won't be my boyfriend when Mom and Dad kill me."

"They won't find out," she says.

"They always find out."

She nods *maybe*.

"And he's not my boyfriend. We're just… having fun."

"That's so grown-up." She lets out a sigh that's pure teenage girl longing. "I can't wait until I'm in college."

"Wait. Stay young forever."

"Don't even! When you were my age… I remember how often you snuck around with guys."

"It wasn't that often."

"It was often enough."

Maybe. I did have a phase. I didn't have sex, but I did have a lot of make out sessions, ranging from OMG to oh, hell no. "Are you seeing the guy you took to prom?"

"Not really."

"You trust him?"

"Yeah, sure. He's sweet," she says. "But don't worry, we're not having sex."

I wasn't worried. Until she said that. "You have condoms?"

"Immy!"

"Seriously, Julie. It's better to be safe than sorry."

"Yes. I have condoms." She flames red. "We're not going to have sex. I'm not ready."

My shoulders fall. I want my kid sister to have a fulfilling life, with everything that entails, but I still worry. Men aren't always the most trustworthy. Women aren't always the most trustworthy.

She's tough, yes, but she's sweet too. She sees the best in people. "He knows that?"

"Oh my god, you're about to go have casual sex."

"I'm ready."

"Ugh. You're the worst."

"That's my job, as your older sister."

"Will you tell me about it?"

"Sure." I give her a hug. "I love you."

"Go. Get laid."

"When did you become a bro?"

"Hello! Softball scholarship!"

That's true. "Be good."

"I should tell you that."

Probably.

I give her another hug, then I say goodbye to my parents, I get into my car, and I leave.

After a few blocks, I stop. I change into a dress. I apply lipstick. I check the time.

A few minutes to eight. The drive is an hour. I'll arrive right on time.

Perfect.

I text Patrick.

Imogen: See you soon.

I add a photo of my legs stretched over the passenger seat. It's not the most graceful image, sure, but there's something about snapping a shot for him.

It's really fucking hot.

Chapter Nine

IMOGEN

Patrick lives just off the happening Abbot-Kinney street, in a new apartment building. He's right on the edge of the bungalow section of Venice Beach (streets and streets of "beach shacks" worth seven figures).

How does he afford his place? He doesn't seem like the kind of guy who comes from money. But then I don't seem like someone who lives on the beach in Newport.

At least, I hope I don't reek of the entitlement people associate with Orange County girls. Not that the stereotypes are fair. I guess that's the through-line, really.

I shouldn't make assumptions about Patrick because he's a tattoo artist who wears jeans. Maybe he pays his mortgage with his trust fund. Maybe he rakes in the dough at work. Maybe he has a side-hustle as an erotica author.

Anything is possible.

His jacket was real leather. I think.

No. No more thinking. I'm here for satisfaction, period, the end.

After I turn off my car, I check my makeup, my dress, my purse. I look cute. No, I look hot. I feel hot. I am hot and I'm ready for this.

Okay, I'm not completely ready. And the stress from dinner is putting a crimp in my sex drive. But, hey, I'm shaking it off.

I read his reply to my text.

Patrick: I hope you're not wearing anything under that.

My cheeks flush. My chest too. My thoughts drift a little further away. And this is just a text. Once I'm actually there, in his space—

It's scary. Not because he's a near stranger I shouldn't trust. Because there's a certain intimacy to being in his space, seeing his life, waking up in his bed.

That's terrifying.

I take another deep breath; I lock my car, and I make my way to his apartment.

He's on the second floor, in the corner, past a gated door and a gorgeous succulent garden.

Seriously, how does he afford this place?

No. That's none of my business. I'm not here to discuss his financial future. I'm here to enjoy his body.

I take a deep breath and I knock.

"It's open," he answers.

It is. I step inside. "Is that safe?"

"Are the hipsters going to jump me?"

"Depends."

"On?"

"Do you have any vinyl?"

He turns to me with a smile. It's a gorgeous smile. He really is handsome. Green eyes, sharp nose, dots of freckles covering his face.

And all his ink; the pieces of his heart on his skin.

I want to trace them.

Because I want to touch him. And because I want to know what they mean.

That is why we're here. Sort of. I'm getting to know his body. He's getting to know mine.

And we do need a certain level of trust for this. A lot, actually. At least, I do.

My shoulders relax. My chest eases.

Bit by bit, I return to my body. I feel the ocean breeze. I smell the salt. And something else, something familiar.

Star anise.

Why does the room smell of star anise and cinnamon? "What are you making?"

"Chai."

"Oh." My cheeks flush. The recipe I promised to teach him. The ingredients I requested. I did send a detailed list, but I didn't expect him to pick up star anise. It's hard to find in normal supermarkets.

Or does he already shop at H-Mart or Woori Market? Maybe he loves stir fry. Maybe he buys sriracha by the pound. Maybe he has a fetish for Asian food and Asian women.

No. He didn't show any signs last time. And those guys never manage to hide the signs. It doesn't happen to me often—they're usually after Chinese or Korean girls, the pale ones with small frames—but there's always one guy at a party who compliments my exotic beauty or assumes I'm either an obedient housewife to be or dragon woman in training.

"You okay?" he asks.

"Sorry. Just remembering this guy who told me he liked spicy women," I say.

"'Cause I bought the star anise?"

"Yeah."

"You asked."

"I know. I just thought—"

"I have a weird kink?" he asks.

"Do you?"

"Not that one." He smiles. "Don't worry, I get it. I've had a few women ask if I'll wear my kilt."

"Aren't you Irish?"

"Yeah. The kilts you see in the movies are mostly Scottish.

Irish kilts are less showy. But I get it. Easy access." His eyes flit to my dress.

My blush deepens. "Do you have any skirts?"

"No," he says.

"You'd look good in one."

"I look good in everything."

"Or nothing," I say.

"That's supposed to be my line," he says.

"I know."

He motions for me to come here.

I move closer, close enough to touch him.

He wraps his arm around my waist and pulls me into a soft, slow kiss. There's heat in it, absolutely, but there's something else too: affection.

Is that a normal part of a friend with benefits? Or is it a sign of danger?

After one second with my lips against his, I don't care what it means. I soak up every drop.

He's a good kisser. Tender and firm and completely intoxicating.

I pull back with a sigh. "I was supposed to teach you."

There are tins of cardamom, ginger, and tea on the stove. Plus, a container, the container of almond milk I requested. Somehow, I'm the only lactose intolerant person in my family. Unable to drink milk in a family that sells Vietnamese iced coffee to the masses (it's mostly sweetened condensed milk, though my parents were ahead of the dairy-free curve thanks to me. They have a very popular, very expensive coconut-milk version).

Their chain is as high-end as Blue Bottle or Philz, which is why they stand out. Really, it's smart business, but hey, now I'm thinking again. And I don't want to keep thinking.

"Are you sure you're okay?" he asks.

"A little disoriented. You're a good kisser."

He blushes. With his skin tone, it's obvious. And it's sexy too.

I've never found a guy's blush sexy before, but Patrick—

Maybe we should stop talking and have sex now. "Do you want to go upstairs?"

"Already?"

"Or wherever the bed is."

"You don't want to try the chai?"

"I'm being rude, aren't I?" I ask.

"I forgive you." He turns off the stove. "Chai? Or upstairs?"

"One sip."

"Good. It's not worth the wait." He scoops a sip into a mug and hands it to me. "You'll still have to teach me."

My fingers brush his as I take the mug. Even though I've felt his fingers inside me, this feels alarmingly intimate. "Thanks."

"Don't thank me until you try it."

I blow the hot molecules from the top. When the tea is cool enough to drink, I take a sip. "Oh."

"Yeah."

"It's…"

"Terrible?"

"Over-steeped." I take another sip. The tea is way too astringent, but the spices come through. The unique licorice flavor of star anise, the spice of cinnamon, the Earthy richness of cardamom. "But not bad for your first try."

"This is try…" He looks to the mugs in the sink. "Four. Make that five."

"I don't drink it this late."

"You might need your energy." He shoots me a wicked smile.

My stomach flutters. My sex pangs. Yes. No more talking. No more thinking. Only this. "I can show you after."

"After…"

"If you're still awake." I slip my hands under his t-shirt.

He feels good against my hand. Warm and hard and real. Concrete.

I don't usually think about sex in these terms, but right now, the feeling is overwhelming.

I'm not all mind. I'm physical too. I use my body for more than getting around and winning races.

"Did you wear anything under this?" he asks.

"Maybe. Where's the bed?"

"You don't like the couch?"

"I like the couch." But I don't wait for the couch. I dig my fingers into his waist and I pull him into a slow, deep kiss.

He hooks his fingers around the strap of my dress. "I've thought about this all week."

"It's been two days."

"Three." He peels the strap down my shoulder. "I've wanted to do this every minute."

He does the same with the other strap, arranging the fabric so it's barely covering my breasts.

"Do you like it this way?" He tugs the fabric a little lower. "Me, stripping you out of your clothes?"

I do. It's a fixture in my fantasies. Not that I've ever admitted it to myself. "Yes."

A little lower. "Or halfway out of your clothes?"

Lower.

Lower.

Low enough to expose my breasts.

There is something about the urgency, the partial exposure. It's really fucking hot. "Yes."

"Are you wearing underwear?"

"Maybe."

He wraps his fingers around my thigh. Slowly, he drags them up my skin. Higher and higher, closer and closer, until his hand brushes my cotton panties. "Too bad." He rubs me over my panties. "This would be a lot more fun with these gone."

I don't respond with words. I bring my lips to his. I kiss him hard.

No patience, no tease, nothing but pure, raw need pouring from me to him.

I'm here, in my body, and I want to soak up every moment of it.

As much as I can, anyway.

It's too overwhelming.

He rubs me again and again, testing different speeds and different pressures, until he finds exactly the one I need.

I tug at his t-shirt.

He works me with the same perfect strokes. Again and again, pushing me closer and closer.

Then he brings his hand to my chest, and I nearly come from the friction—

I like being halfway out of my clothes.

I like him toying with me.

I really, really like the feel of his thumb against my nipple.

He pushes me against the dining room table.

I pull back with a sigh. "Fuck." I dig my nails into his skin.

He works me exactly how I need him, pushing me closer with every brush of his fingers.

Closer.

Closer.

There—

The tension in my sex unwinds. Pleasure spills through my body, waking up every molecule, erasing the stresses of the day.

Right now, none of that matters.

Right now, this is the only thing that matters.

He works me through my orgasm, then he pushes my panties off my hips. "Bed. Now."

I don't want to wait for the bed. I want to do this here, now. I need him inside me. I need it in a way I've never needed anything.

But the table—

That's strange and overwhelming too.

I nod.

He leads me up the stairs and lowers me onto the bed on my back.

I shake my head. "Like the table."

He nods, turns me over. "On your hands and knees."

I get into position.

"Have you tried it this way?"

"No." Zack and I didn't really experiment. For all his talk about creativity, he was relatively consistent in his sexual preferences. And I didn't have the sex drive—or the trust—to ask for more.

Now?

I want this. I want that. I want everything.

"I'll go slow," Patrick promises. Then his hands are on his zipper. The foil packet. The condom.

He brings one hand to my hips and he holds me in place as he enters me.

He stretches me slowly. Then he pulls back and drives into me again.

He stays slow, at first.

Then he moves a little faster. A little harder.

I press my palms into the mattress for stability.

He keeps his hands on my hips, holding me in place as he drives into me again.

He feels good inside me. And I love the way he's handling me, guiding me, responding to my groans.

I lower myself onto the bed.

He rolls my dress a little higher and shifts onto the mattress. "Spread your legs."

I do.

He positions his body behind mine, lifts my hips, drives into me. In one swift motion, he lowers the two of us, so I'm pressed into the bed, the weight of his body sinking into mine.

Again, he starts slow. The mattress barely shakes. But as he moves faster and harder, I have to hold on to the sheets to stay in place. To contain the need racing through my body.

He drives into me again and again, pushing me closer, winding me tighter.

He feels so good inside me. Warm and hard and mine.

I've never felt that before, that overwhelming physical, visceral need to take his body into mine.

But right now—

This really is bliss.

I close my eyes and surrender to the sensation of him driving into me.

The tension in my sex winds tighter and tighter.

His breaths run together.

His fingers dig into my thighs.

Then he's there, rocking into me as he comes, groaning my name into the air, digging his nails into my thighs.

It hurts in the best possible way, like he's claiming my body as his too.

Here. Only here.

But here is really fucking good.

He works through his orgasm then he pulls back, takes care of the condom, rights his jeans.

I push myself up and reach for my panties, but Patrick stops me.

"No way, baby." He takes my hand, so my panties fall to my ankles. "You need to come again first."

Chapter Ten

IMOGEN

For a few hours, the night is easy. I read on the couch. He draws in his sketchbook. We enjoy the silence together. I feel comfortable in his space.

With my head in his lap, and his hands in my hair, I'm not anywhere else. I'm in this perfect moment, soaking in the feeling of his fingertips. This other side of physical touch. Intimate in another way.

We have sex in his bed. It's soft and slow and alarmingly tender. After, we take turns in the shower, and I change into a spare t-shirt and boxers.

He falls asleep in his clean white sheets.

For a few minutes, I settle into the foam mattress. I let the feeling of his space overwhelm me. The soft breeze, the faint smell of salt, the hum of the city streets.

With every passing car, I drift away from sexual bliss. To a place where I worry about Julie's boyfriend (even if she didn't say she has a boyfriend) and Mom ignoring her issues the way she ignored mine. Or maybe Julie is more like me than I can admit. Maybe she's just as good at hiding things.

I climb out of bed, slip downstairs, check my cell. Thankfully, I don't have to invent a reason to check on my sister.

She's already checking on me.

Julie: How was it ;p

Imogen: It's late. Go to bed.

Julie: You're up! Did you just finish another tryst?

Imogen: Why are you up?

Julie: You woke me.

Imogen: Sorry. Don't keep your phone near your bed. Or at least turn it on Do Not Disturb.

Julie: Thanks, Mom, great apology.

Imogen: Sleep hygiene is important.

Julie: I couldn't sleep anyway.

Imogen: Is everything okay?

Julie: No! My sister won't tell me what's going on. Worse, she's pretending like nothing is going on.

Guilty as charged.

Imogen: It's a thing with me and Mom. Not your issue.

Julie: I live with her.

Imogen: Let's talk about it later.

Julie: Please, Immy, I know that means "let's talk about it never," but, sure. If you tell me all about your new boy-toy.

I give her a PG-13 version of events. When she presses, I include a few details. Nothing too explicit. Only the sheer pleasure of being in my body, the way I am when I swim.

Julie: Like a great play. When I dive without thinking. Totally. That's hot.

Imogen: You swear you aren't having sex?

Julie: OMG. Don't even. Hypocrite.

Imogen: I just want you to be safe.

Julie: No. You want me to be an innocent flower, same as Mom and Dad, but I'll allow it this time.

Imogen: Next time?

Julie: No dice.

Imogen: You are seeing someone?

Julie: We're only making out. Don't worry.

Imogen: When you say making out...

Julie: None of your business.

Imogen: What about my details?

Julie: I don't act like you're supposed to wait for marriage.

Imogen: It's only 'cause I know how men are. And you're sweet. I'm not.

Julie: Nice save. Almost.

Imogen: I'll stop. I swear.

Julie: I'll believe it when I see it.

Imogen: Okay, go back to bed.

Julie: Go back to your boy-toy. And come early next Sunday to tell me all about it. Okay?

Imogen: Deal.

She's right. I'm not really worried about her making bad choices. I'm worried she's the same as me, going through the same things I did, hiding them the way I do.

But if I can't lead by example, how can I expect her to share? I'm the older one. I'm the mature, responsible one. I'm supposed to be brave, chart a course for her.

But I'm not.

There's too much in my head. There's only one way to handle it.

I pull out my computer, start another blog entry, and write.

I write for nearly an hour. Until a sound upstairs calls my attention.

"Imogen?" Patrick's sleepy voice floats through the space. "You okay?"

"Yeah. Just insomnia. The chai always does it."

"Come back to bed."

"I don't want to wake you," I say.

"I'm up." He fights a yawn.

"Are you?"

"I can be," he says.

I laugh. "I didn't mean that."

"Are you sure?"

"I am."

"I still want to talk to you," he says.

"I don't have anything to say."

"You can listen to me discuss color theory."

"Yellow, red, blue?"

"That's only the start."

I can't really make him out in the dark. Only the highlights from the moon.

"There are secondary colors, tertiary colors, complimentary colors."

"Complimentary colors? Are there critical colors?"

He laughs. "Yeah. Pink."

"No."

"It's true. People who love pink love to criticize."

"That sounds likely." I nod to my dark pink phone case. We have the same phone, except his case is red. "And what about men who love red?"

"Freaks."

"Really? That's a kind of color?"

"Horny colors, yeah," he says.

"Red is pretty horny."

"Basic color theory."

"They didn't teach that one in my art history class," I say.

"Imogen, you need to know something," he says.

"Yeah?"

"Talking about art is my love language," he says.

"Love languages aren't scientifically tested."

He laughs. "Perfect response."

"It's true. And where did you hear about love languages?"

"Everyone knows about love languages."

Do they? The theory makes a certain amount of sense. People show love in certain ways and they want to receive love in the same ways. They enjoy spending quality time with their partners, performing acts of service for their partners, offering their partners words of affirmation, or giving gifts.

And of course there's the one at play here: physical touch.

Some people show love with touch. Cuddles, kisses, hugs, fucks.

He doesn't mention the typical love languages. He sticks to his unique take. "Horny colors are one thing. If you start talking about pointillism or perspective"—he presses his hands to his heart—"I'll be a goner."

"I'll try to go easy on you."

"I appreciate it." He smiles. "How about a movie if you don't want to talk?"

"My pick?"

"Anything you desire."

"Even something with subtitles?"

"Especially something with subtitles. Remote is on the coffee table. Rent something if you want."

"Rent? Are you made of money?"

"Basically." He laughs and motions… something. Then he slips into the bathroom.

That's it. I need to wrap up… whatever I'm doing here.

I publish my entry, and I close my computer.

Chapter Eleven

"Get In, Get Off, Go Home"
Posted by Hearts and Thorns
Monday
_2 A.M._

I t turns out casual sex is a little more complicated than get in, get off, go home.

Go figure.

But then, how would I know?

I've never had good sex before. Not really. Sure, there were good kissers in high school. There was even the boy in the band (I know, I know, I'm a cliché) who rubbed my thigh over my jeans in a way that made my entire body buzz.

I wanted him so, so badly.

And then I had him—in a high school way—and I had enough. It was fine. We dated a few more weeks. I realized he only had two moves. Great moves, sure, but they still got old.

We broke up without a lot of fuss. I found someone else. Normal high school stuff.

The one time I tried on a relationship (a real, multiple

months, meet the parents kind of relationship), it felt like a swim-suit two sizes too big.

It was useful as an extra practice suit, for creating drag in the pool, but otherwise?

It just didn't fit.

Still, I stayed, for a long time. I didn't know better. I didn't know how we were supposed to fit together. I didn't know sex could be better than okay. (After all, that excitement I felt when I was a teenager came with teenage hormones. And, sure, I wasn't exactly old, but I was old enough).

It's true, I didn't share, but he didn't leave the space for me. He took it instead.

He assumed he knew all there was to know about me.

He said he loved me, but he didn't. He couldn't.

He barely knew me.

He thought I loved the ocean for all the usual reasons—the surf, the sand, the chance to frolic in a bikini.

And, yes, I love the surf, I love the sand, I look great in a bikini.

But that's only part of the appeal.

The Kate Chopin of it all—

He never got that.

Maybe men just can't. Maybe men can't understand what it means to be a woman in the world, even one without a husband or children.

The expectations are still there.

They're still heavy.

And the promise of freedom—

It's enticing.

I'm sure there are things I didn't understand about him, things I don't understand about being a man.

But I never pretended.

I hid.

That's different.

And now, I'm here, trying to dive back into my body, worried I won't do it right.

Because I might fall for this guy.

Because I might screw him up.

Because, maybe, I want to screw him up.

And, maybe, just maybe, I'm a bad role model, again. Maybe the people I love are the same as me—

Weighed down by my expectations for them.

Hiding behind them.

Hiding the places they hurt.

I want to be brave, to lead by example.

But I'm not even brave enough to ask. To look. To see.

And that's the thing—

My ex was right.

I want everything this guy has to offer. For my body, anyway. If I risk my heart, I risk it.

After all, I made this choice knowing what might happen.

Knowing I might get hurt.

I already know how this ends.

I keep everything to myself.

I can't even tell my sister. How would I ever tell him?

Why?

I guess that's clarity. It's not smart, diving in head-first, but I'm tired of doing the smart thing.

And if I fall, well—

I've picked myself up after worse.

Chapter Twelve

PATRICK

This is not an ideal situation.

Imogen is downstairs, and I'm here, hiding in the bathroom, clinging to every word from my online crush.

What the fuck is wrong with me?

There's a gorgeous woman downstairs, a woman who wants to fuck me senseless.

Who only wants to fuck me senseless.

It's obvious. I want the honesty and intimacy I feel when I read *Hearts and Thorn's* posts.

I want to be someone's confidant.

I want to understand.

All this time and I still don't understand—

But it's not like I'm going to figure it out now.

Imogen is here and she needs satisfaction.

Sure, we're never going to be best friends, but we are lovers. A certain kind of lovers. And this type of intimacy is plenty thrilling on its own.

She's open here.

Vulnerable here.

Sexy as hell here.

Less pouting. More making her come.

I leave my cell on my dresser and I move downstairs.

"Hey." She watches me descend. "Did you fall back asleep?"

"Brushing my teeth." Not a total lie.

"Getting fresh for me?"

"How'd you know?"

"I figured the market opened in Australia."

"Is that how the time zones work?"

"Maybe? I don't have them memorized."

"Japan," I say. "That's the market for me."

"Of course. How else could you afford this place?" She lets out a low, throaty laugh as I sit next to her and pull her into my lap. "Hey."

"Hey." I bring my hand to her cheek. "This is really fucking sexy."

"Is it the bad taste in music?" She motions to the Sinful Serenade logo embossed on the black tee.

"They're customers."

"Aren't they a big deal?"

"Pretty big."

"It's not my kind of music."

"How about I play an album and we see how much you rock out?"

"Well, I'm not going to deny I enjoy No Way in Hell. It's a jam. And romantic in its own way." She looks down at me. "Do you really know them?"

"Why? Want an introduction?"

"A threesome."

I laugh. "Is that part of your experimentation?"

"Would you have a threesome with another guy?"

"Maybe."

"Really?" she asks.

"No."

"I knew it. You're vanilla. The red Converse are a lie," she says.

"Oh no, I'm a freak. I just don't like to share." I pull her closer.

"Me either." She looks into my eyes. "You're handsome up close."

"Not from far away?"

"There too." She leans in to press her lips to mine.

"I came downstairs with pure intentions."

"I know." She kisses me harder this time, claiming some part of me, something beyond the physical. "Have you really worn this?"

"No."

"It doesn't really count as your clothes then," she says.

"So you want to take it off?" I play with the edge of the t-shirt.

"If you help."

I run my fingers over the waistband of her bottoms. The soft skin of her stomach.

She shudders as I slip my hand under the t-shirt and cup her breast.

I run my thumb over her nipple and bring my lips to her neck.

She wraps her legs around me. "Is everything okay?"

"Huh?" Are we talking about something? Blood is fleeing my brain at an alarming rate.

"You were upstairs awhile."

"Just something on the net."

"Important?"

"Not as important as this." I run my thumb over her nipple.

She rocks her hips against me. "Patrick—"

I pull the t-shirt over her head.

She shifts and pushes the boxers over her ass. She slides into my lap in only those gorgeous black panties. Cotton. Lace trim. The same style she wore last time.

This is Imogen, to a t.

Practical and sexy and hiding everything I want to see.

I already know what fits her.

I already know I need her.

I rock her body against mine so her clit is against my cock, those two layers of cotton between us, and I bring my mouth to her chest.

I toy with her.

She rubs against me until she comes in those perfect black panties. "Please."

I reach for the box of condoms on the bookshelf.

She helps.

Then she's in my lap, groaning against me, coming on my cock as I suck on her perfect tits. She works me until I'm there, then she collapses in my lap, sweaty and spent and mine.

This *is* what I want.

The beautiful, guarded woman offering something precious.

I've never thought of sex that way. It doesn't have to be special or intimate, but it can be.

With her, it is.

No matter what I do, how I take her, it is.

She shifts off me carefully. "I think you're trying to kill me."

"I think you're trying to kill me."

She smiles, proud and curious.

"Or was that so I fall back asleep?"

"Death. Sleep. Either way, it's quiet."

I love her sense of humor. "Want a drink?" I stand, take care of the condom, bring her a box of tissues for cleanup.

"Water," she says. "But I don't mind if you have something."

"Water is good." I'm not great with moderation these days. Not since Deidre died. I drink until I remember, then until I forget. The next day—

Not fun.

And, yeah, she's leaving tomorrow, but I still don't want to spend all morning nursing a hangover.

"Do you have a t-shirt I can wear?" she asks. "One that's actually yours?"

"Yeah, but I might take you again," I say.

"I can live with that."

I fill the glasses and bring them to the coffee table. Then I head up the stairs and find an old Inked Love t-shirt for her.

She changes into it right away. With only the panties this time.

She looks even sexier in the shirt bearing the name of the shop, but I'm out of juice at this point.

She takes a long sip, settles on the couch, scrolls through a list of classic films. She stops on *The Shop Around the Corner*, decides against it, keeps scrolling. "You don't mind black and white?"

"You realize I'm an artist?"

"And I thought this would get me out of the color theory lecture," she says.

"Oh no. You can't escape."

"What about orange? What does that say?" she asks.

"Were you writing something?"

"Oh. Yeah. Just, uh… thoughts, I guess."

"Thoughts?"

"An essay for a project," she says.

"Already on your homework?"

"Always finishing my homework."

"Do you consider yourself a writer?"

"I guess," she says. "But it's not a career goal."

"Not everything has to be."

"That's not what my parents would say." She laughs. "They don't think psychology is a worthy field of study. And they're not sold on economics either."

"Isn't it all math?"

She looks at me funny.

"It's data, isn't it?"

"It's not engineering or computer science of physics or medicine," she says. "It's funny. Medicine is almost as in flux as 'soft sciences' but pre-med students still act superior. Or maybe it's just my roommate."

"Sounds like painters."

"Looking down on tattoo artists?"

I nod. "It happens."

"To you?"

"Whenever I take a figure drawing class."

"Naked people?"

"It's art," I say.

"Art of naked people."

"I thought you were a sophisticated woman who loved black-and-white movies?"

"And naked people," she says.

I laugh. "Should we watch a French movie?"

"If it's sexy."

"Or an erotic thriller?"

"That's a genre?"

"Yeah? *Body Heat*, *Fatal Attraction*, *The Last Seduction*. A bunch of movies about men screwing shit up by thinking with their dicks."

"Are you trying to tell me something about our relationship?"

"Yeah. You can get me to do a lot of stupid shit if you want," I say.

"By getting you thinking with your dick?"

"Exactly."

"Move a couch?"

"A chance to show off my strength? Of course," I say.

"Teach me to surf?"

"You don't know?" I ask.

"I do."

"I figured," I say.

"How?"

"You're from Newport Beach."

"Can you?" she asks.

"No," I say. "You want to teach me?"

"Not really. I prefer swimming. But I do love the beach. The expanse of the ocean. It's beautiful."

"We're close."

"I would have brought my swimsuit if I realized," she says.

"Next time." I press my palm to her rib, over her new tattoo. "Once it's safe."

"Right. You're very strict with after-care."

"Always."

"You have any erotic thrillers in mind?" she asks.

"Hell yeah. You mind violence?"

"It's not my favorite," she says.

"Okay. I don't think there's anything too gory in this one. But there is some. If you want the nice black-and-white movie—"

"Well, are you up for subtitles?"

"Hell yeah."

"Have you seen *Lust, Caution*?"

"No."

"It's not an erotic thriller, exactly. Or maybe it is. Only it's about the woman. She's a spy of sorts, but she's the one who makes bad decisions because of sex."

"Progressive."

"It is, yeah. Very anti-oppression. And all about the things people hide. Classic Ang Lee. He's amazing."

"You're a movie buff?"

"No. My ex was a film major."

"Lectured you about movies?"

"Mostly *Fight Club*. And those kinds of TV shows about male anti-heroes. We watched the first episode of so many. I think I was sitting there, doing his homework with him. He thought that was a great way to spend time together. But I guess I got a free Intro to Dramatic TV writing class out of it."

"Did you like anything?"

"Some shows were okay, but I never got the "prestige" genre.

All the shows are the same. A man, engaging in violence as a way of expressing himself."

"So you're a *Breaking Bad* fan?"

"I'll leave," she says.

"And Christopher Nolan is a genius?"

"Please stop."

"Did you like anything he showed you?"

"Not really. Is that awful?"

"Yeah, he wasn't paying attention to what you wanted," I say.

She laughs. "I mean, am I awful?"

"For liking what you like?"

"It sounds silly that way. But so many women I know do the same thing. They try to get into the bands their boyfriend's like, try to watch their favorite movies, sit there while guys play video games."

"I don't like video games." They remind me of the guy I used to be.

"Really? A twenty-something man who doesn't like video games?"

"I have to rest my hands."

"Keep them fresh for work?"

"And other uses."

She blushes. It's subtle with her tan skin, which only makes it sexier. "I, uh, started to dive into film after we broke up. There are a few movies I love, but I don't know what you like. I don't want to be like Zack. I want something we'll both enjoy."

"I'm up for anything."

"Really?"

Anything she picks, yeah. I'm sure she wants to watch something substantial. And, these days, I try to open my eyes as much as I can. Invite other points of view. "Anything."

"I'm kinda tired. So something easy, okay?"

I nod.

She picks another old movie. *The Apartment.*

It's good. Interesting.

Perfect really, except for one very awkward moment.

The one that underscores what a fucking mess I am.

Shirley MacLaine's character takes a bottle of sleeping pills. She tries to end her life.

The same way Deidre did.

Chapter Thirteen

PATRICK

Imogen falls asleep on the couch. I cover her in a blanket and let her sleep.

I'm not good conversation at the moment.

The flick's happy ending isn't enough to ease the tension in my shoulders.

There are plenty of reasons to like the movie. The writing is sharp. The acting is great. The point of view is surprisingly modern.

And the scene where the lead tries to end things is understated. Easy to miss. Especially for people who only watch comic book movies.

The person I was, before Deidre.

There's this giant line in my life.

The guy who kicked back with his friends, drinking beer, shooting the shit, ignoring the heavy stuff.

Then the guy who couldn't ignore it anymore—

Who lost his ability to ignore it.

Sort of.

I see it now, but I don't engage. I don't ask Dare if his *I'm hot and dumb* routine is masking an inability to get real. I don't congratulate Oliver on his sobriety. I don't ask Holden how hard it is doing things long distance.

Maybe it's routine. Maybe it's a lack of guts. I don't know, but I know I want more.

I want to bring Imogen to the bed, wrap my arms around her, ask why she loves the movie.

If it means anything to her. If she's had those thoughts, known anyone who did.

That isn't what she wants. I respect that. I do.

And it's not like I know how to be the person she needs, the person anyone needs.

There's a reason why Deidre didn't share this with me. And not just because I'm her kid brother.

I saw it, but I refused to see it too.

She was pulling away, avoiding family dinners, claiming other responsibilities. She said she was exhausted because she was working too hard.

It all sounded reasonable.

But it was bullshit.

In hindsight, it's obvious. At the time, I dismissed everything. I refused to look closer. I turned away from the truth.

After Deidre died, and my parents jumped into "fix it, don't talk about it mode," cleaned up her social media accounts (it was a "tragic accident" not an intentional act of self-destruction), sold her car, closed her accounts.

They didn't talk about it. They don't talk about it.

And now I barely see Molly, my oldest sister, because I can't deal with either option; her denying it or her discussing it.

There's really only one place I find intimacy—*Hearts and Thorns*.

That's how I found her. Deidre followed a bunch of online journals. Hers was the only one that stuck.

For a year now, I've been poring over my sister's passions. The books she dog-eared, the graphic novels she adored, the websites she followed.

Everything offers some insight.

But hers offers the most.

She isn't anything like Deidre, but she still helps me under-stand. And the ability to drink every drop of her words, to watch her recover, lift herself out of the darkness—

It's addicting.

She's an open book and I want to read every page.

She doesn't know me, but she still trusts me with her darkest secrets. And that's intoxicating.

Even though she trusts anyone who stumbles on her site.

It feels different, like I know her, like I understand her.

Maybe I'm delusional, but I need her tonight. I need to swim in an ocean of understanding.

I open my computer, pull up her site, and I read until I'm too tired to read anymore.

―――――

I DREAM ABOUT MY SISTER.

I dream about meeting *Hearts and Thorns* on the beach, reading *The Awakening* together, sharing every place we hurt.

She isn't the formless, shapeless figure she normally is.

She's Imogen.

And she's inviting me to offer something real of my own.

I wake to the smell of cinnamon, a head full of confusion, a hell of a lot of soreness. She was right. She wore me out.

And that's what I'm doing here.

What I'm doing with her.

Maybe I want the kind of intimacy my online crush offers, but I'm not completely oblivious. I get that goes both ways. I understand Imogen only wants me for one thing.

And I plan to enjoy every second giving her that thing.

I move through my morning routine, head downstairs, meet Imogen in the kitchen.

"Morning." Imogen turns to me with a wide, honest smile. "I

got started early. But I can make you another round. I did promise to teach you."

"Can I try?"

She hands a steaming mug to me. "What do you think?"

The mix of spices fills the air. Cinnamon, ginger, cardamom, something like licorice. Not my usual breakfast. I push back when my friends mock my light beer consumption, but they're not exactly wrong.

I'm not a man of exquisite taste. The closest I've ever gotten to a homemade chai is sips of an ex-girlfriend's Starbuck's drink.

This blows that out of the water.

It's stronger, more robust than any tea I've ever tasted. It's spicy, rich, sweet, creamy. "That's amazing."

"Thanks."

"How did you do that?" I ask.

"It's easy."

"You tried my chai?"

"It wasn't that bad," she says. "Just over-steeped and under-spiced."

"Over what?"

"If you boil the tea too long, it gets astringent and bitter. The timing is everything."

"Is it obvious I don't cook?"

"No. You're super ripped."

I raise a brow.

"Don't tell me you eat Taco Bell for lunch. I won't buy it."

"I won't say that."

"Chicken breast and broccoli?" she asks.

"What do you have against broccoli?"

She laughs. "I just mean... I know your body-type doesn't come easily."

"Yeah? And this." I run my hands over her shoulders.

She leans into the touch. "Patrick..."

"You have a fantastic body."

"It's kind of athletic."

"You're an athlete."

"Still." Her eyes flutter closed. "My hips are a little narrow. My breasts are a little small. My shoulders are massive."

"Your shoulders are sexy," I say. "And your breasts are perfect. If you say another bad thing about them, I'll have to lavish them with attention, to make it up to them."

"They are small."

"Sounds bad—"

"It's a fact."

"You're on thin ice, Nguyen."

She laughs. "One of my teammates does that. It never happened in high school. Too many Nguyens on the team."

"My name is Patrick Murphy."

"Is that common?"

"Two of the most common Irish names, yeah."

"So you get it?"

I get it. "Do you like it?" I ask.

"It's kind of cute, yeah. But, uh, the chai… I promised."

"You sure?"

She nods. "I'll have to go after. Class."

"Then show me fast."

"There's no rushing chai. It needs how much time it needs."

"Then fuck the chai."

She laughs. "No, I promised. Here." She strains the pot she's using then she takes me through the process. A cup of water, four tablespoons of leaves, extra spices, a pinch of each, plus a piece of star anise.

It really is shaped like a star.

I'd never seen it before. Never used it before. Apparently, it's common in Vietnamese cooking. It's only used in some chai blends, but Imogen loves the licorice flavor.

Once the tea is boiling, she sets a timer and rests against the counter. "Six minutes. Then we add the milk, let it warm, strain."

"I can make things happen in six minutes."

"Can you?" She smiles.

"You doubt me?"

"No. You just seem to enjoy… taking your time."

"And you enjoy the teasing."

"I do." Her cheeks flush. "But I, uh, I was going to ask about something. Uh… you're really distracting."

"Thanks."

"Right. The books. Are those yours?" She motions to the shelf in the corner. "I just… I've never met a guy who's read *The Bell Jar*. Or *The Handmaid's Tale*, actually. Which is crazy because I almost majored in English."

"You did?" I ask.

"Yeah. My sophomore year, I was considering it. Partly because my parents would hate it. Partly because I love to read and write."

"What happened?"

"I loved some of the books and I loved thinking about them, but I didn't really like doing it in the context of school. Now my economics class? I loved it. It was a whole other way to understand the world. And it was so much more concrete than literature."

"You don't seem like someone who needs concrete," I say.

"Not exactly. But I do need structure."

"A summer fling that ends when the school year starts?"

"Basically."

"So I make you come every Sunday night?"

"I wouldn't say no to that, but before I give in to my lust…"

"They're my sister's." This is it. A chance to share. To open myself to intimacy, to offer her understanding.

I can take it.

But I don't.

"She was an English major. My older sister was philosophy."

"What does she do now?"

Here it is again. *Deidre was a copywriter. Until she died.* "She got a job as a copywriter after school."

"Did you read them? The books?"

"Those two, yeah." Almost all of them.

"Which did you like better?"

"*The Handmaid's Tale*." It didn't offer insight into Deidre's head, exactly, but it did explain a few things. I'm still not sure I understand.

"Yeah, it's a perfect book."

"I liked *The Bell Jar* too," I say.

"Liked it, really? It's sorta heavy."

"You didn't?"

"I can't decide."

"It was heavy, yeah," I say. "But it helped me understand some shit."

She doesn't ask for extra information.

I don't offer it. "This was my sister's place."

"Not anymore?"

"No." How do I explain this without saying it? "She helped me buy it. Well, her and my parents." She left the place to me. And her life insurance covered the mortgage. That was a requirement of the bank—a policy to pay off the loan, in case of the worst. There was a waiting period for suicide, but she was well past it.

"Nice deal."

"I can't complain."

"Does it come with strings?"

"They say it doesn't, but…"

"You still feel like if you stopped going to Sunday night dinners, they'd stop paying your tuition? Sorry. That's me. And I'd never stop. It's just…"

"Unthinkable."

"Yeah. I have a kid sister," she says. "Julie. I can't imagine not being there for her."

"I bet you're a good sister."

"I try." She looks to the shelf. "Is that her favorite book? Your sister?"

I don't know. "She loved all of them."

"Even the graphic novels?"

"What do you have against graphic novels?"

She laughs. "I don't mean it that way. I just don't see a lot of people who read 'literature' also reading graphic novels. I never really got into them, but I tried. I read all the words too fast. I forget to see the pictures."

"Maybe you need to slow down."

"Probably."

"Borrow one," I say.

"Maybe next time."

"Next time?"

"Unless you don't want me to come over again."

"I do."

"Good. I don't know about every Sunday night, but I do… I do like this," she says. "And the chai is almost done."

Right on cue, the timer beeps.

She turns off the stovetop. "We can let it cool. Strain it after."

"After is good." I carry her to the bedroom.

Chapter Fourteen

IMOGEN

The sex is fantastic. It really is.

For the entire drive to my place, and the walk to campus, I'm completely lost in lust. I miss the first half of the lecture, use my laps to imagine all the things I want to do with Patrick, text Julie on the walk home.

Again, I don't offer any explicit details. But I let her know I'm having fun and I respect her desire to have fun, so long as she talks to me and lets me warn her off bad guys.

She rolls her eyes (I can see it, even in text) but she agrees. I almost text Patrick a *thanks* or *how about another round, tonight?* But I resist the temptation.

Yes, I want to mount him again. I want to try all sorts of things with him. But one day at a time.

It's too easy to get mixed up, to make sex into something else. And he's the kind of guy who likes to keep things easy.

He's not going to want to dive into my fucked-up head. It's not exactly great pillow talk. *Hey, did you realize I got this tattoo to celebrate the one-year anniversary of my suicide attempt? To celebrate being here, and being alive yes, but to celebrate the attempt too. Yeah, that's fucked up, isn't it?*

I mean, it was a promise to myself—

And I'm going to do a wrist tattoo next, to promise my forearms I'll never try that method (not that I could handle it. There's a reason I'm not studying medicine). But, hey, sometimes it's whatever's handy.

Yeah.

That's really hot.

I put my cell away as I step inside.

Jade is in the kitchen, fixing a grilled cheese sandwich (the extent of her cooking skills) and dancing to cheesy pop music. She loves cheesy pop music, not that she'd ever admit it.

She turns to me with a blush, caught. "Hey." She grabs her cell and turns the music off.

"You can keep it." The over-the-top cheer is grating, but I need it right now. I need to push my other thoughts away. At least, while we're both here, in the main room. Jade and I are roommates, not confidants. I don't have confidants, sure, but I'm happy to keep spilling my guts to strangers.

"I wasn't feeling it," she says.

"Uh-huh."

"You want a sandwich?"

"You don't have to bribe me. I won't tell anyone you love ABBA."

"I listen ironically," she says.

"If you say so."

"Only one? You eat a lot after you swim." She notes my wet hair and my post-swim sweats. "Where do you put it?"

"Huh?"

"You eat like a linebacker."

"Thank you…?"

"We should study you."

"What's to study? When I swim a lot, I eat a lot. It's not complicated."

She shakes her head *if only you knew*. "How many?"

"Two is fine," I say.

"I thought so." She turns back to the pan, humming ABBA as she works.

It's kind of adorable. She's usually in *I have to be tough to survive med school* mode. Or *I don't have feelings, I have fuck buddies* mode.

I like seeing the other side of her.

It feels honest.

Maybe that's what I need to do with Patrick, with Julie, with anyone, share more of myself.

How can something so hard sound so easy?

I put my stuff away and take a seat.

She switches to humming Duran Duran, finishes the sandwiches, brings lunch to the table.

"Seriously, Imogen. I know how to kill," she says.

"Aren't doctors supposed to do no harm?"

"I'm not a doctor yet."

"Good loophole." I cut my first sandwich in half diagonally. "Thanks." Perfectly toasted bread, sharp cheddar, just enough butter to keep everything rich. Yum. "Really, these are great."

She cuts her sandwich in half. "What happened with the hot tattoo artist? Are you boning?"

"We have an arrangement, yes."

"And last night, right? You usually change after you swim. Today—" She motions to my UCLA sweats. "Those don't smell fresh."

"Sorry."

She motions *don't worry about it*. "How was it?"

"Good."

"Good is not a detail."

"Did we agree to share details?"

"This experiment was my idea."

"Right."

"Yes! You could write an entire paper on it. The Hookup Experiment. Can a casual fling lead to great sex? Can great sex lead to more? Is Imogen vanilla or is there a kinky freak under the swim cap and goggles?"

She has a point-of-view. I have to give her that.

"You don't look excited," she says.

"I'm in awe of your wisdom." And, well, she's not wrong, exactly. I'm not doing a great job as a scientist. I know I'm experimenting with Patrick, but I haven't set out to answer a specific question.

What do I like? What do I want? Can casual sex ever stay casual?

All of the above.

All of the above is good.

"I am a genius, yes." She laughs again. "But one question: Will he be here all the time?"

"Sometimes, I guess," I say. "I think I'll be there more."

"'Cause you don't have to keep it down," she says. "I have great soundproof headphones."

"Uh-huh."

"And I don't mind the noise. My roomie freshman year had this sugar daddy with a college kink. He was always there. In our room. When I was there. So a few sounds from next door are no big deal."

That's disturbing. "Are you okay?"

"It was no big deal."

Really?

"Keep me posted on the experiment. It's a good one." She finishes her sandwich, stands, brings her dish to the sink, blows me a kiss. "Or if you need advice on anything. I'm experienced. Outfits, positions, anal. Anything."

"I appreciate that." As disturbing as her offer is, I might need advice, and I trust her more than I trust strangers on the internet.

It's not consistent. I share my soul with strangers on the internet.

But humans aren't rational creatures. That's really the core lesson in my courses.

People! They don't make sense!

After I finish lunch, and wash the dishes, I give in to my temptation to text Patrick.

Imogen: Are you free later this week? I could go for another round.

Patrick: My place or yours?

Imogen: Yours. If you don't mind.

Patrick: Happy to host.

Imogen: Tomorrow.

Patrick: Can you make it that long?

Maybe.

Imogen: I'll survive.

Patrick: Will you?

Imogen: Will you?

Patrick: Survive, yeah? But I won't be thriving the way I would if I heard you come.

How is he so sexy?

Patrick: You want to sleep over?

Imogen: Maybe. I have a big project. If I get enough done.

Patrick: You can say no.

Imogen: I'm saying maybe.

Patrick: I get off work at eight. Meet me at Inked Love.

Imogen: Can I park at your place? I hate looking for parking in Santa Monica.

Patrick: We can meet there.

Imogen: No. Inked Love is good.

Patrick: Are you going to get another tattoo, already?

Imogen: If I am?

Patrick: You better let me do it. I don't want anyone else touching you.

Imogen: I have another one.

Patrick: I try not to think about that.

Imogen: Really?

Patrick: Really. Wear a dress.

Imogen: Are you going to fuck me at the shop?

Patrick: Do you want me to fuck you at the shop?

Imogen: Yes.

How did I write that so fast? My cheeks flush. My chest too.

I don't know if I'll survive waiting until tomorrow.

I might die of desire right here, right now.

Patrick: Anything else?

Imogen: Is that not enough?

Patrick: I will fuck you in front of my friends if you ask. But I imagine that's a lot.

Imogen: It is.

Patrick: You like being on display, huh?

Imogen: I think so.

Patrick: I know just the thing. Trust me.

Imogen: Trust you?

Patrick: Yeah. We'll move as fast as you want. But wear a dress or a skirt. So we can keep our options open.

Imogen: What options?

Patrick: Me, getting you off, in public.

Fuck.

Chapter Fifteen

IMOGEN

For a few hours, the thrill of potential public sex races through my body. I write experiment notes in my paper journal.

Part one: Casual sex. Excellent but overwhelming.
Part two: slightly less casual sex. Excellent, still overwhelming, but less.
Part three: public sex. Am I out of my fucking mind?

Bit by bit, my lust fades. My normal concerns take over. By the time I park in Patrick's complex, I'm the same confused, heavy version of myself.

I walk along the beach, to take in the beauty of the water, to remember how it felt to sit here thinking *this is the last time I'll ever see the ocean.*

That was my first thought when I came-to. *At least I'll see the ocean again.*

Maybe I should celebrate it, the way I did with my tattoo. Yeah, this is a mess, but it's my mess. It's part of me.

But so is my blossoming desire. And why not focus on that for a few hours?

The walk goes quickly. The tattoo shop sneaks up on me. It fits perfectly into the bustling main street. Blue Bottle, only with less java and more ink.

The bell rings as I step inside. Familiar sights and sounds greet me—red and pink string lights, white walls, framed art, the buzz of a tattoo gun mingling with conversation and alt-rock women.

Luna, the teammate who recommended Patrick, is at the counter. She looks different in her street clothes. She looks incredibly cool, actually.

Her light hair is cropped short, and she's rocking a sheer top, a leather skirt, and a perfect shade of red lipstick.

She looks like the kind of girl who knows what she wants, but then I do too.

And I do. In some ways.

I know I want this. A night with Patrick. A night in my body.

Now that I'm here, the other details feel less important. He's taking over again. The intoxication of this arrangement.

"Hey!" Luna waves. "You look hot. I love that dress."

"Thanks." My cheeks flush. "It's weird seeing you in clothes."

"Isn't it?"

I meet her at the counter. "You're not playing Billie Eilish?"

"I know. It was painful. And I still think she's better than Fiona Apple—"

"Not possible," I say.

"But I figured you'd like this." She motions to the speakers. The song is familiar. Feist.

"Patrick didn't veto it?"

"Oh, has he forced you to listen to classic rock yet?" She sticks her tongue out. "And I thought my boyfriend had bad taste."

"Oh?"

"Grunge." She shakes her head. "And not the good part, the riot grrrl part. Nirvana. And Pearl Jam. Like they can be deep with a name that means semen."

Yuck.

"Oh… what are you doing this weekend?" she asks.

"Studying."

"Summer school?"

I nod.

"If you want a break—" She looks to Patrick. "I'm having a welcome home party for Oliver and Holden. And I could really use some support on the music."

"What are we talking?"

"Mostly Hole and Garbage. He's not exactly adventurous. But, hey, it sounds like grunge and my adoring audience wants it."

"So Regina Spektor is out of the question?"

"Ah, that's your type?"

"My type?"

"The confessional female artists with a unique style."

"It's not the only thing I like."

"Olivia Rodrigo?"

"She's no Fiona Apple, but I appreciate the attempt."

"Hole?" she asks.

"Of course."

"Michelle Branch?" she asks.

"You're going way back."

"Oh yeah. That's where the good stuff is, when pop-rock was still trying to assert itself."

"Are there any pop-rock artists getting radio play?"

"Only on the 'rock' stations!" She shakes her head *ridiculous*. "I wish you controlled our music. I have to be 'fair' and 'take requests.' But it's just… not good. Chase and Forest love pop-punk from the early two thousands. Dare loves The Beach Boys for some reason. And Tricky only wants the most boring, basic classic rock."

Tricky. His friends call him Tricky. That's adorable. "That bad?"

"Yeah, it's like listening to K-Earth all day."

"So do you play *Happy Together*?"

"I should," she says. "It would be better than the Rolling Stones and The Eagles. I got the point of those songs ten years ago."

"Really? When you were, what, nine?"

"Ten," she says. "Maybe you can teach him some taste. He has expanded a bit in the last year. But we do keep it pretty bland here. Nothing that will scare a client."

"Do you have something in mind?"

"Maybe." She looks to Patrick as he stands. "At the very least, you could get him to request Celebrity Skin. Or some songs from the nineties and eighties that are actually good."

"You talking about me?" Patrick moves closer.

"The world doesn't revolve around you," Luna says.

"Maybe we should ask a physicist to double-check that."

She blows him a kiss. "I probably shouldn't flirt in front of you, huh? Bad habit. It drives my boyfriend crazy. He gets all protective and…"

"Would that work with Patrick?" I ask.

"Is that what you like?" She bites her lip. "Sorry. I forget normal manners with these guys. They're like teenage girls. No, they're way worse than teenage girls."

"It's okay." It might be something in the water. Or the air. I already feel freer, less in my head. Or maybe that's Patrick's presence. "I'm not too into green guys."

"I wouldn't think. Not his MO. Not like this anyway. I don't know the rest. I, uh, I'll stop before I'm in too deep."

"I think you're past that point," I say.

She laughs. "Well, if I'm gonna get wet, I might as well—"

"Get laid?" Patrick meets us at the counter.

"You could hear that, huh?" she asks.

"You asking about my sex life, yeah. I heard that," he says.

"No. I'm asking Imogen. She's interesting. You're…"

"We are exclusive," he says.

"But I'm sure she's been with people before you. Unless—" she turns to me—"It's totally cool if you haven't. I don't anti-slut shame."

"I have," I say.

"See." Luna turns back to me. "Who was the best? You know, leaving Patrick out."

"That doesn't seem fair," Patrick says.

"I specifically don't want to hear about you," Luna says.

"I don't have any great stories. Sorry," I say.

"Really? Nothing juicy. Even a little? My boyfriend is still out of town," she says.

"You are extra thirsty," Patrick says.

She flips him off.

"Well, my ex, my only serious ex… we had some pretty emotional sex before he went abroad. I knew it was the last time and I thought he did too. But he wanted to try long-distance and I didn't," I say.

"Emotional how? Was it intense? That connection you feel in your soul?" Luna asks.

No. I was relieved. "It was kind of like… I could be more selfish, knowing it was the end. I could take only what I wanted."

"I love a greedy woman," Patrick says.

Luna holds out her hand *stop*. "Tricky, it's not about you. I know that's a hard concept."

He scratches his head, playing dumb.

"It's okay. I'm teasing him 'cause I know how much he likes you." She shoots him a knowing look.

He returns one that says *don't overstep*. "If you're done attempting to extract free audio porn from my girl."

"No. I'm not done," Luna says. "I have way more questions."

"You're done." Patrick wraps his arms around me and pulls me into a tight hug. "Hey."

"Hey."

"You look good." He presses his lips to mine. "Hot as fuck."

"You too," I say.

"Give me five to finish. And let me know if Luna keeps asking intrusive questions. I'll have the other guys cut her off." He kisses me again. Then he pulls back and takes his customer through checkout and after care speech and walks him to the door.

"The other guys?" I ask.

"There might be a lot of free audio porn," she says.

"Free is free."

She nods *right*. "I told Tricky you're smart and cute and way too good for him, so he should hold on to it, but he's not that bright."

"We're just having fun," I say.

"Fun is good. As long as you come Saturday. Please. Otherwise, I'll have to hear Lithium twenty-five times."

"That is hard," I say.

"And it will be really low-key. Mostly people from the shop. Barely any alcohol. The guys here do talk about sex, a lot, but they mostly gossip and pontificate on art. Including Kurt Cobain's brilliance." She sticks out her tongue.

I don't go to parties, normally, but this doesn't sound too bad. "I'll see what I can do."

Patrick returns to the desk, finished. "Are you messing with her?"

"Inviting her to a party," she says.

"Generous," he says.

"No," she says. "I already want Imogen to myself too. She's way more interesting than you are."

"You didn't invite me to this party," he says.

"Hmm. Must be an oversight. Don't worry. Your girl has a plus-one," she says.

"You wanna go?" Patrick asks.

"Please," I say.

"To the party?" he asks.

"If we can have sex first," I whisper.

"No. After," he whispers back. "Now. Do you want to get dinner? Or do you want to go back to my place?"

"Is that even a question?"

Chapter Sixteen

PATRICK

Is that even a question?

Imogen's voice echoes through my head as we walk down Main Street. I barely notice the hip restaurants, the string lights, the mix of tourists and locals.

I want her so badly I can't think. It's ridiculous.

She stops in front of a French restaurant and studies the yellow glow of the lights. "I have no idea what kind of food you like."

"You know I like chai," I say.

"Who wouldn't like my chai?" Her lips curl into a small smile. It lights up her gorgeous face. It makes my heart thud against my chest and my stomach do flip-flops.

She's beautiful. She really is.

"Are you okay?" She tilts her head to one side. "Don't tell me you're still drained?"

"Huh?" I ask.

"From Sunday," she says.

"Sore, but not drained," I say.

"Yeah." Her smile widens. "Where?"

"Are you gonna rub it better?" It's easy, keeping this to sex. It's what I do. I hide from heaviness.

"Here? On the street?" Desire flares in her eyes.

"Behind the restaurant." I nod to the French bistro.

"In Santa Monica? We'll get arrested," she says.

"Once we cross the line into Venice," I say.

She laughs. "That will do it."

"Against the matcha shop on Abbot-Kinney."

"Screw *I love you so matcha* when you have *I need to screw you so matcha*," she says.

"Is that on your Instagram?"

"It should be."

"You have an Instagram?" I ask.

"Only the one I made to message you."

"It was empty."

"I know."

"We could fill it," I say. "With pictures of you."

"I'll get kicked off."

"They can be PG-13."

"I'll think about it." She shifts into casual conversation. "Do you like matcha?" She looks to my hand, but she doesn't take it. Instead, she resumes walking and nods for me to follow.

I do. "When it's sweet enough."

"You have a sweet tooth?"

"I can't take much bitter."

"But you drink coffee," she says.

"With cream and sugar," I say.

"And the Bud Light?"

"You didn't even see it," I say.

"You didn't deny it," she says.

"It's not as bad as it sounds."

"Maybe." She laughs. "I don't drink beer. I have no idea what's good or bad."

"It's not the worst, but it's not great either."

"Do you like beer?"

"Not anymore." It reminds me of the guy I used to be. It reminds me of the nights I spent trying to drink myself into oblivion. That takes a lot of beer. Way too much beer. "What do you drink?"

"Gin and tonic," she says. "But only one or two."

"That's smart. You stay clear-headed."

"Yeah. And… well, you know how some people are happy drunks and some people are mean drunks?" she asks.

"And some people are horny drunks?"

A laugh spills from her lips. "Is that you?"

"Are you going to ply me with alcohol to find out?"

"No. I couldn't bring myself to buy light beer. Or… what do you drink now?"

I don't, mostly. "Whatever sounds good."

"You're very agreeable."

"That's a nice way to say I don't have taste."

She laughs. "Well, you're helping me find what I like. Maybe I can help you find what you like too."

"I've never had a proper gin and tonic."

"No."

"Is it that surprising?"

"It's such an iconic drink," she says. "But it's not really at college parties."

"You go to many?"

"Some," she says. "Especially my freshman year." She stops at the light. The last one before the big stretch of nothing before Abbot-Kinney. "I didn't feel that connection everyone else seemed to feel."

"They weren't playing your music?"

"You heard me and Luna?"

"Enough," I say.

"I didn't have the heart to tell her I kinda like The Beach Boys."

"You are from surf city."

"That's Huntington Beach."

"Exactly," I say.

"Damn. That was good." She laughs. "It's more my dad. He

got into American culture for a while. All those artists from the sixties. Action movies. Baseball. Only the baseball stuck, but I still have these happy memories of my parents dancing to *I Get Around*. They, uh, they're not as happy now."

"I'm sorry."

"We, uh, we should go to the party," she says. "For an hour or so."

"Make out on in the backyard?"

"I'm okay with that," she says. "I have to admit something."

"Yeah?"

"I thought about you last night." She blushes. "When I touched myself."

"I tried not to—"

"Think of me?"

"Fuck myself. I like to wait."

"How long?"

"As long as I can."

"Days?"

I nod. "But I didn't make. I was too excited. Had to take the edge off this morning."

"The edge—Oh. Do guys really do that?"

"Are you kidding? In high school? I was a minute-man."

"You admit that?"

"Why not? It's true. I learned. I had a few relationships. I started to enjoy waiting. It was a challenge, to see how long I could go, if I could make it."

"So it is a kink?"

"I don't know. Maybe. Probably."

"I did say I'd try it."

"Yeah, but not tonight."

"No, not tonight," she says.

"Does that mean you're ready?"

"To try doing this? In public?"

I nod.

She passes the matcha shop, a trendy boutique, a hip vegetarian restaurant. "Have you ever done this? Had sex in public?"

"In a car," I say. "In another room at a party. At a bar. Not sex, sex, but someone came. I was drunk though… I don't know if I'd have the nerve sober."

"You're the scared one?"

"You're the brave one," I say. "You're the one who invited me to her place."

"I wasn't brave. I was horny."

"My ego."

"You satisfied."

"That's better." I pull her closer. "We can start with something easy. Kiss in public. Touch under the clothes."

"Now?"

I stop in front of the bar I picked for this. "If you're ready."

She takes my hand and leads me inside.

Chapter Seventeen

IMOGEN

I 'm officially crazy.

No, I've been officially crazy for a while now. I'm officially unofficially crazy.

I'm in a bar in the hippest part of the Westside, ready to reveal myself to Patrick.

Sure, I'm not ready to reveal my feelings? But my boobs?

I can show those off in front of strangers.

Thankfully, the place isn't too crowded. There are a dozen patrons, spread over the long bar, the pool table, the booths along the wall.

There—the corner booth. It's not totally private, but I can only see a portion of it from the entrance.

"Do you want a drink?" Patrick asks. "It doesn't have to be alcoholic."

I should resist the chemical temptation, but I need the liquid courage. "Gin and tonic."

"You sure?" he asks.

My stomach flutters. My sex pangs. My want is tinged with affection. He's concerned with my well-being.

He cares about me.

I want him to care about me.

It's different than it was with Zack. It feels real. Honest.

Because I'm different than I was with Zack. I'm giving him a chance.

And, so far, he's acing every opportunity.

My love of chai. My two-drink maximum. My inability to spend the night impromptu because I need my prescriptions.

Seriously, how are TV and film characters constantly having casual one-night stands? Do they tote their drugs in their bags along with fresh pairs of underwear?

"Just one." I motion to the booth. "Can you claim it? I need to, um… remove some items in the bathroom."

This dress is perfect. It helps that it's the nicest thing I own. Well, the nicest comfortable dress I own. Short, black, low cut, breathable.

Sexy yet practical.

And somehow perfect for this—

If I push the dress aside, I reveal my bra. If I pull it up my hips, I reveal my panties.

But I'm not going to meet him at the booth with either of those.

I find the women's bathroom in the back, lock myself in a stall, do away with my bra and panties.

While I'm here—

I pull out my cell and angle the picture just right, so I'm not totally exposed.

Snap.

I send the picture to Patrick before I lose my nerve.

He answers immediately.

Patrick: You're going to make me drop these drinks.

Imogen: Bud Light on the floor?

Patrick: Two gin and tonics.

That's kind of sweet, him ordering my drink. Or maybe it's dirty. I'm not sure anymore. I'm already losing touch with conscious thought.

He does puts me in touch with my body like this too.

That's good to know.

Patrick: Show me.

Imogen: From here?

Patrick: If you trust me with it.

I do, actually. I probably shouldn't, but I do.

I hang my purse on the hook behind me, then I angle the phone a little lower, so it's catching my lips, my jaw, my neck, my chest.

My exposed breasts.

Snap.

Again, I send before I lose my nerve.

Again, he replies right away.

Patrick: Fuck. I might come in my pants at this rate.

Imogen: That's no fun.

Patrick: I'll make it up to you.

Imogen: You ready?

Patrick: Are you?

I'm not sure.

Patrick: We can do this another way. From here.

Imogen: In the bathroom?

Patrick: At my place, separated by the wall.

Imogen: No. I want to do it here.

Patrick: Meet me at the booth.

I right my dress, gather my purse, check my reflection in the mirror. It's not too obvious I'm not wearing a bra. And, hey, no visible panty lines. That's a benefit of going commando.

The breeze between my legs makes me feel exposed in the best possible way.

This is already a five-alarm fire. How am I going to actually bare my skin in public without dying of desire?

Maybe this is what people mean by friends with benefits. We have a regular relationship. I trust him.

I apply another coat of wine-red lipstick and I step into the bar.

The room feels quieter. I can make out snippets of conversation, smashes of pool balls, the indie rock song flowing from the speakers.

And there, Patrick, sitting in the booth.

He stands and holds out his hand.

I meet him in front of the wood table.

He wraps his arm around me. "You're driving me out of my mind."

I don't know what to say, so I lean into his touch.

He slips his hand over my hip, my ass, all the way to the hem of my dress.

Without underwear, his hands are so, so close.

"Do you want the inside or the outside?" he asks.

"Inside seems safer," I say.

"Less revealing, yeah."

And less sexy, too. But safer is good. At least this first time. "Inside."

"After you." He makes space for me.

I slide into the booth.

He slides in after me.

He's close, his jean-clad leg against my bare thigh, his pine soap in my nostrils. And that smell that's him mixing with the gin and tonic and the ocean breeze and whatever cleanser the bar uses.

"Fever Tree," he says. "I asked."

"That's the good stuff." This must be good gin too. Who would waste premium tonic water on ten-dollar Trader Joe's gin?

He looks to my glass. "You don't have to drink."

"I know." I raise my gin and tonic. "But thanks for reminding me."

"Any time."

We toast. I take a long sip. Mmm. The perfect mix of bitter quinine, botanical gin, tart lime.

And it's cooling. Not cooling enough. But what could be at this point?

"How do you like it?" I take another sip.

"It doesn't taste like Pine-Sol."

"Cheap gin can."

"That was my first experience, yeah. My only experience, really."

"Is gin too British?" I ask.

"No. Maybe. I've never asked my parents."

"Are they both Irish?"

"I don't want to talk about my parents."

Right. "I don't want to talk about your parents."

He motions to the drink. "It's sweet. Unique. Subtle. Sure of itself. Perfect for you."

"That's how you see me?"

"Absolutely."

I've never really thought of myself as a cocktail. And I should probably question the whole objectifying nature of it, but I love the idea of Patrick drinking every drop of me too.

"Put down your drink." His voice shifts to another tone. A deeper one. More commanding.

I do.

"Show me."

"Already?"

"Yes."

I glance around the room. No one is watching. And his body is blocking me, for the most part.

I bring my hand to the neckline of my dress. Slowly, I pull the fabric aside, revealing my breast.

His eyes glue to my skin. "Perfect."

"Really? Not too small?"

"We talked about this."

"I know. It's just… the women who are presented as sexy are always—"

"Blondes with fake tits?"

"Yeah," I say.

"It's not the size." He cups my breast with his palm. Rolls his thumb over my nipple.

A groan falls from my lips.

"It's that. The way you react to me." He does it again, only softer, so softly I can barely feel it.

"Patrick—"

"Yeah, baby?" He does it again. Again.

"Please."

"Please…"

"I need to touch you."

"Is that part of it?" He runs his fingers over the over side of my dress, tracing the neckline up and down. "Do you want to touch me in public?"

"Yes."

"Fuck me in public?"

"One day."

"Now?"

"This."

"This," he agrees.

Patrick traces the neckline of my dress again and again. Up and down. Up and down. Up and down.

The song shifts to something else, a mumbly indie rock jam. It's not sexy, not really, but in the circumstance, it feels sultry. It feels right.

He scoots a little closer.

He traces the line again.

Then he pushes both sides of my dress open. He covers one breast with his hand. He curls the other around my neck and he leans into a slow, deep kiss.

It starts softly. His lips on mine. The taste of gin and sugar and quinine.

My lips part. His tongue slips into my mouth and dances with mine.

He leads.

I follow.

I release a little more control. Because I trust him with my body. I trust him to lead. Sure, it's more sexual than anything, but that's something.

That's a lot.

He toys with my nipple as he kisses me.

I kiss him back; I melt into his body; I give in to the desire buzzing through my body.

I stop fighting, pushing, trying.

I feel every raw drop of perfect, agonizing need.

He teases me again and again, then he moves to my other breast and toys with me there. All the time, his lips stay locked to mine. He kisses me harder and deeper, claiming more of me, promising more of him.

It feels like we go forever. For hours.

Finally, he comes up for air. He pulls back, but he leaves my dress where it is, leaves me exposed to him in the crowded bar.

He takes a long sip of his drink.

I do the same with mine.

He rakes his eyes over my body, studying every exposed inch. "You like this?"

"Yes."

"Being on display?"

"Yes."

"Good. I like to watch."

How can the simple words make my sex clench? Did my new meds turn me into a freak? Or am I finally in touch with the sexual side of myself?

I don't even care.

I only care about finding more satisfaction.

"I'm going to watch," he says. "Later."

"Later?"

He nods. "But now—" He curls his hand around my leg, just above my knee.

He's cold from the glass, but that only makes me hotter.

"Now…" He traces a line up my leg. "Now you're going to come on my hand."

I nod.

He pulls me into another slow, deep kiss.

I part my legs to make way for his hand.

I part my lips to make way for his tongue.

He kisses me hard. I let him lead, but I kiss back, pouring every bit of need into the gesture.

His thumb finds my clit.

His other hand goes to my chest.

He toys with my nipple as he rubs me with perfect, slow strokes.

Again and again.

Then a little faster.

A little harder.

Exactly what I need.

I slip my hand under his shirt. I dig my fingers into his skin. Then my nails. Until my gesture is hard enough, he groans against my lips.

He keeps the same perfect rhythm.

Every stroke pushes me closer to the edge. I'm not sure how I take more. I'm already so keyed up, so ready, so consumed by need.

The tension winds tighter and tighter.

So tight I'm sure I'm going to break.

But I don't.

I unfurl.

Pleasure spills through my body as I come. My sex pulses. My toes curl. My nails dig into his skin.

Bliss fills every cell.

The world is a big, beautiful place of want and need and the best kind of satisfaction.

He kisses me, rubbing me through my orgasm.

When he finally pulls back, he rights my clothes and brings his thumb to his lips.

He sucks the taste of me from his digit.

It's the hottest thing I've ever seen.

I barely manage to pick up my drink, to bring the glass to my lips. "Now?"

"Now, you wait until I'm ready to take you home and have my way with you."

Chapter Eighteen

IMOGEN

Patrick nurses his drink until the last ice cube melts. Finally, he stands, helps me out of the booth, leads me to the street.

The short walk to his apartment feels like a million miles.

I don't wait.

The second he closes the door, I push him against the wall.

He responds quickly, pulling a condom from his pocket, pushing my dress off my shoulders, peeling my skirt up my waist.

I undo the button of his jeans and rub him over his boxers.

"Fuck." He breathes into my air. "You're going to make me come."

"Fuck me." I can feel him through the fabric, hard and thick and ready for me.

I need that.

I really, really need that.

"Now." I push his jeans off his waist.

Then the boxers.

He nods, rips the foil packet with his teeth, rolls the condom over his cock.

Then he switches our positions, pins me to the door, lifts my hips.

He drives into me with one hard, deep thrust.

It's intense. If I wasn't so keyed up, it would be too much. But I am and it's not and I feel wild in the best possible way.

I arch into him.

He digs his nails into my hip, brings his lips to my neck. He sucks on my tender skin as he drives into me.

Again and again.

With perfect, slow, steady strokes.

Again, I wind quickly. I'm already wracked with desire. More desire than I thought was possible.

And I have more.

He drives into me again.

I slip my hand between my legs, rub myself as he drives into me.

Again.

Again.

The perfect mix of penetration and external stimulation.

The perfect mix of him and me.

Again.

Again.

Then he's there, thrusting through his orgasm, raking his teeth against my skin, digging his nails into my hip.

His pulsing pulls me toward the edge.

Then I fall over it.

It's harder, more intense, an agonizing mix of pleasure and pressure.

I come with intense pulses. Bliss spills through me again, consuming every other thought, consuming every ugly thing in the world.

I see stars.

Actual stars.

When I'm finished, I collapse.

He catches me, carries me to the couch, helps me out of my dress.

I sink into the cushions.

He rights his boxers. Then he sits and removes my boots and socks, one foot at a time.

"Have I told you how much I love these?" He nods to the boots sitting next to the couch.

"That particular pair?"

"You in combat boots."

"You've only seen me in them twice."

"I pictured you in only the boots after our appointment."

"Really?"

He nods. "I like you in everything, but these… with that dress."

"The one you threw on your floor?"

He laughs, picks up the dress, drapes it over the couch. "It's sexy as hell. But, more, it's you."

"You barely know me."

"I know enough."

There isn't a single objection in my brain. Yes, he mostly knows this side of me. But he knows me better than anyone here.

And all I want to do is get to know him better, let him know me more. It's not love, but it's more than lust.

"Then why are you keeping me naked?" I ask.

"That's sexy too."

I laugh. "Reasonable."

"I'm smart sometimes," he says.

"You have moments."

"You want to wear the dress?"

I have spare clothes, pajamas, but I want to wear his again. "Do you have a shirt?"

"Of course. One minute." He leans in and presses his lips to mine. "Don't move."

"Oh, I wasn't going to move."

He stands. "I wore you out."

"Mm-hmm."

He beams with pride, and he races up the stairs. I'm not sure how he has the energy, but he does.

The couch is so soft and comfortable and inviting.

He returns with a t-shirt, boxers, and a smile. "You're cute when you're shy."

"Cute?"

"Sexy."

My cheeks flush. "It's the dirty talk. It always makes me blush." It's a little early to use the word always, but, hey, this is the start of a pattern.

"And I have to think about baseball so I don't come too fast."

"That's a real thing?"

"Baseball?" he asks.

"Guys thinking about it so they… last longer."

"Yeah, baseball is boring," he says.

"But the bats are so phallic."

He laughs. "Not in a sexy way."

"The men with their hands around the bats, swinging? And the tight pants. Have you seen Mike Trout's ass?"

"You're an Angels fan?"

"I'm from Orange County."

"You want to go to a game?" he asks.

"Maybe. I used to go with my dad. He tried to get us into softball. Me and Julie. She took to it like, well, like I took to swimming."

"Like a fish to water?"

"Right. A metaphor. Uh, simile. Analogy? I think you emptied my brain. I forgot."

He smiles. "How old is she?"

"Seventeen. A senior next year. She's varsity. And she's getting scouted by all sorts of schools."

"A softball scholarship?"

I nod. "We have money, but not Ivy League tuition money. My parents got really lucky with their business. They didn't do the usual 'authentic restaurant' thing. Well, they kinda did, but they packaged it more like a Vietnamese Blue Bottle. Expensive iced coffee and pastries for hipsters."

"That's smart."

"Yeah. They were really smart. And lucky too. They work hard, but there's always luck."

"I get it."

"They expanded all over Orange County. They have an actual chain."

"A pastry and coffee chain?"

"Yeah," I say.

"But you drink tea?"

"I like tea."

"And you like that they don't like it?" He sits on the couch and presses his finger to my chest. "You're a rebel."

The spot between my breasts, over my heart.

I'm naked on his couch and he's touching my chest and, somehow, it's all affection.

I do like him.

I do like this.

It's not just an appreciation of his skills or a desire to screw him again. It's more.

"It may have occurred to me," I say.

He smiles. "And cake? Do you like that?"

"It's sugar and flour. No nuance."

"Mm-hmm. That's it. All of it." He offers a plain white t-shirt.

"Because it's see-through?"

"Didn't consider that." He holds up his crossed fingers.

I sit up and shift into the t-shirt. Then the pair of boxers. They're a little big on me, but they're comfortable that way.

"That is why you got into tea?"

"Everyone thinks it's because I'm Asian. Even in Orange County, where people should know better." I shake my head. "But my parents rarely make tea. They're always pushing coffee. So I… it was that at first, but I really do love it."

"The subtlety?"

"Yeah."

"I have bad news."

"Oh?"

"I'm not a subtle chef."

"Really? I'm shocked."

"Don't bring the Bud Light into this."

"You said it."

He laughs and presses his lips to mine. "You thought it."

"No."

"Is that our first lie?"

"Really." I stand and stretch my arms over my head. "I'm not thinking anything."

"Forgot your own name?"

"And yours. Who are you, anyway?"

"Mister O."

"Oh my god." A laugh spills from my lips. "Are you always this cheesy?"

"Basically." He stands and pulls me into a hug. "Come on. You need to save yourself from my cooking skills."

"I eat grilled cheese sandwiches for lunch. I'm a normal college student," I say. "Sorta."

"You don't cook?"

"Sometimes," I say. "Not often."

"Do you want to?"

"Now?" I move into his kitchen. It's nice. Modern. This entire place is nice. But then he didn't answer my question last time. How does he afford it?

I guess that's a little personal. Money is more taboo than anything in the US.

"No. I want to take a nap then go for round three," I say.

"Greedy."

"Always."

He smiles. "I don't have bread—"

"Of course you don't."

He raises a brow.

"You're very…" I motion to his biceps. His chiseled torso. "Ripped."

"Thank you." He laughs again. "That's not why."

"Sure it isn't."

"I don't eat it fast enough."

"Uh-huh."

"I have my own cheese delivery system," he says.

"Oh?"

"Quesadillas."

"The Californian version of grilled cheese."

"I think that's avocado toast."

"Where's the cheese?"

"Exactly." He puts a pan on the stove, turns on a burner, gathers ingredients. "I use corn tortillas."

"Authentic."

"Tasty."

True.

"Salsa roja or verde?"

"Verde."

"Excellent choice." He places four tortillas on the pan. "Now, if you'll prepare for dinner." He motions to the table. "Unless this is too much cheese."

"You're in luck. I ate real food for lunch."

"Oh?"

"A salad. With avocado."

"And I'm the California boy?" he asks.

"You have freckles."

"You're a competitive swimmer."

"You live in a loft," I say.

"You go to UCLA."

Hmm. What else do I have? "You have Cold Brew in your fridge."

"You drive a Prius."

Damn.

"And you love the beach."

"Everyone loves the beach."

"Talk to Oliver," he says. "See what response the beach gets."

"Which one is Oliver?"

"You haven't met."

"Oh, Luna's boyfriend? I'm sure he's happy enough to watch her run around in a bikini."

"He is a man."

"See. He likes it in his way," I say.

"That doesn't count."

"So you don't want to watch me run around in a bikini?"

"Oh, I do, but I don't concede the point."

"Let's call it a tie," I say.

"I think we both know the truth."

"You wear Vans," I say.

"And you don't?"

"Vans were founded in Anaheim."

"Exactly."

Damn. He's good. "Okay. You win. I'm the true Californian."

"Don't worry. I have avocados in the fridge." He shoots me a knowing look.

"I…" I can't lie. "I love avocados."

"I know." He smiles.

I melt.

———

WE TALK ABOUT NOTHING OVER DINNER. WE WATCH AN OLD movie. We fuck on the couch, shower, dress.

I fall asleep in his bed.

And I sleep well. Easy.

In the morning, I feel rested and refreshed and alive.

I want more. I want everything. But I have school and I'm grateful for the distraction too. I don't trust myself to stay here and not fall for him.

Still. I don't want to wait until next weekend. I want something soon.

So I leave a note.

Have to run to class. Then read a bunch. I saw the details on the party from Luna. Let's stop by for an hour. Meet you there? Saturday at seven? Then back here? Or maybe on the balcony.

XO,

Imogen.

P.S. TEXT ME TONIGHT AND I'LL HAVE A PICTURE FOR YOU. BUT only if you say please.

Chapter Nineteen

PATRICK

Before Deidre died, I took one thing seriously: work. (Not that I showed it).

I craved one thing: mastery of my work.

Okay, yes, I craved the usual things. Candy and freedom and beautiful women. But I never craved a specific, beautiful woman. And once I was old enough to flirt, well, I didn't have any trouble attracting women.

Add the tattoos and the freckles and the ability to cop my grandmas' accent (a lot of women have a thing for Irish guys, for some reason), and, well… I always knew I could find someone if I was so inclined.

Even when I had girlfriends, monogamous relationships, I knew those women were interested in me. I knew we'd get together and enjoy each other soon enough. I didn't crave them. Or savor their touch. Or feel an intense need to text them right away, to demand pictures.

With Imogen?

I need to respond to her offer, to tease her, to test her, to adore her.

All morning, my cell burns a hole in my pocket. I make it all the way to work, and through set up, before I give in to my desire to reach her.

Patrick: Not tonight. Today. Text me when you're ready.

She replies right away.

Imogen: I don't see the word please.

Patrick: Are you free?

Imogen: Leaving class.

Patrick: Going to swim laps?

Imogen: Maybe. Maybe not.

Patrick: A picture of you in your practice suit says yes.

Imogen: What if I'm not going? What do I get?

Patrick: A picture of me in your practice suit.

Imogen: You'll stretch it out.

Patrick: Brutal.

Imogen: Do you have any idea how quickly I run through these?

Patrick: Are you always this pragmatic?

Imogen: Yes.

There's another side to her too. The girl who wonders about my dog-eared copy of *The Bell Jar*.

But, hey, I'm not going there.

This isn't a time for ugly things.

This is the most beautiful thing in the world.

Patrick: How about a picture of me in my swimsuit?

Imogen: Deal.

Patrick: Deal.

She sends a handshake emoji.

I reply with one.

The shop's bell dings. My client. There isn't time to flirt, but I don't put my phone away.

Imogen: I am on my way to swim laps. But if I ask for the picture later, I expect it.

Patrick: I don't have a pic in a swimsuit.

Imogen: You could always send less.

Patrick: Really?

134

Imogen: If I ask. I'll be home in an hour and a half, give or take. Free in two. Jade might be home, but…

Patrick: Text me when it happens. I'll reply when I can. At work.

Imogen: Tease.

Patrick: Always.

I put my cell away; I greet my client; I fall into the rhythm of work.

A badass hammerhead shark.

A small Latin quote.

A musical note behind a woman's ear.

I don't listen to my clients' stories the way I usually do. I talk to them, yeah. I set them at ease, distract them as well as I can, but I don't *hear* them.

My thoughts are too tuned to Imogen.

What does she think about while she swims? What she wants to do to me? What inspired her to read *The Bell Jar*?

I want to know everything.

All of it.

Finally, I find a twenty-minute break. I stand, stretch, text Imogen.

Patrick: Please.

Imogen: Ten minutes. And I need the magic word.

Patrick: Pretty please.

Imogen: Guess again.

Patrick: Avocado?

Imogen: Bingo.

A laugh spills from my lips.

Luna taps her fingers against the counter. Loudly. She clears her throat even more loudly.

"Yes?" I slide my cell into my pocket. Check the time on the wall clock. Ten minutes. I don't need lunch on my break. I need this. I can go hours without food if I have this kind of nourishment.

"Is that Imogen?"

"Why do you ask?"

"She was here last week."

"And?"

Luna looks around the empty shop and slides onto the counter. She pushes to the front. Dangles her long legs off the edge.

She looks cool and effortless in her crop top, shorts, and high-top sneakers, but we both know she's buzzing over her boyfriend's imminent arrival.

"You didn't look very casual," she says.

"So?"

"Tricky, don't play dumb. I'm a woman who's gone two weeks without."

"Two weeks is nothing."

"Maybe if you're not getting something good," she says.

"And when you were single?" I ask.

"When you're single, the world is your oyster. There's possibility at every corner."

"A whole world of dick to unlock?" I offer.

"You tease, but yes. I don't want to see them all, but I know I can, anytime I want."

I can't argue. She's a knockout. I'm sure she can find a dozen willing guys via bar, party, or hookup app. And I understand her feeling too. When I was single and wanting, I felt a different hunger. A general sense I knew I could sate with effort.

Right now, knowing I have to wait another nine minutes to tease Imogen?

It's torture.

"You two haven't had phone sex?" I ask.

"That only made it worse."

Another laugh spills from my lips.

"See. That's what I mean. You laugh because you love me and love my pain."

"Sure."

"And you laughed the same way just now. So… is that her?"

"Yes," I say.

"It's serious?"

"No," I say. "Not for her."

"But for you?"

"No comment."

"And your online friend…"

"We're not friends," I say. "I read her journal. That's it. Do you tell Oliver about your fantasies of Michael B. Jordan?"

"That's not the same."

"Isn't it?"

"You're emotionally attached."

"I don't even know her name."

"Still. Don't you think Imogen should know you have feelings for another woman?"

I don't have feelings for her. But that's bullshit. I do. "No. It's the same thing."

"That's just sex."

"Yeah, and your boyfriend is a man. He'd want to know."

She shakes her head *no way*.

I nod *yes way*. Though I don't have the confidence I normally do. I don't like the idea of Imogen reading some guy's online journal, falling in love with him through his words. I hate it. "We're not serious. It doesn't matter. But I appreciate you looking out for her."

She shoots me an incredulous look. "You do like her?"

"Don't spread the news," I say. "She's been clear about what she wants."

"Your dick and only your dick?"

"Basically."

"And you're really okay with that?"

"With a fling with a gorgeous woman? Yeah."

She looks at me like she doesn't believe me, but she doesn't call me on it.

My cell buzzes in my hand.

"I have to take this," I say.

"Casual, huh?"

"Phone sex date."

She blushes. "Here?"

"Where else?"

"I'm not listening to you come."

"Then turn up the music."

Chapter Twenty

PATRICK

A Billie Eilish song flows through the bathroom door. It's not my idea of sensual, but it feels right all the same. Besides, I'm not here for me.

I'm here for her.

Imogen: It's not as sexy as it sounds.

She attaches a picture of her, dripping wet, in her practice suit. A shot by a friend, teammate, coach. I don't know, but I adore it, instantly.

Not because it bares skin, though it does (the swimsuit is cut way up her thigh, showing off her long legs).

Because it's an insight into her life.

I do like her. A lot. And I don't care what that means tomorrow.

I need to do this now.

It's different than with other women. I don't want to stay on the sidelines, unwilling to lose myself in the absurd experience of talking someone off, participating without really participating.

I don't want a moment of detachment or inhibition.

I want to feel every second of this.

Patrick: Agree to disagree.

Imogen: You think I look sexy in my practice suit? Really?

Patrick: I prefer you out of the suit, but yeah. You look hot.

Imogen: With the swim cap?

Patrick: You're not wearing it.

Imogen: I'll show you my true form, but it might be a boner-killer.

Patrick: Not possible.

Imogen: Is that a dare?

Patrick: If you want to see it that way.

She sends another photo.

A selfie in her blue swim cap and goggles, from the top of her head to the bottom of her chest.

It's not sexy in a traditional sense, but the insight into her life?

Patrick: Hot as fuck.

Imogen: Really?

Patrick: I guess I have a fetish.

Imogen: We don't need a lot of roleplay skill for that one.

Patrick: You want to roleplay?

Imogen: Maybe. I haven't thought about it.

Patrick: Do you have a scenario in mind?

Imogen: Do you?

Patrick: A few. But I want this, now. Me and you.

Imogen: Me too.

Patrick: Is that from today?

Imogen: It is.

Patrick: How often do you swim?

Imogen: During the season, five days a week. Sometimes six. In the off season, I swim after class every day. Well, every day I have class.

Patrick: How many days is that?

Imogen: Three, right now. I'm not sure what I'll do in the fall. I won't have as much time. I won't have as many chances to hit the water.

Patrick: But you need it?

Imogen: I do.

Patrick: What do you love about it?

Imogen: I can't put it into words. It just feels right. It feels like home.

Patrick: I know what you mean.

Imogen: So many of my teammates don't go to the pool or the beach. A lot of people on my high school team went to college, stopped swimming entirely. I can't imagine that. I know life gets in the way, but when I have to go a few weeks without a pool or a large body of water... I don't feel like me. Do you have anything like that?

Patrick: Sketching.

Imogen: You can do that anywhere.

Patrick: Yeah, but to really get into it, fall into the zone? That's different.

Imogen: And you have to make the mental effort. You have to let your guard down and be honest with yourself.

Exactly.

How does she know that?

Imogen: It's the same when I write. I try to journal every day, to keep up with my thoughts.

Patrick: You seem to have a lot.

Imogen: I do.

Patrick: I like that about you.

Imogen: Thanks.

Patrick: Sorry. You didn't text asking for conversation.

Imogen: As long as you don't leave me waiting.

Patrick: Are you alone?

Imogen: In my room.

Patrick: Show me.

She sends a picture of her legs stretched over the sheets. It feels different than last time. Deeper. More intimate.

Patrick: What are you wearing?

Imogen: Uh-uh. Your turn.

Patrick: I'm at work.

Imogen: Can someone see?

Patrick: Do you want someone to be able to see?

Imogen: Yes. But it's scary.

Patrick: I'm somewhere private. I can change that.

Imogen: Where?

Patrick: Your turn.

She sends a picture of her pajamas—a UCLA tank and the matching blue shorts—on the ground.

Patrick: What's left?

Imogen: I lack lingerie.

Patrick: I don't need fancy lingerie.

Imogen: Maybe I do.

Patrick: I can buy you something.

Imogen: That's sort of a boyfriend task.

Patrick: Not if it's for sex.

Imogen: Maybe. Jade does say her lingerie is from gentleman callers, and she'd never consider a serious relationship.

Patrick: You've seen her collection?

Imogen: We're not that kind of roomies.

Patrick: There go my threesome fantasies.

Imogen: Really?

Patrick: No.

Imogen: Have you ever considered it?

Patrick: A threesome with two women?

Imogen: Don't tell me you haven't. I won't believe you.

Patrick: Imagined it, sure? Watched some manufactured porn? Also, yeah. Looked for something more believable… again, yeah.

Imogen: Did you find it?

Patrick: Do you want me to send links?

Imogen: I don't know. Will it scare me?

Patrick: Not the more realistic stuff. Unless porn scares you.

Imogen: I've never watched.

Patrick: Never?

Imogen: Okay, I have, but never on purpose, on my own, for stimulation. A friend showed me in high school. And there was this college party my freshman year. A bonding experience for all the girls on my floor watching some over-the-top, high-production value stuff.

Patrick: Did you like it?

Imogen: No. It was fake. And weird. Aggressive. Do you watch a lot?

Patrick: When I was younger.

I didn't always see through the bullshit. That's another thing

I lost, another thing I'm glad I lost, but it's strange. I barely recognize the guy I used to be.

Patrick: Not much, anymore. I got tired of how fake it felt.

Imogen: Aren't there amateur videos?

Patrick: A lot of those are fake too.

Imogen: Manufactured authenticity?

Patrick: Exactly.

Imogen: Is there anything real?

It's a good question.

Patrick: If you look hard enough. Do you want me to find something for you?

Imogen: You'll suffer through a bunch of porn for me?

Patrick: That's how much I like you.

Imogen: What a sweet fuck buddy.

Patrick: I'm generous that way.

She sends an eggplant emoji.

Then a water drop emoji.

She's funny. She really is.

Imogen: I prefer to use my imagination.

Patrick: Oh?

Imogen: Or a book. I don't sit there, reading with one hand, but I find inspiration and then…

Patrick: Go on.

Imogen: I touch myself.

Patrick: When was the last time?

Imogen: Last night.

Patrick: What did you think about?

Imogen: I replayed our tryst in the bar.

Patrick: Which part?

Imogen: Every part. Especially your hands on my skin.

She's good at this.

I'm trying to tease her and she's torturing me.

Patrick: How did you fuck yourself?

Imogen: My hand on my clit.

Patrick: Do you have toys?

Imogen: Yes, but they wouldn't feel like your hands on my skin.

My blood rushes south.

Why did I wear jeans? The denim is too tight.

Imogen: I thought about this too. How it would go. How it would feel to send you a picture. To hear your voice. Or for you to hear mine.

Patrick: I want to.

Imogen: You're somewhere private?

Patrick: Yeah.

Imogen: Can you go somewhere public?

Patrick: You want me to hear around other people?

Imogen: Yeah. I want to torture you too.

So she knows the effect she has on me.

Patrick: What if I want to fuck myself?

Imogen: You can wait.

I want to wait. Is it that obvious?

Patrick: Pictures first.

Imogen: What do you want to see?

Patrick: You. In your bed.

Imogen: I need a mirror here, for angles.

Patrick: You want to go to Target? I'll buy one.

Imogen: That's domestic. Target.

Patrick: It's dirty. Buying a mirror for sex in front of all these people shopping for laundry detergent.

Imogen: When you put it that way…

Patrick: If you stay over after the party.

Imogen: Bribery?

Patrick: Or before if you'd prefer. We can meet there instead of my place.

Imogen: I'll consider the bribery.

Patrick: It could be for my place.

Imogen: I'm considering it.

Patrick: Picture. Now.

She sends a snapshot of her legs stretched over the bed.

Then a higher one.

Purple fabric stretched over her hips.

The long line of her torso.

A matching bra covering her perfect tits.

And then her face, her lips the perfect shade of berry, her eyes on fire with need.

Patrick: Take off the bra.

Imogen: Done.

Patrick: Show me.

She sends a photo of the bra on her sheets.

She doesn't trust me.

It's fair.

But it's—

The buzz of my cell interrupts my thoughts.

There it is.

A picture of Imogen, from her nose to her belly button.

Only Imogen.

Her bare skin against the dark pink sheets.

Patrick: You're gorgeous.

Imogen: Thank you.

Patrick: I'm hard enough to cut glass.

Imogen: Are you ready to call?

Patrick: Take off your panties.

She sends another picture of her underwear on her sheets.

Then just her.

She is torturing me. She's torturing me in the best possible way.

Patrick: Two minutes.

Imogen: I'm not waiting two minutes.

Patrick: Thirty seconds.

Imogen: Fifteen.

There's no way I'm going to let the flag fall while I do this. I can't walk around advertising the state of affairs, but I can stay discrete—

I slip out of the bathroom.

Luna shoots me a suspicious look. "That fast?"

"No."

She looks to my crotch without a hint of shyness. "You know, I, uh… I'm going to get some coffee."

She grabs her sweater and leaves.

I find my sketchbook, hold it over my waist, step outside the shop.

There's nobody to greet customers.

But fuck it. I'm in public. There are people. People who will see me doing this dirty shit.

I call Imogen.

She answers right away. "That was three minutes."

"Had to get into position."

"I don't forgive you."

"I'll make it up to you," I say.

"How?"

"Take you to another bar. A nicer one this time."

"Will you dress up?"

"I can wear slacks and a collared shirt," I say.

"I'd like to see that."

"Next week. Name a night."

"What if you're working?" she asks.

"I'll take you after."

"That will be late."

"You want to talk practicalities, or you want to come?"

"Both," she says. "Tell me about this place—"

"I went once. With my sister Molly and her girlfriend."

A woman walks by me. Looks at me funny. She knows I'm hiding something. Maybe she knows what I'm hiding.

It must be written on my forehead.

Patrick Murphy is desperate to get off Imogen Nguyen.

I push my back against the wall, pretend to reach for a cigarette.

She shakes her head and moves along.

I've been here a million times, but I'm seeing the street in a whole new way. It's a great place for this. And a terrible place for this.

Perfect.

She's evil in the best possible way.

"Sorry. Almost had company," I say.

"People can see you?"

"Tons."

"Are you hard?"

"Very."

"Where are we?"

Right. I need to get back to getting her off. "A secluded bar in Hollywood, on the balcony. Great view of the city. Plenty of space to strip you naked."

"Completely naked?"

She wants to keep some of her clothes on. That gets her off. "No. You'll wear some tight dress, nothing under it."

"Yeah?" Her breath hitches.

"I'll push the straps off your shoulders. Pull the skirt to your waist. So you're grinding against me."

"Is anyone around?"

"No one can see."

"Then?"

"You unzip my jeans. I pull you onto my cock. Fuck you right there."

"With my nipple in your mouth."

"And your hands in my hair."

"Fuck." A moan falls from her lips. "Then?"

"I hold on to your hips, guide you over my cock again and again, until you're groaning my name."

"Fuck, Patrick—"

"And I come inside you."

Something falls in her bedroom. "Shit. I'll put you on speaker."

"Don't apologize."

"Is that the only place?"

"You need more than one?"

"I need everything."

How is she so fucking sexy? It's not fair. "A party in the hills. In some huge mansion. A friend of a friend. No one we really know."

"With a pool?"

"Yeah. The main party is in the house. The backyard is quiet. A few couples talking or drinking. But no one is swimming."

"No?"

"And I'm going to make you wait. To torture you for the chance in the water. I peel your top over your chest and toy with you until you're panting—"

A moan falls from her lips.

She's close now.

I need to push her over the edge.

"Then I toy with you some more. Unzip your jeans, roll them to your waist, push you on one of those plush lounge chairs."

"Fuck me?"

"Not yet."

She huffs.

"I make you wait. I slip a finger inside you. Then two. Three. I stretch you wide."

"Fuck."

"Then, when you can't take it anymore, I unzip my jeans—"

"Yeah?"

"Push you to your knees. You take me into your mouth. Try to toy with me the way I'm toying with you. But I won't have it. I put you back on the chair and I slide into you."

"Tricky—"

She's never used my nickname. It's impossibly sexy. And impossibly intimate. And I want every ounce of it. "Come for me, baby."

She releases her last inhibition.

Her breaths run together as she moves faster, falls closer.

Then she's there, coming for me, groaning in my ear, torturing me the way I'm torturing her.

She's raw and free and exposed.

And it's hot as hell.

"Perfect," I say.

"Do you have time?"

"I like it this way."

"I come for you?"

"I watch you," I say. "And you wait until I want to watch you more."

"What if we were at the party? And I did go down on you?"

"You don't have to."

"If I want to."

I'm not going to say no to that.

"People would be watching you."

"Us."

"You wouldn't stop me," she says.

Probably not. "Try me."

"A dare?"

"You heard me."

"You think I won't?"

"At Luna's party?"

"Okay. Not at Luna's party." She laughs. "But somewhere else? I will."

"Then we should do it."

"Do it…"

"I'm invited to a lot of parties. Part of the job," I say. "We can go after."

"I don't want to wait."

"Then a bar. Before. Like the one I mentioned."

"Only if I can wear a crop top and jeans."

She's evil. "I'll pick you up at six."

"I'll get you off at seven."

Chapter Twenty-One

IMOGEN

Saturday morning, he sends his test results. Recent. All clear.

I send mine.

And now, I'm equipped with truly tantalizing knowledge that I can safely go down on him. He can safely go down on me. We can have sex bareback if we want.

How am I supposed to think of anything else?

I try, really. I finish my homework. I get ahead on my reading. I give up on reading and watch TV. I call the TV a failure and change my outfit three times.

This crop top or that one?

The dark wash jeans or the black ones?

Jade talks me into a blazer and wedge shoes. I let her do my makeup, so I stay distracted. It's the most stereotypically girly thing I've ever done. (Julie is not a winged eyeliner and berry lipstick kind of girl).

Patrick arrives exactly at six. After the usual introductions (my pre-med roomie Jade, my new date Patrick), I kiss him hello, head to his car, and endure the slow, agonizing, perfect torture of driving to a mysterious bar where I'm going to torture him.

———

THE PLACE DOESN'T MATCH MY MENTAL IMAGE, BUT IT'S beautiful all the same. The top floor of a hotel in Hollywood. High ceilings, modern couches, wide windows.

And a perfect view of Los Angeles from every angle. The hills, the Hollywood sign, the skylines of downtown and Century City, the sunset over the Pacific.

Gorgeous.

The people here match. They're all beautiful and effortless, a mix of truly carefree outfits and California casual (jeans and polos or button-ups for guys, sundresses and wedges for women). In my crop top and jeans, I fit into the cool, youthful atmosphere.

I don't just feel stylish. I feel badass.

Or maybe that's my plan to have my way with Patrick.

Probably my plan to have my way with Patrick.

He presses his palm into the small of my back. There are too many layers of fabric in the way—the blazer, the stretch denim of my jeans. I need his hands on my skin.

I need my hands on his skin.

Now.

I force myself to take a deep breath. I try to recall a single word of our conversation in the car (something about music… maybe). I focus on my surroundings (there's air-conditioning in here, but it isn't keeping me cool).

"Do you want a drink?" Patrick leads me toward the bar. "A soda?"

"A gin and tonic," I say. "Just one."

He nods with understanding and leads me all the way to the bar, cool and confident and totally at ease.

Is he really this carefree about our plan?

I guess most men would be happy to hear *I want to suck you off on the balcony*. Especially after my insistence on taking things at my own pace.

He is more experienced. Maybe he's done this kind of thing a lot. But he hasn't done *this*. He hasn't agreed to help anyone else experiment to figure out exactly what they like.

That's ours.

Patrick makes small talk as he orders. He and the bartender discuss their tattoos (of course, he's a tattooed hipster) and the weather. Isn't it a beautiful night? And it's nice how the heat fades along with the sun.

Really, this is a classic summer evening. Warm but not hot. Comfortable for jeans or dresses or taking off your clothes on the balcony.

I'm not doing a great job distracting myself. But why distract myself? I'm not a man. I can't blow my load early. And I'm not here for me, either.

I doubt Patrick will let that stand, but I'm not scared about that either. I don't know why, but I trust him here. I want more here.

The bartender delivers our drinks. Patrick closes the tab. I consider offering to pay, but I'm too slow. Besides, my parents taught me not to argue with men or elders who offered to pay.

Which feels weird, especially as an adult woman. When I let men pay, they get ideas about what that means. They think it entitles them to my body. But, hey, I'm the one using his body for my satisfaction. Sorta.

The point is, we're enjoying each other's bodies.

What's it matter who pays for our gin and tonics if we both enjoy ourselves?

As long as it feels fair.

"I'll get the next round," I say.

"You want two rounds?" he asks.

"Next time," I say.

"The ones at the party?" he teases.

"I brought tonic water," I say.

"You're sweet."

"No. I want the tonic water I like."

He laughs. "Sweet. And strategic."

The balcony is around the corner, past a B-list celebrity and their entourage and two men in suits sipping brown liquor.

"Do you think they're lost?" I ask.

"Visiting from New York, maybe." He glances at the guys again. "Or agents."

"For actors?"

"Or entertainment lawyers, maybe. That's what Molly does."

"Your sister?"

"Oldest sister, yeah. She said we were here to celebrate her engagement, but when her fiancée went to the bathroom, she started lecturing me on my career path." He laughs. "She wanted to make sure I wasn't apprenticing just as a rebellion against our parents."

"What did they want you to do?"

"Anything stable," he says. "Yours the same?"

"More or less," I say. "They want better than what they had, even though they're really successful. Only they don't really get psychology or economics. It's too theoretical. Not practical enough. I think they'd prefer if I was getting a degree in accounting."

"Have you tried it?"

"A little. I ran their books in high school. I can do the basics, but I can't do anything more sophisticated."

"There's sophisticated accounting?"

"There are all sorts. But I didn't get very far. It was too dry. I like the space in psychology, the complexity of the mind, the surprises. Human beings believe they're logical, but they're really not. We're more animal than we want to admit."

"Oh?" He raises a brow.

My cheeks flush.

Patrick settles on a low couch in the corner. It's turned away from the other men. Private, but not as private as the booth in the bar.

Is he daring me? Fucking with me? Trying to carve space for actual conversation?

No. That can't be it.

What man turns down a blow job for conversation?

"I took a class last year." In the middle of everything. Maybe that was it. I was trying to punish myself. Or I was trying to be the person my parents wanted me to be. I don't know anymore.

"It, uh—" This is not a sexy topic. I need to move back to a sexy topic. Or at least a less fraught one. "I wish I did like accounting. Or something else more practical. Wouldn't that be nice, to have a passion for computer programing?"

"Economics seems pretty in demand."

"Not in the same way, but it is."

"Do you ever think about writing?"

Do I talk about it that much?

"I bet you're good."

"Based on what?"

"How you text."

"That seems like a flimsy basis."

"I'm not the scientist."

I smile. "As much as I love the feeling of losing myself in words, I love this too. I love being a scientist. And I don't really want to make a creative passion my career. I don't know how you do it, actually."

"Work as a tattoo artist?"

"Take something yours and sell it. Not that there's something wrong with selling it—"

"But you couldn't do that with your writing?"

I nod. "I'm not judging."

"I didn't think you were."

Right. He doesn't jump to that assumption the way other people do. I like that about him. "You're curious about people."

"About you."

"It's very scientific of you."

"The scientific people I know aren't curious," he says. "Only

Luna. The others are nerdy guys who think they know everything, because they're more educated than I am."

"I know that kind of guy."

"In your classes?"

"Everywhere, yeah." I like that he isn't that way. "Don't you have to apprentice to work as a tattoo artist?"

"For about two years, yeah."

"That's an education."

"It is and it's hard. But I understand it's not the same. It's not as intellectual."

"Intellectual is over-rated."

He smiles. "Really? You believe that?"

"Intellectual people."

"I don't know. I like them."

My cheeks flush. "We, uh, we were talking about you. Your job. Selling your work."

He nods *if you insist.* "It's hard to sell my work sometimes. Clients don't always want something great. Sometimes, I come up with an amazing design and they ask me to get rid of everything interesting about it," he says. "But I still have my sketchbook. I can still draw for myself, design a piece for myself or a friend. And I've put some of that on my skin. Who else can say that?"

"Can I see?"

"This one is obvious." He pulls up his t-shirt to show off the Latin quote on his ribs. "But it's mine."

luctor et emergo

I struggle and I emerge.

I know that one. It was on my shortlist for my first tattoo. What has he been through that inspired him to pick those words?

I want to know.

I want to touch him, trace the lines, absorb every ounce of his experience. "It's beautiful."

"Thanks."

"Is that your favorite? Of yours?"

"I can't pick."

What does it mean? How did you struggle? What happened? "Of the designs you've done for clients?"

"Yours."

"Really?" I ask.

"No. But I do love it."

"You promise?"

"Cross my heart and hope to die." He drops his shirt. "But it doesn't always go that way."

I take a long sip of my drink. It cools my temperature. It slows my thoughts. "And you have to do it, because that's the job?"

He nods.

"A family friend is in that position. She always loved acting, practically ran drama club, tried out for every play. She was great and she got lucky too. A friend of a friend offered her a role on a show with a last-minute 'diversity push.' She's not waiting tables anymore. She's following her dreams. And she makes good money, but she doesn't have her outlet anymore. And she's not performing Tennessee Williams. She's on sitcoms playing the dragon woman neighbor. Or she's on dramas as the Asian sex worker. She has chances to do real work, but most of it is bullshit."

"I get that."

"I guess it's different, being the one in control."

"Kind of," he says. "I'm the one crafting the design, but I have to put my clients' needs first. I enjoy the challenge, most of the time, but sometimes—"

"People are difficult."

"Yeah. And I'm not constantly doing badass, unique sleeves. I'm drawing hearts on wrists—"

"Hey."

He smiles. "It is one of my favorites. I promise." He slips his hand under my jacket and presses his palm against my ribs. The spot where he adorned my skin.

The design is beautiful. A rose stem wrapped around a heart, shedding petals on the ground.

Our collaboration. I shared a lot with him, online, before I met him. (Via Instagram, of course). I told him I wanted something that would prove I survived hard things, that I wasn't afraid to face anything.

It was very…

Over the top.

But that was perfect.

"And this too." He runs his fingers over the edges of my blazer. "May I?"

I set my drink down.

He helps me out of my blazer, and he traces the Latin quote on my forearm.

The evening breeze brushes my skin, but I don't feel a chill. Then his fingers are tracing the words and I'm on fire.

"It's simple," he says. "But it's beautiful."

"It's not yours."

"I know. I hate it."

"You're jealous?" I ask.

"Someone else marked your skin forever."

"A woman. Does that make a difference?"

"Will you think I'm a pig if I say yes?"

"Maybe," I say.

"Yes." He leans in and presses his lips to my upper arm. "It's you, too."

How does he know?

He barely knows me.

But he's right.

Veritas lux mea

Truth is my light.

He traces the lines of ink again. "You want to talk about it?"

"No," I say. "Is that okay?"

"I know you didn't come here for conversation."

Right.

"I just like talking to you."

"More than you like fucking me?"

He moves a little closer. He honors my silent request to shift back to sex. "It's harder to get you talking."

A laugh spills from my lips.

"Maybe that will be my kink with you, talking about feelings."

"That's going to be a hard one for me to satisfy."

"I bet." He brings his hand to my cheek and pulls me into a deep kiss. "But I'm happy to keep exploring this one."

Right. "You're not going to fight me on this?"

"See if I can make you come first?"

"Mm-hmm."

"What kind of guy do you take me for?"

"A gentleman?"

"Of course."

"Does that mean you will or you won't?"

"There's only one way to find out."

Chapter Twenty-Two

IMOGEN

Despite my status as a Division One swimmer, I'm not that competitive. I've never dreamed of Olympic golds or spots at Nationals. I've never wanted to be the best, only the best version of myself in the water.

This is different, somehow. Because this is a game. Because we're evenly matched. Because I win even if I lose.

But this time I really want to win.

"You realize I'm a college athlete?" I ask.

"I've heard that."

"You doubt me?"

"Invite me to a game," he says.

"A meet," I say.

"Invite me to a meet then."

"The season is over."

"Next year," he says.

"They're boring."

"It won't be boring." He pulls me into his lap. He picks up my blazer. "It might be easier in this."

My chest flames. My stomach. My sex. Affection and need surge through my body. He wants to watch me swim. He wants to be here next year. He wants to help me into something that will make it easier to expose my breasts.

I'm not sure which part is scarier.

No. That's easy. The thought of him being here next spring. That's a long relationship. That comes with expectations of other kinds of intimacy.

This—

The biggest danger here is an arrest as a sex offender. That's nothing compared to sharing my secrets.

"If you won't be too hot." He offers the blazer.

I slide it on.

Patrick pulls me into a slow, deep kiss.

My body responds with gusto. Every part of me is awake and alive and every part wants him.

I don't care if he has the upper hand. I don't care if he wins. I don't care about anything besides my skin against his.

I turn toward him.

He traces the waist of my jeans. Right to left and left to right.

He circles the button with his fingers. He brings his hand to my crop top and rolls it up my chest, one inch at a time.

Until I'm in his lap, exposed.

Patrick pulls back with a needy sigh. He takes a long, long moment to look at me. He stares with wonder, like this is the first time he's ever seen me, like I'm the only thing he's ever wanted.

Right now, I feel it.

Anyone else, it doesn't matter.

This is what matters.

I turn a little more toward him.

He brings one hand to my chest, cups my breast with his palm.

"I have to ask you something," I say.

"Now?"

"Now." I sigh as he toys with my nipple. "I like this. Trying to make normal conversation while you touch me."

"Me too." He presses his lips to my neck. "I like torturing you."

"But this is about sex."

"Oh?" He brings his other hand to my hip. Adjusts me so I'm right on top of his hard-on.

Fuck, that feels good. I need it. Now. "We're both safe."

"Yeah." He moves to my other breast and toys with it.

I rest my head against his chest. This feels good. Too good. I can't hold on to conscious thought. It's impossible. "Have you ever?"

"Have I ever…" He toys with me again and again. Shifts my body, so I'm upright, so I'm perfectly exposed to him. "Done this? No."

My chest warms. My sex clenches. I'm his first here. I want this to be ours too. But—"That's actually… fuck."

"Yeah?" He slips his other hand between my legs. Rubs me over my jeans. "Lie down and you come on my face."

"Not here."

"It's not that private." He runs his fingers over the seam of my jeans. "I get it. I'd prefer that to this, but I don't care, as long as I get you off."

"Tricky—"

"Say it again, baby—"

Fuck. "Tricky, I… I want to go bareback with you."

"Fuck." His fingers curl into my inner thigh.

Even with my jeans in the way, I feel the sharp pinch. And I love it. "Not here. We don't have the privacy."

"Let's get to the bathroom. Right now."

"You would?"

"Fuck yeah," he says. "You're on birth control?"

"An IUD." My mom insisted when I went to college. She said I needed to be safe, all the time, just in case, and I agreed.

"Bathroom. Now."

"Tricky!"

"I'm not kidding."

"Is it even a single stall?" I ask.

"Fuck if I know."

"Maybe after." I turn toward him. "I still want to do this."

"I'm not sure I can concede." He runs his fingertip over the seam of my jeans again.

"You don't have to," I say. "But if we go somewhere else, you can… we can…"

"I can eat you out?"

"I meant—"

"I know. But that's what I want."

"More than bareback?"

"Yeah."

"If you're not ready, I get that." He runs his fingertip over me again. Resumes toying with my breasts. "If you are—"

"I am."

"Okay. Let's go now."

"No." God, his hands feel good on my skin. I could stay here, on the brink, forever. It's the best possible torture.

He undoes the button of my jeans.

"Tricky—"

"Tell me to stop if you want me to stop."

No. I don't want him to stop. I shake my head.

He undoes the zipper.

But my jeans are too high-waisted. There's no way he's getting what he wants here.

I can get what I want.

Everything I want.

I wrap my fingers around his wrists and bring his hands to my chest.

He cups my breasts with his palms, toying with me again and again.

I shift off him, so I'm more exposed, so I can bring my hand to his inner thigh.

He groans as I rub him over his jeans.

He turns toward me, moving closer, pulling my body toward his.

He kisses hard as he toys with me. Again and again.

And I tease him back, running my hand up his thigh, moving closer and closer to where I want to be.

He groans as I undo his button.

Then the zipper.

"Imogen—" He kisses me as I slip my hand into his boxers. "Fuck."

He feels good. He always does, but being here, in public, knowing I'm the one exposing him here—

It's really fucking hot.

I stroke him again.

I push his jeans out of the way.

And then I bring my lips to his neck.

He cups the back of my head and he guides me to exactly where I need to go.

Victory.

But I'm not a sore winner.

I don't brag. I wrap my hand around him. Then my lips.

He tastes good. Like soap and Patrick.

It's been a long time since I've done this. I've never really loved it, but right now I'm on fire.

The power, the control, the feeling of him under my thumb.

And the intimacy too—

The generosity of it—

Everything.

I tease him with a few flicks of my tongue.

Then I find the pressure he needs, the pattern.

He presses his palm into the back of my head, guiding me over his cock.

He brings his other hand to my breast. Toys with me as I take him.

Again and again.

That perfect cycle of his need and my desire.

He pushes a little harder.

Lifts his hips.

Groans way too loudly for the setting.

But that only winds me tighter, urges me further.

I move faster, harder.

He holds me right where he needs me.

Then he's there, groaning my name as he comes in my mouth.

I wait until he's spills every drop, then I swallow hard. I rise. I check our surroundings.

No one here.

No one saw.

Or they didn't care.

I start to right my shirt, but he shakes his head.

"Keep it that way." He does the button of the blazer, covering me, but just barely.

It's obvious I'm halfway out of my clothes under here.

And it's incredibly, painfully hot.

"You ready to go?" he asks.

I shake my head. "I have to finish my drink."

"No way, baby. You don't get off that easy." He fixes his jeans, pulls me into his lap, slides his hand under my jacket. "We can stay as long as you want."

"Yeah?"

"But I'm going to do this the entire time." He cups my breast and toys with my nipple. "I'm going to wind you so tight you burst."

"You promise?"

Chapter Twenty-Three

IMOGEN

Patrick toys with me for ages. It might be ten minutes. It might be ten years. I'm not sure. I only know how badly I need release.

When we finally leave, he doesn't pull into the bathroom. He doesn't stop me in the elevator.

He leads me all the way to his car and just when I'm sure he's going to drive to his friend's party without a word, he pushes me against the passenger side door.

He unzips my jeans, slides them to my hips, slips his hand between my legs.

He winds me tighter and tighter.

I come fast.

I'm too revved up already.

I buck against him as I come. Pleasure spills through my pelvis. It's almost too much. It hurts.

But the release—

Fuck.

I collapse against the car.

He catches me and rights my clothes. "Hey." He looks at me with pride in his green eyes. Pride and affection. "You good?"

"What?"

He smiles. "I thought so."

"Can we go back to your place?"

"If you ask really nicely."

"That wasn't nice enough?" I ask.

"No magic word."

"Avocado?"

"That is it. But you have to say it after the request." He cups my cheek with his palm, runs his thumb over my temple. "It would be more fun to go to the party. Make you wait until after."

"The party?"

He chuckles. "Luna's party. For her boyfriend."

"Who?"

"Maybe I need to take you home. Put you to bed?"

I nod.

"Well, you know how to request it…" He opens the car door for me and helps me into the passenger seat.

I gather my bag, secure my seat belt, settle into my surroundings.

The low hum of the electric engine. The mumble of music. A new pop artist Luna recommended.

She's not bad, actually.

Not Fiona Apple, but not bad.

And we're moving.

Right.

I let the music and the surroundings wash over me. For a few songs, we sit in comfortable non-conversation.

Bit by bit, blood returns to my brain.

I still want to drag Patrick to my bed and fuck him bareback. But I can wait. In theory.

We breeze down the ten.

Patrick raises a brow as we near my exit.

I shake my head. "If you can make it, I can."

"Baby, you have no idea how long I can wait."

"I have some idea."

He laughs. "Maybe. I can go easy on you. Talk about something else."

"Us? Talking about something besides sex? I'm not sure about that."

"It's a wild theory, yeah."

"I like the music," I say. "It was a good suggestion."

"Thank Luna."

"I will. But I wanted to thank you too." It's sweet, him trying to find music I'll like, listening to music I like. I'm not sure a guy has ever done that for me before. "I appreciate it."

"My pleasure."

"Do you like it too?"

"At first, I thought it was a little slow," he says. "But once I surrendered to that, I loved it."

"It is mellow."

"But in a thoughtful way. I feel like I'm staying up late, talking to a friend. Or even reading the singer's journal."

Huh.

"She's honest in a brave way, but she doesn't underline it."

"That's specific."

"I know."

"But kinda dead-on. Did you come up with that?"

"Am I not clever enough?"

No. It's just… something. I'm not sure. I don't think there's enough blood in my brain yet. "Have you ever read someone's journal?"

"Have you?"

Kind of. "Not really."

"I stole my sister's when I was younger," he says. "I didn't get any of it. It was too grown-up."

"What did she say?"

"She was pissed, but she didn't tell our parents."

"I'd never tattle on my kid sister," I say.

"That's what I thought at the time, that she'd never narc. And that's probably true. But I think it was more, too. She didn't want our parents to know she kept a journal. She didn't want to give them the opening. Now that I look back, there was stuff in there, normal teen girl stuff—"

"You're an expert?"

"From what I hear," he says. "Crushes, kisses, hating her body or wondering if she wasn't good enough."

That is normal teen girl stuff. Why do we accept our own self-loathing so easily? It's terrible.

"I thought she didn't want Mom and Dad to know about the kissing, but now… I'm not sure."

She didn't want them to know about everything stirring inside her. "You rebelled by becoming a tattoo artist? At least your sister worried about that."

"Molly, yeah."

"It wasn't Molly's journal?"

"No. Deidre's. She was closer to my age. Molly is the oldest. And she's the high achiever, but she's rebellious in her own way."

"As a lawyer?"

"She studied philosophy."

That is a common plan for philosophy majors. "Deidre?"

"She was the good girl, for sure. Straight As, college scholarship, volunteer sessions at my parents' church."

"They're religious?"

"Catholic, yeah."

"Oh."

"Oh?" he asks.

"I don't know. It sounds right."

"The Catholic guilt?" he asks.

"Not exactly." Not guilt as much as rebellion. "Strict parents with rules. Mine were the same. My sister had issues, but she always fell in line. Whereas I… I guess I fall in line, in the end." Sorta. "But I fight it more."

"You don't seem like someone who falls in line."

"Maybe not anymore." Sorta. "I had this moment where I realized it was my life and I could only live it for myself."

"Good realization."

"I think so," I say.

"Is that what your tattoo was about?"

"Which one?"

"Either."

"I guess both were about that," I say.

"They suit you."

"Thanks." My cheeks flush. "Did you apologize? To your sister?"

"Eventually," he says.

"I can't imagine my kid sister reading my journal. I'd feel so... exposed."

But it would be a relief, too. Because I wouldn't have to explain all this to her.

She'd know.

She'd get it. Or, at least, she'd have as much insight as I can give her.

Is that why I keep my online journal? A secret hope Julie will stumble on it and understand?

A secret hope someone will stumble on it, understand, realize it's me, love me.

Maybe. It's an impulse more than anything. A desire to understand myself, to feel understood.

"But maybe it would be good in some ways," I say. "If she read my ugliest thoughts, if I didn't have to worry about whether or not I should share them with her, if she saw me at my worst and loved me anyway."

"You don't think your sister loves you?"

"I know she does. But there's plenty I don't tell her."

"Maybe you should."

Maybe.

"It would make sense, if you did like something about it."

"Huh?"

"Someone reading your private thoughts," he says.

"It would?"

"You are an exhibitionist."

"I am, aren't I?"

"Is that really a question?" He laughs.

It's an easy laugh. Sex is easy for us. Less fraught. And I need to talk about something less fraught. "Okay, yes, it's pretty obvious. But you?"

"Baby, don't tell me you're not sure if I enjoyed that."

"I know you enjoyed it."

"Good."

"But I'm not sure which part."

"Every part," he says.

"You liked being watched?"

He nods.

"Watching?"

"Fuck yeah."

I like to be watched. He likes to watch. It's a match made in sexual Heaven. It's almost too good to be true. Except for my total inability to take our relationship outside the bedroom. Well, the metaphorical bedroom. "Would you ever want to watch me with someone else?" Where the fuck did that come from?

"No. I don't like to share."

I nod.

"But on your own, with other people around… maybe."

"Where would we do that?"

"A sex club."

"Do those really exist? Or are they just a thing in the movies?"

"No idea."

"Damn. And here I thought you ran the biggest sex club on the West Coast."

"No, that's the other Patrick Murphy."

"The one?"

"I'm sorry. We can't all have Irish first names and Vietnamese last names."

"Imogen is Irish?"

"Hell yeah, it's Irish."

"So that's why you like me," I say.

"No, it's your tits."

A laugh spills from my lips.

Sex. Yes. This is easy. And easy is good. And, yes, I'm afraid of feelings, but at least I can admit it, here, to myself, in his car, while I contemplate how long I need to stay at his friend's party before I drag him back to his place.

Probably an hour, minimum.

That's another two until we're alone at his apartment.

"I liked the pictures." He interrupts my dirty thoughts. "And sending me to somewhere public while I talked you off… that was evil."

"Thanks."

"I've got plans for next time."

"I look forward to it."

"And for tonight," he says.

"Additional plans?"

"Oh yeah."

"I never took you for the planning type," I say.

"I guess you don't know everything about me."

Chapter Twenty-Four

IMOGEN

As we park, Patrick gives me the quick rundown of the dynamic at Luna's party.

In theory, the party is in her boyfriend, Oliver's, honor. Since Oliver and his best friend, Holden, were visiting Oliver's sister, Daisy at Berkeley. (Like me, she's staying to take summer courses).

Daisy is also Holden's girlfriend and Luna's best friend.

There's a lot of in-dating, apparently. Holden and Daisy got together first, on a four-person birthday trip to Mexico. That, understandably, made Oliver upset. (I should object to him deciding who his sister should date on feminist grounds, but, as an older sibling, I get it. Apparently, Holden was known for not taking things seriously, especially relationships).

Then, a little while later, when Luna's parents announced their divorce, she ran to her best friend Daisy's place for comfort. A sort of habit, since they were old friends. Only things were different now. They were in college, Luna at UCLA, Daisy at Berkeley, and who was at their house but Oliver, Daisy's brooding older brother.

Apparently, he promised Daisy he'd stay in their childhood

home for her first year of school, so he always knew where to find her. He did. Even after Daisy discovered their relationship. (She took it in stride, apparently).

But Luna didn't stay. She went back to her parents' place. They're crazy rich. Rich enough, they don't need to sell the house to split assets in the divorce. One of her moms (she has two moms) is using her newfound freedom to travel the world (she and Luna are touring Southeast Asia together in August).

Her other mom works all the time, so she's not usually here.

And Mom agreed to a small party, as long as we keep things relatively quiet. And no underage drinking, of course. Which would normally be a non-starter at a party of twenty-somethings, only Luna's boyfriend, Oliver, is a recovering alcoholic.

Patrick tells me more, but I don't absorb it. I nod, I double-check my top (now in place), I follow him to the house.

It's a gorgeous place. Modern and huge (by Southern California standards) with a perfect mix of clean white and bold color. Red pillows, orange throws, canary yellow mugs.

We move through the empty, and impeccably clean, living room, to the bustling backyard.

That, too, is the perfect mix of modern and homey. Orange patio chairs, glass table, string lights and lanterns illuminating the space.

There are only a handful of people here and no one is visibly drunk.

It's not the night of debauchery I imagined. It's actually kinda… nice.

"Hey." Luna jumps to her feet when she sees us. "Thanks for delivering my new best friend, Tricky. And thanks for these, Imogen." She takes the bottle of tonic water, sets it on the patio table, and pulls me into a hug.

He nods hello. Excuses himself to the bathroom, to wash up, after getting me off.

Fuck, I'm hot. Even though it's a cool evening. Even though

I'm in front of a teammate. Especially because I'm in front of a teammate.

I'm a filthy pervert.

Who knew?

"Won't your current best friend get jealous?" I release her and redirect my thoughts to less dirty places. Say, anywhere.

"She's not here." She motions to the quiet groups of people mingling. "No adorable blonde with a look that says 'it's time to leave and go read.'"

"My kind of girl," I say.

"You're going to make me jealous." She motions to the table inside. Then to the cooler by the row of succulents. "Do you want something to drink? We do have a bottle of wine open. And my mom has gin in the fridge. Or are you more of a vodka girl?"

"Gin."

"Me too." She smiles. "But you'll be the only one with a cock-tail. Which I respect."

"Do college students ever drink cocktails?"

"Wine and coke, yeah."

A laugh spills from my lips. "Or Trader Joe's vodka and the cheapest jug of fruit punch available."

"I'm not sure which is grosser." She sticks her tongue out. "Sorry. I'm completely bourgeois. But at least I know it, right?"

"Are you kidding? I grew up in Newport Beach."

"Fancy schmancy. And you're slumming it with Tricky."

"Slumming it? Have you seen his place?"

"No, actually. He's never invited me to his new place." She moves to the cooler, grabs two cans—a diet soda and a La Croix —and offers them to me. "I don't mean like that. Gross. No offense. He's objectively handsome, but he's like a brother. And he's totally smitten with you, so even if I had ideas—"

Is he really?

—"I'm also tragically in love with my boyfriend. Tricky doesn't have parties. That's all I mean."

"Really? He seems like a party guy."

"He's social, yes. He attends. He drinks Bud Light."

"So I hear."

"But he's been less around for a while. Family stuff, I think," she says.

Right. He mentions his sisters a lot. But there's something off about it, something I can't quite explain.

"But then we're not here to talk Tricky. We're here to have fun. What do you drink?"

"The soda is fine." I take the diet.

"Or the wine, if you want," she says.

"This is good, but thanks. Sorry we're late. We, were uh…"

"I can imagine." She laughs. "Don't worry. I'm not judging." She motions to the couch where a tall man with dark hair is chatting with a slightly less tall guy with dark hair. "Have you met Oliver?"

The taller guy turns to me and nods a hey.

"Ollie! That is no way to greet a party guest!" Luna huffs.

He smiles.

"You did that on purpose?" she asks.

He shrugs *maybe I did, maybe I didn't*. "Oliver." He stands and offers a hand.

I shake. "Imogen."

"Patrick's new girl?" he asks.

Luna clears her throat.

Oliver just laughs. "She hates when I do that." He turns to me. "It's nice to meet you, Imogen."

"I am seeing Patrick."

"My condolences," he says.

"He's not so bad," I say.

Oliver makes that *maybe* motion.

"He's just grumpy because Patrick flirts with me," Luna says. "Or he did, a lot, before you two were serious."

"We're not really serious." I think.

"Using him for his body, huh?" Oliver asks.

"Basically," I say.

"Smart move." Oliver looks to Luna. "That's why she's here."

"No. It's really tragic, but I love the grumpy asshole," Luna says.

"Grumpy? Am I a Muppet?" He pulls her onto the couch, into his lap, in one swift moment.

"Mm-hmm." She wraps her arms around him. "Coffee monster."

"Pussy monster."

"Ollie!"

"You deny it?"

"Well…"

He presses his lips to hers. "I missed you."

"I missed you more," she says.

"Damn. They've been like this all night." The other guy shakes his head and stands. "Dare."

He looks familiar. About the same height and build. Dark features. Similar *I'm ridiculous* attitude.

"Darren," Oliver corrects. "He thinks he sounds tough going by Dare."

"Aren't you making out?" Darren, uh, Dare asks.

Oliver nods *good point* and does, in fact, return to making out.

Dare shakes his head *you're ridiculous*. He looks to the sliding glass door behind me, checking for something. For Patrick, I guess. "It was your boy who earned me the name. He's Tricky. I'm Dare. You know, 'cause he has to trick girls into kissing him. And I have to dare them into it. I guess it doesn't sound clever now. But when we were thirteen…"

"You've known each other that long?" I ask.

He nods. "Friends since middle school."

Really? Patrick doesn't mention Dare often, but then what do I know about old friends?

"He's been happier lately," he says. "I'm glad to see that. He had a hard time after his sister... he never talked about it, but it was obvious."

"His sister?" I ask.

Surprise spreads over Dare's face. "He didn't tell you?"

"I don't know," I say.

He looks behind me, again. "Yeah. Deidre. She... I don't know how much I should say."

I don't reply.

"She died."

Everything clicks together. The past tense, the frequent mentions of his older sister in present tense, the shelves packed with books young women love.

The apartment was his sister's, and she gave it to him.

As an inheritance.

"He was a wreck. Not that he showed it," Dare says. "But he was saying no to invitations. Or saying yes and drinking too much. I think... I don't think he really started to see the light until recently."

"We're not serious," I say.

"You sure?" he asks. "'Cause the change in his mood... it's not the extra sunshine. It's you. He likes you."

"I like him too."

"It's nice to see. That's all." Dare looks behind me. "But I've said too much already."

Someone slips through the door.

Dare motions to the footsteps and mimes zipped lips. "Just telling your girl she should drop the zero and find a hero."

Patrick wraps his arms around me. "A hero, really? You know one?"

"No. I thought you might," Dare says.

They laugh in a familiar way. It's a routine of theirs. It's comfortable for them.

A couple in the corner notices the commotion. Another tattoo artist looking guy and a curvy woman in thigh-high boots and a short black dress.

She whispers something in his ear and they stand, meet us in the center of the backyard.

They're a little older, in their late twenties maybe, and she looks even more stylish up close. Dark lipstick, heavy eye makeup, a tulle skirt. A goth princess.

Wait—

I know her.

"You're Princess Skye," I say.

She lights up. "I am." She offers her hand. "And you're Imogen."

"Sorry. I must sound like a fangirl. You just… I love your stuff."

"Thanks." She smiles. "It's a little weird being a 'plus-size influencer.' It forces me to really objectify myself. But I'm the photographer, so it's fun in its own way."

I follow her because she wears awesome outfits (mostly lingerie).

And I follow her because I see the way I want to expose myself in her pictures.

Not because I want to support a plus size Asian influencer.

I mean, that's there too. But my true motives are all for my own sexual gratification.

My cheeks flush. "I love your style. That's all. And your pictures are hot."

"They're really fucking hot," the guy says.

She leans into his chest. "If you ever wondered about the anonymous male model—" She looks up at him with a smile. "Hey. Stop distracting me with your sex appeal."

"What am I doing?" he teases.

"That. Exactly," she says.

Patrick shakes his head. "They're obsessed with each other. It's disgusting."

"It's called love," Skye says. "One day you'll understand that. Maybe one day soon." She rises to whisper in her boyfriend's ear then she turns to me. "We're going to bounce, but I'm glad I met you. We should do something. Drinks. Or karaoke."

"The beach?" I offer.

"A woman who loves the beach." She rests her hand on her chest. "After my heart." She nods a goodbye and leads her boyfriend out of the space.

"I've seen her naked," I say. "Well. Almost naked."

"I've seen her pictures," he says.

I imagined myself in her pictures.

I got off on the thought of showing my body to thousands of strangers. Or non-strangers. After all, people know who she is. They develop a sort of relationship with her.

It's like my site, only visual.

Patrick brushes my hair behind my ear. "We can do that, you know."

"Post on Instagram?"

"Yeah. A secret account. Just for us," he says.

"Isn't that against the terms of service?"

"I didn't mean pornographic." He laughs. "But we could do that too. Somewhere else. Somewhere racier."

"Would you really?"

"Yes." He presses his lips to my neck. "We can start with the tamer ones."

"Okay."

"That was fast."

"I know," I say.

"You're not going to make it to my place," he says.

"I will too."

"I don't think so." He leads me back to the couch, sits, pulls me into his lap.

We pry his friends from their make out session and I ask for all the dirt they have on Patrick.

They share stories. Silly ones. Dirty ones. Ones about him obsessing over his work.

Nothing about a sister.

Or bad decisions after he lost her.

Or any other places he hurts.

They keep it light and easy and I hate it.

I want more. I want to know. I don't care that it's messy and complicated. I want that part of him.

Chapter Twenty-Five

PATRICK

By the time we leave, Imogen is exhausted. She falls asleep on the five-minute ride to my place, stirs for long enough to brush her teeth and change into her pajamas.

When I help her into bed, she looks up at me with hazy eyes. "Hey Tricky."

"Hey." Something swells in my chest. Pride. Affection. Need.

She's so beautiful. And I want this side of her. The open, vulnerable side.

"Your friend… he mentioned something," she says.

"They're idiots. Don't listen to them."

"Maybe." She laughs, but there's something off about it. "About your sister—"

Shit.

"She died?"

"Yeah."

"This was her place?"

"Why do you say that?" I ask.

"It's expensive."

That's true.

"Did she own it?"

"Most of it."

"But that wasn't the main thing. I mean, as far as I know, your parents pay your rent."

"They don't."

"I'm sorry. It wasn't an accusation. I just meant… there's a lot about your life I don't know. That I didn't want to know. But this…" She rolls onto her side. "I wanted to know. And he mentioned it and I thought about the dog-eared copy of *The Bell Jar*…"

Does she know everything? How the hell does she know everything? My parents buried the details and I sure as fuck didn't tell anyone.

"What happened?" She lets out a yawn. "No. It's okay. You don't have to tell me. I just… I guess I was surprised by how much I wanted to know. I think… I think I like you."

"Yeah?"

"But I'm not good at sharing. I'm not good at feelings. This might be the only place I can really be open for a while."

"Okay."

"You sure?"

"Yeah. Go to bed." I press my lips to her forehead.

She laughs. "Okay. Good night, Tricky."

"Good night."

She rolls onto her side and drifts to sleep.

For a few minutes, I watch her. I push my other thoughts aside. I try to stay here, in this moment.

I should feel at ease.

I should be bursting with joy.

Imogen wants more. She wants something real. She wants me.

But my sleep is uneasy.

The morning is too quiet, too awkward, filled with the silence that takes up all the space. The silence that always comes after *I'm sorry about your sister.*

I say nothing about Deidre. I suggest a video-session next

weekend. She agrees enthusiastically and says goodbye with a kiss.

But I don't find distraction in mental images of us tangled in my bed.

I don't find distraction in my run, my shower, my lunch.

I don't find distraction until my phone pings with a notification.

An entry from *Hearts and Thorns*.

I did a bad, bad thing...

Chapter Twenty-Six

"Criminal"
Posted by Hearts and Thorns
Sunday July 2, 4 P.M.

I did a bad, bad thing.
Maybe I am channeling Fiona Apple too thoroughly. Because I have been a bad, bad girl.
And not in the fun way.

Okay, in the fun way. In a very, very fun way. A way I won't put into words because they could be used against me in the future case of The People vs. Hearts and Thorns for the charge of public indecency.

But hypothetically, if I was in public, with my top undone, his hands on my skin, and my entire body tuned to his—it felt so fucking good, and I want to be there so fucking badly. It's more than filling a strictly physical, medication-inspired need. It's spiritual. In a physical way, yes, but the way swimming is. I need it in my core.

I want him, physically.

And yes, the connection there is amazing.

But it's not just post-orgasm affection.

I want to fuck him all night *and* wake up in his bed. I want to screw him in the shower *and* eat oatmeal on his couch. I want to—

Well, you get the idea.

But it doesn't matter.

It's impossible.

His sister died by suicide.

I shouldn't know. Or maybe I should. What are the rules of social media these days? I follow him on Instagram, sure, but this wasn't on his page.

I had to go looking.

It wasn't hard. I knew her last name, after all, and I knew her likely friends, and I knew where to look.

But I couldn't stop. I found too much.

It was bizarre, reading the thoughts of a dead woman. The familiar, comforting, terrifying thoughts.

But it's not because I've betrayed him. (Have I betrayed him?)

It's because this is where he hurts.

And I can't be the person who tears at the wound.

Maybe that's an excuse. Cowardice. Maybe one of my friends will mention my history and he'll find out.

But then, no one knows.

Only my parents and they—

Well, they have their story.

I have mine.

I have an excuse. It's almost a relief.

But it's not.

Because I like him. All of him. And I want all of it, with him.

It's not fair to decide for him.

But I'm not deciding for him.

I'm deciding for me.

Chapter Twenty-Seven

PATRICK

F uck.

Chapter Twenty-Eight

PATRICK

The hearts and thorns tattoo on her ribs.

The references to swimming.

The Fiona Apple lyrics.

Has it been obvious all this time?

I scan old entries. The excitement about a possible tattoo a week before she contacted me. The desire for sex the night she booty called me. The excitement after our first attempt at exhibitionism.

And that's only what she's written since I've known her as Imogen.

All the other hints, the pieces of her I collected?

I should have seen it.

How the hell did I miss it?

The woman I've been following all year, the woman who makes me laugh and cry and understand, is the woman who wants to screw me senseless.

Imogen is Hearts and Thorns.

I don't put my phone away. I don't text her with a confession.

No, I do something much worse.

I read her entire online journal, cover to cover.

I pore over every word.
I fall in love with her.

Chapter Twenty-Nine

IMOGEN

Usually, my thoughts are the safest place to be Sunday evenings.

Today, they're dangerous.

Today, instead of trying to stay out of the fray, I try to enter it. But I can't latch on to a single word. There's too much swirling inside me.

Patrick's sister died by suicide. She overdosed.

With a more lethal medication (obviously).

She lived alone. She didn't need to work out careful timing or think up some place no one would find her.

She was lucky. Unlucky, I guess.

I am grateful to the rent-a-cop who tried to kick me out of the strip mall parking lot. He saved my life.

I should be more grateful, probably, but I'm not. It's too messy. Don't get me wrong. I'm glad I'm here. But I wish it was different, easier.

There's something odd about knowing I had the guts to go through with it, knowing I could now correct my mistakes. It's terrifying and comforting in equal measure. It's different now. I know how hard it is to come back. I don't want to go through that again.

I work—hard—at treatment so I don't have to go through that again.

Weekly therapy during the school year and a regular prescription aren't enough to fix me, but they keep me steady.

Julie pulls me out of my thoughts with a soft kick to my shin.

Slowly, my surroundings come into focus. My food is barely touched. Dad is in the kitchen, pouring another drink. Mom is staring at me.

"You said you love the micro-economics class," Julie says. "So I figured you're acing it. She's such a show-off when it comes to math, isn't she?"

"I'm doing well so far." Are we talking about grades? That's an easy enough topic. No subjectivity. Either I have an A or I don't. "The summer session moves quickly."

"It would be fun to do something together," Julie says. "In the two-week break between summer session and fall, right?"

Right. She asked and I… did something.

"Mom still doesn't see the appeal of San Diego," Julie says.

"It's only an hour drive. Why stay?" Mom asks.

"It's beautiful," Julie says.

Really? Mom wants to travel to somewhere besides Julie's softball games? That doesn't sound like her.

"Or Cabo San Lucas," Julie says.

"Expensive." Mom shakes her head.

"TJ would be cheaper," I say.

Julie laughs. "Right? And all the guys go for the strip clubs."

"What guys?" Mom asks.

"The seniors at school," Julie says. "They talk about the easy women."

"Boys at your school hire prostitutes?"

"Mom! They're dancers, not prostitutes. And the term is sex worker," Julie says.

Mom mutters something in Vietnamese. That's a bad sign. Around middle school, she decided we needed to integrate, to become "normal" and she stopped speaking to us in Vietnamese.

She still cooks traditional food, but she and Dad watch American movies, listen to American (and British) music, and try to love American pastimes.

Thus all the baseball and Julie's love of softball

And I guess swimming is normal enough for the area.

"We're not in Vietnam," Julie says. "Things are different."

"Things for women are the same everywhere," Mom says. "Don't talk to those boys."

"They're posturing," Julie says.

Mom shakes her head. "They mean it. They don't know."

"Okay. No dancers," Julie says. "Only authentic tacos and cheap Valium."

Mom's eyes darken.

My throat tightens.

"Are you done, Mom? Julie and I can clean," I say.

Mom mutters another Vietnamese phrase. I don't catch this one either. My skills are beyond rusty.

But she doesn't explode or lecture. She shakes her head. "Finish first. You're getting too skinny." She stands and leaves.

To the deck, on her own.

"She's smoking out there," Julie says.

"We'd know."

"We do know." She motions to herself. "We're here. But you're right. She vapes."

"No way."

She shrugs *see for yourself* and steals a bite of my stir-fry.

I lean to the right, but I can't see the deck from here. So I stand, sneak around the table for just long enough to see Mom outside.

She doesn't look like the stern woman who tries to paper over my pain. She looks overwhelmed and scared and impossibly small against the sunset.

I hurt her.

I hurt her so badly she shut down and pretended it didn't happen.

I should sympathize, I know. No, I do sympathize. But I can't access that empathy when I'm surrounded by the cold front, while I'm busy fighting with myself, reminding myself what really happened.

"When did she start smoking?" I return to my seat.

"Start? When she was fourteen. She never told you this?" Julie asks.

"No," I say. "When did she tell you?"

Julie clears her throat.

"You were smoking?"

"Pot is legal," she says.

"Not for minors," I say. "Oh my god, that was your vape pen?" Wait, Mom caught her with pot and talked to her about smoking? "You actually… discussed it?"

"Yeah, we talk," she says. "She tells me what's going on. Unlike some people."

"Are you kidding? I gave you plenty of R-rated details."

"Not what I mean. You're different. You've been different…" She doesn't mention the last year. Or the year before that. "Did something happen?"

"Huh?" I pick at my stir-fry. It's too cold and the flavors are too dull. I'm far away. I barely notice the ginger.

"Did something happen with your boyfriend? You're spacey today."

"Sorta."

"A fight?"

"No." I eat another piece of chicken.

"Seriously, Immy, I never thought Mom would be more communicative than you."

Did Mom tell her? No, she'd say something.

"Don't make me compare you to Mom again," she says.

"It's not good for us," I say.

"I know." She motions *so say it*.

"What if I don't want to talk about it?"

"You get to lecture me about sex. Why can't I lecture you about whatever this is?"

"I like him." I can tell her that. "I thought I could keep it strictly sexual, but I like him, and we just… I have to end things."

"Because you like him?"

"For a lot of reasons."

"Sounds like there's one reason," she says.

Maybe. I am scared. That is true. But look at Mom. I destroyed her and I'm still here.

With what happened with his sister—

How could he ever love me? Trust me?

How could I ever trust him to see that side of me?

"It's not going to work," I say.

"Because…"

"His sister…" What can I say that won't give me away? "I found something about her, something I'm not supposed to know."

She raises a brow. "Is she a porn star?"

"No."

"An assassin."

"No. She died."

She frowns. "Oh. That sucks. But what does that have to do with you? Is this really because you went digging for something he didn't tell you, because everyone does that?"

"No. It's just… we're not compatible."

"Because…"

"I can't explain it," I say. "But I know."

She taps the table with her fingertips. "I know what you would tell me to do."

"You do?"

"Oh yeah. Easy. Talk to him."

That is good advice.

"If you're sure you're going to end things, what's the harm in an actual conversation? Or is that the harm? Are you scared you won't end things and fall in love and get your heart broken?"

I am. But it's more than that. It's so much more than that. "It's complicated."

"Oh my god, Immy! You're the one who told me 'it's never complicated. Don't trust a guy who says things are complicated. That means he's hiding something.'"

Why did I teach her so well? "Okay. It's not complicated. If I want things to continue, I need to open up with him, and I'm not ready to do that."

"You're scared?"

I say nothing.

"Seriously? You're better than that. And how bad could it be? You're like… the golden child."

"What? You're the golden child."

"You have straight As. You got a scholarship to UCLA!"

"You're going to get a full ride to an Ivy."

"And those schools are three thousand miles away. If I get offered a scholarship at Stanford and I don't go there…"

"Mom has said that?"

"She doesn't have to say it."

"She wants the best for you."

"She wants the best for you too. She just… doesn't know how to do that. Aren't you the one studying psychology?"

"It's different. She's softer with you."

"Maybe. But only because I give her the opening."

What does that mean?

Julie doesn't expand or ask me to explain further. She shifts the conversation to the adventure novel she's reading as we finish dinner and clean. She waits until I'm on my way out the door and she launches a counter-attack.

"Talk to Mom sometime," Julie says. "She misses you. She won't admit it, but she does. I know something is there. So don't bother denying it."

"Okay."

"You won't deny it?"

"I'll talk to her."

"Will you tell me what it is?"

I shake my head.

"Should I worry?"

"I love you." I pull her into a hug. "Be good."

"Text me when you get home. And after you talk to him. Whatever you decide to do. Even if you chicken out."

She releases me and she shakes her head *I know you didn't answer my question*, but she doesn't call me on that either.

She's right.

She always is.

And the best way to do this is quickly.

Like a Band-Aid. I don't want to wait and let it attach.

I owe him an in person breakup.

I slip into my car and I text Patrick.

Imogen: Hey? Can I stop by on my way home? We need to talk.

Chapter Thirty

PATRICK

My phone sits on my desk, mocking me, baiting me, daring me.

I stare at Imogen's text for the better part of an hour. I consider claiming exhaustion or plans or a desire to discuss things tomorrow.

But I don't.

I reply.

Patrick: I'll be here all night. You okay?

As if I don't know why she's rushing here after her family dinner.

As if I don't know every single one of her secrets.

This is a start. A step in the right direction.

I'm capable of doing the right thing. I am.

This is fucked.

This is totally and completely fucked.

A sketch doesn't clear my thoughts. I need more. A drink. But I cleaned the place out a few months ago, when Dare made an offhand comment about how I was putting him to shame. I was. I was drinking too much, hiding from too much. And she inspired me—

Imogen, as Hearts and Thorns.

She faced her pain head-on. She worked through it. She dealt with it.

I wanted to be able to do that too. I wanted to be a better version of myself. The kind of guy who does the right thing in this situation. Who doesn't stop and question himself. Or try to ease the knots in his neck with booze.

But I'm not.

There's a bottle of vodka in the back of the freezer. Here for dates. Not that I hosted many. Too much bullshit. After Deidre died, I couldn't take any more bullshit.

I fill a glass with ice, a leftover bottle of Imogen's tonic water, enough vodka to relax my thoughts.

But the drink tastes like her. The unique bitter flavor of quinine on her lips. The two of us, in that bar, drinking gin and tonics, Imogen offering me all the trust in the world.

I didn't know.

She trusted me, and I trusted her, and neither of us had any idea.

We can hold on to that.

Somehow.

I ditch the booze. Pour a glass of water instead. Drink with greedy sips.

She knocks.

Almost an hour exactly. No traffic on Sunday nights. An easy drive up the 405. Plenty of time to think about how she wants to break this to me.

I take a deep breath and I answer. "Hey."

"Hey." Her voice is soft.

I'm not supposed to know why she's here. But I can still read her, tell something is wrong.

Nobody texts *we need to talk* if they're expecting an easy hang.

"You okay?" I lead her inside.

She closes the door behind her. "Long dinner, you know?"

I nod.

"Do you see your family often?"

"Not as much as I used to," I say.

She shifts her weight between her legs.

"Do you want something to drink?"

"Water. Thanks."

"Sure." I pour her a glass, refill mine, lead her to the couch.

She sits on the other side of the cushions. There's distance between us. A new distance.

She's preparing to do this, to do the right thing.

Of course she is. I know her. As Hearts and Thorns, sure, but I know her.

She follows the wisdom of her tattoo to a T.

Truth is my light.

She's always fighting for honesty, fighting to do the right thing.

But then—

She keeps this to herself too. She doesn't explain the details exactly, but she admits she hasn't shared her history far and wide.

She holds it close, keeps it safe.

"I don't really know how to say this." She takes a long sip and sets her water on the coffee table. "With my ex, it was… I thought I made things clear, but I didn't."

"What things?"

"I thought so much on the way here," she says. "I went through so many possibilities. My sister, she accused me of being a coward, and I think maybe she's right. Because I'm terrified of what this means."

"Slow down."

"I like you." She turns to me. "A lot."

"I like you too."

"But I… this isn't a good idea. The two of us."

"It's not?"

"It's not." She presses her palms into her quads.

"Why not?" *I've been following your site for a long time. I just put the pieces together. I'm not a crazy stalker, I swear.*

Sorry. I know you don't like when people use the word crazy casually.

Two years ago, I would have rolled my eyes. I would have run from understanding. Now, I know better.

I love the way you take it back. You're right. You've earned it.

I know what happened last year and I don't care.

It doesn't scare me. I promise.

"I did something I shouldn't have done," she says. "After I heard about your sister. I just thought… with the books she had and the way you talked about her… I looked for information and I found things I shouldn't have found. I know what happened. I know she died by suicide."

I don't know what to say.

If I didn't know she knew, what the fuck would I say?

No.

That doesn't matter.

The situation is the same.

"I'm sorry you lost her that way, Patrick," she says.

"Thanks."

"But I… I don't know how to explain."

"You don't have to explain," I say.

"No, I want to. Because I know how it is when people find something ugly and they get scared and run away. Like it changed you."

"Yeah."

"And it isn't that. I'm not afraid of your pain." She looks at her hands. "No, that's not true. I am. I'm scared of what it means."

Is she going to tell me? "I'm glad you know."

Surprise fills her dark eyes. "You are?"

"It's not an easy thing to bring up. But it feels good, sharing it, like I'm not hiding anymore."

Her eyes stay glued to mine.

"My friends don't know. And my parents don't talk about it. They're ashamed. Suicide is a mortal sin, you know?"

"No. Sorta. Not the religious part, but the whole idea that people attempt suicide as an act of malice, and not because they didn't see another option." She rubs her thumb with her forefinger. "I don't even believe in god, but I don't know... if there is some creator, why would she fault us for trying to end our suffering?"

"I don't know. I don't believe anymore."

"You don't?"

"I'm not sure I ever did," I say. "But after Deidre, I couldn't keep pretending. I couldn't go to church on Easter and Christmas. I couldn't look at my mom's rosary without raging."

"You rage?"

"Yeah."

"I can't imagine that," she says.

"It's more stewing, I guess. I get mad, but I stay in my head. I think about how fucked up the world is."

She watches me carefully.

"It was so tempting, to believe that story, that she was selfish or weak or somehow at fault. Because then I wouldn't have to ask myself what I missed, what I could have done to help her, what part I played."

"It's not your fault."

I should object, but I don't.

"She... I guess I don't know your relationship, but if it's anything like the one I have with my sister... that was probably the only thing keeping her here."

"She was living for me?"

"She wouldn't want to hurt you," she says. "She'd hate that she was hurting you. Even if she was too depressed to see it, if she felt like a burden or a failure, if she knew you'd be sad but she believed you'd be better off without her..."

Did she really feel that way?

"I'm sorry... I... excuse me." She stands and moves toward the downstairs bathroom. "Restroom."

"Sure."

She locks herself in the bathroom and runs the water.

I stand, stretch, try to remind myself to do the honest thing.

Is that the right thing? I don't know, but I know it's what she would want.

Don't freak out. I know.

Don't leave.

Please.

I need this connection.

But that's the problem.

I can't lose her.

Not the Imogen I know here. And not the one I know there either.

If she changes her site, stops writing—

That's too big a loss. Not just for me.

For everyone who finds understanding in her words.

The bathroom door opens.

Imogen moves into my main room.

I call on my conviction, but it evaporates the second her dark eyes meet mine. There's only thing I want.

To erase the pain on her face.

She's so fucking hurt and I'll do anything to stop it.

"I'm sorry." She wipes a tear away. "This isn't how this is supposed to go."

I move toward her.

She meets me in the middle of the room. She lets me wrap my arms around her. She sinks into my touch.

"I'm sorry," she says it again.

"You don't need to apologize."

She shakes her head against my chest. "I do. You lost her and I'm freaking out."

"It's okay."

She shakes her head into my chest again. "I'm a mess. I tried to warn you. Or maybe I didn't. I'm not good at this."

"Everyone's a mess."

"I came here to end things."

"I know."

"But I don't want to," she says.

"I don't want you to."

"I just… I can't explain, Patrick. I'm sorry. I wish I could. But I can't be the person you need."

"How do you know what I need?"

She pulls back enough to look at me.

"I decide what I need," I say.

"But…"

"And I need you, Imogen. I do."

"But—"

"No buts. I care about you. I want you in my life. What else matters?"

Chapter Thirty-One

IMOGEN

I *want you in my life. What else matters?*
The words are on the tip of my tongue.
The truth is so close.

I attempted suicide too. I swallowed a bottle of pills too. I set the whole thing up, so it would look like an accidental overdose, so my parents would have a story they could handle.

But I didn't time things right. Or maybe I timed them wrong on purpose. I don't know anymore.

I'm glad I'm here.

Alive.

In your apartment.

Connected.

That's the problem. I'm too connected. And there's nowhere to go if I don't tell him.

This is the perfect time.

The only time.

I have to be brave, to give him the chance to digest this information, decide what he wants to do with it.

I can't stay unless I tell him.

I can't leave unless I tell him.

"You don't have to say anything else," Patrick says.

I shake my head.

He rests his palm on my cheek, wipes a tear with his thumb. "You don't. Whatever it is, you don't have to tell me."

I did the same thing.

I'm sorry.

I'm stealing your pain, making it about me. I hate when people do that. It's the worst thing in the world.

"If you want to go, I won't stop you," he says. "But I don't want you to go."

"But—"

"You want to be here?"

I nod.

"I want you here. Don't over-think it." He wipes another tear with his thumb. "Whatever it is, we can talk about it. Or not talk about it."

"You're that agreeable?"

"No. I like your tits that much."

A laugh breaks up my tears.

His voice shifts back to a serious tone. "I haven't talked about my sister with anyone. This is new for me too. I'm scared too."

"You are?"

"Terrified."

"I don't want to hurt you," I say.

"You're not going to hurt me."

"Really? If I end things now, it won't hurt?"

"Okay, yeah, it will. But that's the cost of a relationship, isn't it?" he asks.

"You sound like my sister."

"She must be a smart kid."

"She is." I rest my head on his chest. "I have my own problems."

"Everyone does."

"I don't know if I can share."

"It's not a race."

"You're this calm about it? Really?"

"I'm not calm." He rests his hand on mine. "I'm shaking. But I don't want you to go and that's bigger than anything."

"Anything?"

"Anything I can imagine. And I've got a great imagination."

Maybe.

But even with this right in front of his face—

Most people never imagine this possibility.

Patrick laces his fingers with mine. "Stay. At least tonight. You're upset. You shouldn't drive. I'll sleep on the couch."

"No."

"Imogen—"

"No. I don't want to go. You're right. I just… I don't want to mislead you."

"You want to be here?"

I nod.

"You like me?"

"Yes. But this isn't casual anymore. And there are things I should tell you. Important things."

"Is there someone else?" he asks.

"No."

"Then you don't need to tell me. Not yet."

"Really? That's the only secret that would hurt you?"

"No. But I'm a man. And I'm not better than my instincts," he says.

"Me either."

"I think you are."

"I'm really not. But I… I don't want to talk anymore."

"Okay." He releases my hand.

I grab his wrist. "No. I want to not talk. If that's okay with you. I know everything with your sister must be complicated and I want to listen, I do. But right now, I can't. And I respect it if you need space or if you need an ear, I just—"

"Kiss me."

I don't hesitate. I bring my lips to his. I kiss him hard and fast.

My need pours into him.

His need pours into me.

It's different than our other kisses. Charged with the desire to come closer, let our walls down, connect mentally and emotionally as we connect physically.

It's different than it was with Zack too. I didn't love Zack. I didn't trust Zack. I didn't want to show Zack the places I hurt.

It wasn't his fault (not entirely). I never gave him a chance.

But this—

I'm trying.

Patrick wraps his arms around me. He guides me to the stairs.

We struggle up them.

I pull my tank top over my head.

He does away with his t-shirt.

Then my bra.

He pulls me onto the bed and wraps his arms around me. He explores my body with his hands.

He's not just finding the places that make me purr.

He's exploring my heart and soul too.

The same way I surrender to my physical needs, I surrender to these.

I close my eyes and I soak in the sensation of his hands on my skin, his lips on my neck, his breath in my ear.

The slow, tender movements.

The softness.

The intimacy.

We lie together, kissing and touching, for a long, long time. Then he brings his lips to my chin and kisses a line down my body.

All the way to my belly button, then just below it.

He undoes the button of my jeans and rolls them all the way to my feet. Then the cotton panties.

The feel of his lips against my thigh.

He explores me with his tongue, testing me with long, slow strokes and hard, fast ones.

He licks me up and down.

Then he finds the spot where I need him and he tests me there.

A little harder, a little higher, a little faster, a little slower.

There.

I dig my hands into his hair. "Fuck, Tricky. Don't stop."

He gives me exactly what he needs. He works me with perfect, steady flicks of his tongue.

Soft and wet and perfect.

My eyes close.

My hips buck.

My hands knot in his hair.

The rest of the world fades away until all I feel is anticipation. His soft wet tongue against me, his hands against my thighs, his movements winding me tighter and tighter.

Closer and closer.

Until it's almost too much to take.

Then I'm there, groaning his name as I come, my entire body wracked with bliss.

The entire world, a place of pure, white bliss.

He works me through my orgasm, then he presses his lips to my thigh. Only he doesn't move on. He gives me a moment to catch my breath then he brings his mouth to me and he drives me to the edge again.

I come hard and fast. It's too much, too painful, but it's not enough either.

I need more.

I need him inside me.

"I'm ready," I tug at his hair.

He kisses his way up my body and reaches for something on his dresser. The condom.

"No. I'm ready," I say. "If you are."

"You sure?"

"Yeah. If you're not—"

"I am," he says.

"Then please."

He nods and undoes his jeans.

I push them off his hips then wrap my hand around his cock. There's a visceral, physical pleasure to the sensation, but there's more too.

A desire to feel every part of him.

To connect without anything between us.

He kisses me as he does away with his jeans. It's a little strange, tasting him on my lips, but there's something sexy about that too. The full circle of pleasure.

He brings his hands to my hips and holds me in place.

I wrap my legs around his waist.

His tip brushes my sex. His skin against mine. Nothing in the way.

He teases me again.

Again.

Inch by inch, he slides inside me.

All of him against all of me.

I'm wet and ready. My body stretches to take him easily. And without the layer of lubricated latex—

He's so much closer.

The sheer intimacy of it overwhelms me.

The need.

The trust.

The satisfaction.

Maybe I can't share my past, but I can share this. Fuck, how I want to share this.

I wrap my arms around him.

He pulls back and sinks into me again. Slowly, patiently, like he's savoring every perfect inch.

I rake my nails against his back.

Again.

I groan against his lips.

Again.

I pull him closer with my thighs.

His body feels so good against mine. The weight of it. The warmth.

And feeling of him driving into me again and again—

This is a whole other tier of bliss.

This is everything.

I rock my hips to meet him.

We move in time together, our bodies coming closer and closer, the two of us tangled as one until he's close.

He starts moving faster, harder. His breath speeds. His thighs shake.

Then he's there, groaning against my neck, pulsing inside me as he comes.

It's more visceral.

It's way fucking hotter.

The feel of his orgasm pulls me toward the edge. But I'm not quite there. I dig my nails into his back, savoring the sounds of his bliss.

He pumps through his orgasm, then he untangles our bodies, he turns me onto my side, and he positions himself behind.

He slips his hand between my legs. "Can you take more?"

"Please."

And he rubs me exactly how I need him.

I come quickly, tugging at the sheets, groaning his name as the tension in my sex releases.

When I'm finished, I move his hand to my waist and I dissolve in his arms.

This feels good.

Way too good.

But, right now, I don't care.

I don't care about anything but feeling his body against mine.

Chapter Thirty-Two

IMOGEN

We lie there for a long time. Eventually, I rise, shower, change into one of Patrick's shirts and a pair of his boxers.

I didn't plan on staying the night.

I didn't plan on screwing him.

I didn't plan beyond *I'm ending things*. And now I'm here and I'm continuing things and I don't know what the fuck I'm doing.

Just like when I tried to end everything. I had no idea what to do when I woke up. All of a sudden, I had this huge life I didn't know how to handle.

I didn't regret my attempt. It was the only option I saw.

Maybe my faith in systems is too strong, but that was how I saw it. Of all my available choices, there was only one guaranteed to end my pain.

With treatment, I realized there were other options. They weren't guarantees, but they didn't come with the same opportunity cost.

I really sound like an economist now. Life as opportunity cost. But that's why I love economics. Everything makes sense when it's broken into opportunity costs, profits, losses.

Add the psychology of behavioral economics and all of a sudden, people actually make sense.

But how does that knowledge help me now?

I'm here and I have this huge connection I don't know how to handle.

There's some dark humor here, but I'm too tired to find the pieces. The start of an entry forms in my head as Patrick showers.

Turns out I'm not great at ending things.

Intentions, sure?

But the results speak for themselves.

There's too much swirling in my head. I need to write. But I don't want to dig through it yet. I want to stay here, in the comfortable space of his room.

Because I like him.

Because I like fucking him.

Because he understands. In some strange way, he understands.

Maybe I was wrong. Maybe this is an asset, not a liability.

Or maybe I'm full of it.

That's a strong possibility.

He emerges from the bathroom wrapped in a towel, wet hair sticking to his forehead, water rolling off his chest.

He looks good here. And, more, this feels personal, like we're really in each other's lives.

Experiment notes: Subject went off-script with social media dives. Add new rules, to forbid these kinds of things, and repeat with a more compliant subject.

Or maybe give up on the whole separating sex and love thing.

Focus on the what-do-I-like instead.

"You okay?" He adjusts the towel.

My eyes flit to his crotch instinctively.

He smiles. "I can drop it."

"I've seen it before."

"My ego."

"That's not what I mean."

"I know," he says.

"We can talk. If you want. Or you can talk. I can listen."

"About Deidre?" he asks.

"Or anything," I say.

He moves to the dresser, dries, pulls on a pair of boxers. "Is that what you want?"

I don't know what I want. "I want to sleep."

"Good news." He motions to the bed.

"I can't. Not right now. I'm too wired."

"My ego again."

"Tricky—"

"I know." His voice is soft. "Someone told you last night?"

"Dare, yeah. He was worried about you."

"Really?" Surprise streaks his face. "Darren worries?"

I nod.

"He's never said anything." He runs a hand through his hair. "Dare is like me. He's always been like me. He runs away from hard, complicated things."

"You were middle school friends?"

"Yeah, instant friends. Deidre called us Rosencrantz and Guildenstern."

I can't help but smile. "She really was an English major."

"Yeah. Even when we read Hamlet in high school, well, when I read the SparkNotes, I didn't get it."

"They're on the outskirts."

He nods. "She had to explain it to me. They're the comic relief. They're not part of the main events. They're not making things happen."

"You were watching your own life?"

He nods. "I was hanging back, watching, never taking anything seriously. I had problems, sure, but nothing that forced me to introspect. Hell, until I discovered drawing, I never even sat in silence. I was always filling the space with something. TV or music or dumb jokes with a friend."

He leans against the dresser, lost in thought, two feet away. Close and far at the same time.

I want to wrap my arms around him. But I want to stay here too, listening, giving him space, letting him come to me.

Is this love?

I don't know. But it's something.

Patrick continues, "When I got older, I started using women and alcohol to fill the space instead. I knew something was missing, deep down. And sometimes it caught up to me. I had these moments where I felt a pang of longing I couldn't place. I'd feel this sense of falseness, that everything was bullshit, but I chased it away with another drink or another fuck."

"I know what you mean."

"You avoided introspection?" he asks.

"When things were too hard," I say. "I tried to fill my time. I tried to stay too busy to really get into my head. But I picked the wrong sport. An hour and a half in the pool is a lot of time to think, even if I'm exhausted afterward."

"What were you running from?"

"The same things you were." Sort of. "The things that were too heavy and complicated for me. I thought it was cool to be a damaged artist. To cultivate misery."

"Like Sylvia Plath?"

"Yeah. It seemed romantic, how she—"

"I know she killed herself. Everyone knows that."

"You knew before your sister?" I ask.

"No," he admits. "But I found out when I started reading her stuff."

"Right. I guess most thoughtful young women go through that phase, where they admire the women with guts. It's fucked up, but it…"

"It is a gusty thing to do," he says. "It doesn't help anyone to pretend otherwise."

It is. I hate when people say it's cowardly. It's not like

depressed people are any less afraid of death. But this isn't about me. "Do you think of her as brave?"

"She was always brave, yeah."

"But not brave enough to talk to you?"

He looks to the floor. "I wouldn't have heard her if she did. I don't know if she tried to talk to Molly… but Molly is like me. She hides from the heavy stuff with work, but she hides all the same."

Maybe we all do.

"How did you run from stuff?"

I owe him this much honesty. "I didn't have the nerve to really dip into self-destruction. Or maybe I was too sheltered. People at my school weren't having wild sex or buying drugs off the street. They were making out and stealing their parents' wine. And we'd get caught, get in trouble, get too scared to do it again."

"It's not as fun as it sounds."

"I know. I had my phase where I went through guys like it was going out of style. Not sex."

His shoulders fall.

"You really are a man, huh?"

"I told you."

"You've been with other people," I say.

"Yeah."

"But you're jealous I've been with other people?"

"I don't like thinking of some guy taking advantage of you."

"That's kind of sweet." A little possessive but sweet.

"And if you told me you were jealous of all the women I fucked, I'd tell you not to be. 'Cause it never meant anything. I wouldn't let it mean anything."

"Never?" I ask.

"No. It was always bullshit. After Deidre, I tried to go back to my routine. I had a few casual flings, but I didn't enjoy them. I could feel the falseness. There was no honesty there, no vulnerability. It was all pretense."

"And that's why you liked me?"

He nods. "'Cause you were straight with me. No bullshit."

"I don't like bullshit either."

"I know."

"I don't have to talk about the other guys," I say. "If it bothers you."

"Do you want to talk about it?"

"I guess there isn't much to say. Guys were always willing."

"Of course," he says. "You're gorgeous."

My cheeks flush. I'm not gorgeous, really. Conventionally attractive enough? Sure. Athletic? Absolutely. But I'm not a knockout by any definition of the word. "I did have fun, sometimes, experimenting. But I wasn't there, really. I would check out of my body, go somewhere else. And then I'd think about why I wasn't enjoying myself enough."

"Always?"

"No." My cheeks flush. "Sometimes, if the guys were talented… I had moments, you know. Never the acts themselves, but the anticipation. I guess I… I've always had these impulses."

"That's nothing to be embarrassed about."

"I don't want to push things to sex," I say. "I want to talk to you."

"I promise not to jump your bones." He stays glued to the dresser.

My lips curl into a smile. "For how long?"

"Five minutes."

A laugh spills from my lips. "That's a long time for you."

"I can even make it ten."

"A new record," I say.

"I can wait as long as you want."

"You get off on it."

"Yeah," he says. "But that's not what I mean."

"I guess sex and love are tangled for both of us, huh?"

He nods. "I've had girlfriends before, but it was the same as everything else. It was surface level. I liked them and they liked me but we didn't share anything meaningful."

"Even sexually?"

"Sex doesn't have to be intimate," he says.

"No. It doesn't. But it is with you."

"I like it."

"I do too." I sit up straight. "Was that the biggest way you hid from yourself?"

"No. I drank too much. Then, when Deidre died, I drank way too much. I wanted to forget. But I only felt it more... until I drank enough, I passed out. I didn't run to understanding her. I hid from that for a long time too."

"What happened to change things?"

"There wasn't one big moment. It was a bunch of little things, adding up. I was here, surrounded by her stuff all the time, in her space, feeling her absence."

"You took over her lease?"

"Mortgage," he says. "She left it to me. Not an official will. A note. Enough nobody fought it. Or maybe... sometimes I think they let me have it as a bribe, so I'd stay quiet."

"That must hurt."

"I'm used to it."

"Do you want to talk to them about it?"

"I don't know. I can't force them to face it. I'm still trying to understand it myself."

"I'm sorry," I say. "I know how hard that is when your parents want to deny your reality. I... I'm really sorry."

"Thanks."

"Is that why you read her books? To understand?"

"Am I that obvious?"

I nod. "Did it help?"

"It did. And it didn't. I can see what she was going through now, how she felt, but I still don't get it. There's something that just doesn't make sense to me. How she could leave me that way? How she could hide this from me? I *know* it's not about that. I *know* she was too hurt, she probably thought she was doing me a favor. I know, but I can't quite wrap my head around it."

"Do you have to?"

"I don't know." He sits on the bed next to me. He sits close enough our legs touch. "It gets kind of exhausting, thinking about her in these terms. I annoy myself for making it about what I could have done, how it affected me. She deserves better. She deserves to live in my memory as the person she was too."

"What was she like?"

"Witty. She always had a literary reference. For a while, she threw out Shakespeare quotes as quips. I never got it. Our parents hated it. Molly hated it. But that only encouraged her."

"A troublemaker?"

"Yeah." He smiles. "She was like you. In her head a lot. I always wondered what she was thinking, what it was like to have such deep, interesting thoughts."

"You looked up to her?"

He nods. "She stood up to our parents, she stood up for me. Hell, she stood up for people who needed it. She ran the Amnesty International chapter at our school and she volunteered to teach at community centers. She always said it was for her, too. That she did it 'cause it made her feel good. But sometimes I think… she was doing what I did, staying busy to stay away from her ugly thoughts."

"We all do it."

He nods. "She had refined tastes in literature. Even the graphic novels—she only read the acclaimed books. But her taste in music?" He shakes his head. "She loved the worst shit."

"Aren't you all classic rock, all the time?"

"Sure, I don't have taste, but at least I don't have bad taste."

"Isn't that worse?" I ask.

"Hey." He nudges me.

"What did she like?"

"The cheesiest sensitive dude songs."

"Softboys?" I ask.

"Yeah, that's it." He laughs. "Molly was always tossing 'soft-boy' memes in our group chat."

"The three of you had a group chat?"

"It was mostly the two of them, but I jumped in sometimes. Deidre was funny. She gave as good as she got. It's not like Molly had better taste. She loved the same stuff Chase does."

"Chase?"

"Our shop manager. Even though he's a dad now, he still listens to the music he liked in high school. All these toxic dudes whining about their ex-girlfriends. And Molly loves that too. They'd fight about who was a bigger traitor to feminism. Molly would insist she was laughing at the misogyny, depriving it of its power. Deidre would say her favorite bands seemed like they were doing concept albums, to try to prove Margaret Atwood right."

"Men are afraid women will laugh at them. Women are afraid men will kill them."

"Yeah," he says. "I learned a lot through them."

"Bossy older sisters are the best."

"You'd say that." He smiles. "They had these epic fights about it, but it was in good spirit. Molly thought it was better to face anger and know. She thought it was honest. At least the guys she listened to were upfront about being assholes. And, well, she never really admitted it, but I think she felt that anger too. With her girlfriends. She hated that she identified with all these possessive assholes. Fuck, that was a long time ago."

"Did you have a take?"

"I couldn't really talk. It's not like classic rock is filled with feminist manifestos. And I didn't pay attention to the lyrics anyway."

"You cared about that stuff?"

"It's not that I cared or didn't," he says. "It was normal to me, to talk about it, consider it. That was something older sisters did. And I internalized their lectures. Their voices popped into my head all the time."

"I know what you mean."

He smiles and raises his voice an octave. "'Patrick, are you really listening to *My Sharona*? Isn't it about a super young woman! What a creep. Listen to something else. Maybe try a female artist.' Then they'd start arguing that neither of them listened to enough female artists."

"And everyone sat around listening to Fiona Apple."

"The happiest ending, yeah." He laughs. "Sometimes. But never Fiona Apple."

"Terrible," I say.

"Very." He laughs. "They'd have a sorta badass girl artist off. See who could find someone better. Then they'd go back to their usual stuff."

"Fiona Apple didn't stick?"

"No, but Deidre added more female singer-songwriters to her rotation. And Molly added riot grrl stuff."

"And still, despite all these options, you kept listening to AC/DC?"

"I didn't think about music much."

I actually gasp.

"Sorry," he says. "I know it's sacrilege to people who love music, but I just… I didn't get it."

"Do you now?"

"I'm starting to," he says. "But I'm a work in progress."

"Maybe we should play something now."

"Let me guess? Fiona Apple."

I laugh. "I like other artists."

"Uh-huh."

"I liked the woman Luna found. She was good," I say. "It was sweet, you were listening to stuff I'd like."

"We can play something if you want."

"Later," I say. "Tell me more about her."

He rests his head on my shoulder.

My entire body buzzes. It feels so good, having him close, sharing this way.

"She would have liked you," Patrick says.

"How do you figure?"

"She hated that I was always dating 'ditzes.'"

"Were you?"

"No, but I wasn't dating intellectual women. I was trying to avoid heavy shit. And smart girls want something real. Even when it comes to casual sex. I couldn't handle real. I think that was why she hated it, because she saw that, because she knew I could do better."

"She expected a lot for you?"

"It felt like it. But now… I think she wanted me to be the best version of myself."

"She sounds like a good sister."

"She was, yeah."

"I'm sorry you lost her," I say.

"Me too." He pulls me closer. "But it feels good to do this, to just talk about her, the person she was."

"Then keep talking."

He does.

―――――

WE STAY UP LATE, UNTIL WE'RE BOTH TOO TIRED TO TALK, TO move.

We climb under the covers, tangled together, listening to each other's breath.

And, slowly, I fall asleep in his arms.

I wake up in his bed.

I rise, I brush my teeth and wash my face, I fix a chai.

Patrick meets me in the kitchen. "You have to go? Class?"

I nod.

"What time?"

"I have two hours."

"Should we make them count?" he asks.

"How are we going to do that?"

Chapter Thirty-Three

IMOGEN

"**I** have a crazy idea," Patrick says.

"Sex in the ocean?"

He laughs. "Crazier."

"Sex under the Santa Monica Pier? Then masturbation in the Santa Monica jail?"

"Even crazier," he says.

"Trying to bribe the cop who arrests us with sex?"

His laugh is easy. "Not that crazy."

I strain the chai and fix two mugs.

His fingers brush mine as he takes one. "We could listen to one of Deidre's albums, one you'd like."

"Does she have vinyl?"

"An Apple Music playlist."

"Modern," I say.

He motions *sorta*. "Or we could do Fiona Apple. If you pick the album she'd like the most."

"*Criminal* is the broadest, but I'm not sure it's what she'd like, based on what you've said."

"It won't put me in the mood," he says.

"No? Thinking about your sister doesn't turn you on?" Late sister, but, for some reason, it feels wrong to mention that.

He wants to remember her, celebrate the person she was.

And I want to do that too. Because she led him, she helped him, she left him.

Because if he understands her, maybe he'll understand me too.

Are my motives pure or evil?

I don't know anymore. I don't care. I want to be here. I want to skip school and lie in bed listening to singer-songwriters and reading and making love.

Maybe there's a better term, something less cheesy, but fucking isn't accurate anymore. We're closer. More intimate.

"We could also get arrested at the pier," he says.

"I'd miss class."

"Damn. If only."

"If only." I laugh. "Okay. How about I fix us oatmeal and you pick an album. We can eat and listen. Talk or not talk."

"Oatmeal?" he asks.

"Oh, you're an oatmeal hater?"

"Is that a deal breaker?"

"It's just kind of obvious," I say. "Like making a joke about pineapples on pizza."

"Californian."

I raise a brow. "And you'd turn down a slice of pineapple pizza?"

"We've established my lack of taste."

"Try it. Once."

"All right, once. If I don't like it, I'll make you eggs next time you're here," he says.

"You cook more than quesadillas?"

He nods. "Scrambled eggs too."

"Anything else?"

"Burgers. Salad. Grilled chicken."

"What do you eat?" I ask.

"When I'm not eating quesadillas and eggs?"

I nod.

"A lot of rotisserie chicken. Takeout from places near Inked Hearts. My parents send me home with leftovers when I see them. Molly too. Beef stew, mostly."

"It keeps well."

"And they make it well. I can't complain."

"Stew is easy," I say. "I could teach you."

"You like stew?"

"Who doesn't?"

"You don't eat anything plain. Even that oatmeal. You'll drown it in cinnamon."

"Well, I do make Japanese Curry, but that is a stew."

"Aha."

"I can do stew," I say. "Plain, boring stew."

Again, he raises a brow.

"Plain, not boring stew."

"I can, actually," he says. "Deidre taught me a few dishes when I moved out. She didn't want me to survive on ramen and Cheetos. But I… I haven't made it in a while. Or Shepard's pie. Or sheet pan chicken. Sheet pan anything."

"We could do it together, if you want."

"Yeah?" His shoulders soften.

"Whenever you're ready."

"You're sweet," he says.

"Maybe I like chunks of beef."

"Obviously." He flexes a bicep. Laughs at himself. "Sorry, that's Dare's bit."

"It works for you too."

"Yeah, but it's lame," he says. "Even for me." He moves to the coffee table and opens his laptop. "Do your best with the oatmeal."

"I always do."

He looks through his sister's song library.

I fix oatmeal on the stove. It isn't my absolute best, but it's solid. Soft and chewy with the extra crunch of walnuts and sweetness of raisins.

A woman's voice fills the room. Then a piano melody.

It's familiar. The artist was popular way back when.

"Christina Perri." He moves to the table. "She played this album to win one of her song-offs with Molly."

"Did you pick the winner?"

"No. They didn't give a fuck what I thought."

"So, what, they fairly judged each other?" I sit next to him.

"So they said." He picks up his spoon. "Thanks, Imogen. Really."

"It's nothing."

"Fixing me breakfast at my place. It's something."

My cheeks flush. "You're welcome."

He studies a scoop of oatmeal with suspicion, shrugs *here goes nothing*, and brings the spoon to his mouth.

I watch his expression change. Hesitation. Surprise. Satisfaction.

"Not as bad as I expected."

"You like it," I say.

"I like it." He takes another bite. "I don't love it, but I like it."

"That's how it starts."

"Oh?"

"Have you ever noticed? Nobody just likes oatmeal. They make it the butt of every joke or they love it."

"I'm surprised you like it."

"Too plain?"

He nods.

"But that's why I love it. I can add whatever I want. It's a perfect base, like white rice."

"Anything? Even eggs? Or cheese?"

"Savory oatmeal," I say. "Some people are into it."

He looks at his bowl. "No fucking way."

"I prefer sweet, but I've tried it."

"With what?"

"Green onions, eggs, sesame seeds. It works better than you'd think."

He shakes his head *disturbing*.

"It's like rice or bread. Nobody thinks it's weird we put jelly on toast and eat roast beef sandwiches."

We fall into silence as the song shifts to the next. It has the same sound. Soft, emotional vocals, melodic piano, all this openness and easy vulnerability.

It doesn't sound like his description of his sister. But maybe that's why she loved it. Because she wanted to feel a connection with anyone she could find, even the songwriter.

"Did your sister like guys?" I ask.

"Yeah," he says. "She always said it was unfortunate. Molly came out young. And our parents… I guess it doesn't make sense, now, how quickly they accepted it, but they did, and I was too young to wonder about the contradiction, how they could support a church that said my sister was a sinner and support her too, but they did."

"Are they close?"

"Molly and my parents? Kinda. She was always headstrong, same as Deidre, but different, you know? Deidre would stand up for other people. Molly would fight for herself."

"I know what you mean."

"She's never said it, but I think she's always felt it," he says. "That divide between their faith and her. She stopped going to church after she came out and they never asked. But now… I wonder if it was their suggestion."

"Parents are hard. With my mom… I know how hard things are for her. I see it. Fuck, I saw her smoking."

"Smoking?"

"Vaping." I laugh. "My stern, totally in control all the time mom… vaping. And she looked sad, scared. I wanted to feel for her. I did. But then all the ways she hurt me came rushing in."

"You feel both at the same time?"

"But my hurt wins," I say. "Or at least… I can't bring it to her. I can't talk about it."

He nods. "I get that."

"Is she okay, you think? Molly?"

"I don't know. She acts tough and she'd never confide in me. She's older. In her early thirties."

"How old was Deidre?"

"Late twenties."

"You really are the baby," I say.

He nods. "Molly sees me that way. It's kind of nice, having a sister who's so much older and wiser. But she knows it too."

"She sounds badass."

"She is."

The singer's voice catches my thoughts. She's hurt, vulnerable, raw. It's commendable.

But there's something else about it—

It feels too easy. She's running toward her big, hard feelings, not struggling to grapple with them.

Do people really process that easily?

Fiona Apple makes more sense to me. Her hurt is laced with self-destruction.

Maybe that's why his older sister likes music by angry guys. It's more honest. Anger is easier for most people, especially men.

"Where are you going, baby?" he asks.

Baby. He's never called me that here. I like it. I like it too much. "I guess I was thinking about your sister. The, uh, soft-boys. Maybe that's what she liked about it, this guy being vulnerable with her. That's hard to find in real life. It's hard for everyone, I think, to find someone who truly shares with them."

He looks at me funny.

"But men aren't as primed to think about it."

"We're not."

"And so it's easier for women to fall for these guys who share their hearts. Or even… these guys who share their anger. Because it's honest."

"It's fucked up."

"But that makes it feel more honest."

236

"Don't convince me to respect those assholes." He shakes his head. "I have to hear them nonstop at Inked Love."

"Anything I'd know?"

"Nah. Old stuff. Chase and Forest are older."

"Anything I'd like?" I ask.

"It's no Fiona Apple."

My lips curl into a smile. "I like other artists."

He raises a brow.

"I do."

"Okay. After this, it's your turn."

"Okay, but only if it's your turn next time."

"My turn?"

I nod. "To play me something you love. Not your sisters or someone at the shop. You."

"Can it be something I hate instead?"

I laugh. "If you can't think of anything you love."

"Fair." He offers his hand.

I shake.

And we fall back into silence. For the rest of the album. Then the one I pick.

I go back to an old favorite, something I loved before I realized I wanted to self-destruct. A Michelle Branch album with the perfect mix of honesty and melodic piano.

He listens with me.

I explain how I discovered it. A friend's older sister. She had the best taste in music. She seemed to know everything about boys, clothes, movies, music.

And she did.

But she knew the world the same way I did. Went down her own path of self-destruction. High functioning alcoholism.

I don't mention that.

Or the music I fell for after this.

Instead, I sit with Patrick and remember the girl who played *Hotel Paper* on repeat, the girl who wanted to share her poetry with the world (not that I ever managed to write decent poetry).

She's still there, inside of me, somewhere.

And being here, in this open, honest space, I want to find her. Only I don't want to share with the world.

I want to share with him.

And that's scarier than anything.

————

After, I gather my things, we kiss goodbye. I think of Patrick on the drive back to my apartment, as I shower and dress and rush to class.

For an hour and a half, I study micro-economics. I think about my experiment, wonder what the hell this means. Not because I need to save this for posterity.

Because that's how I understand people.

I can break it down, sure.

The opportunity cost of exclusivity.

The mutual gains of exclusivity (safe, condom free sex).

The mutual gains of shared labor. (Pooling resources is more efficient).

It all makes perfect sense.

But where do I explain the feeling in my chest? The free fall of falling for him? The desire to spill my guts? The fear of pushing him away.

Sharing secrets leads to trust.

Trust leads to additional cooperation.

Cooperation leads to the best outcomes.

It all makes sense, but none of it explains the feelings coursing through my veins.

After class, I pull out my cell, ready to text him, check on him, plan more time together.

But I have something else to address first.

A text from Julie.

Julie: So? Are you single? Did you chicken out? Or did you tell him everything?

Chapter Thirty-Four

IMOGEN

Did I chicken out?

I didn't end things, but I didn't confess either.

How the hell do I explain this to Julie? What do I owe my kid sister?

She isn't like me. She doesn't live in her head, obsess over books, pour her thoughts onto blank pages. She's a social butterfly. She can discuss anything with anyone.

I can't.

Our family can't. We haven't.

I don't know what to say, so I stick with the truth. What I'm willing to share, at least.

Imogen: I didn't end things.

Julie: !!

Imogen: I talked to him. We dealt with it, like adults.

Julie: Yeah, you're a bastion of maturity, staring at your phone all night, needing your high school sister to talk you into conversation.

Imogen: I know, right?

Julie: Seriously, Immy, where are the details!

Imogen: What details?

Julie: "We handled it like adults" isn't a real description of events. What really happened?

Everything. Nothing. There are a million places to start.

My depressive phase, my attempt, my inability to broach it with Mom, to confess to anyone.

That's the problem with Patrick too.

Or maybe it's not a problem.

It stopped feeling like a problem last night. But maybe that's the sex talking. Or something else.

Imogen: I want to tell you, I do. But it's his. It's not mine to share.

Julie: What you found about him?

Imogen: Yes.

That's not totally true, but it's true enough.

Imogen: It's between the two of us.

Julie: I guess that's sweet, that you're keeping his secret.

Imogen: It means I'll keep yours.

Julie: Trust me. I know you keep secrets.

Is it that obvious?

Julie: I guess everyone does. I didn't mean it as an accusation. I'm just worried.

Imogen: You don't need to worry about me.

Julie: I do.

Imogen: Not with him.

Julie: Especially with him. I remember you and Zack. What a train wreck.

Imogen: It wasn't that bad.

Julie: Maybe for you. But for him? Did you know he texted me for a while?

Imogen: What?

Julie: Not in a sleazy way. It was just about the internship at his dad's company at first.

That's vaguely familiar.

Julie: Then, you ended things, and he wanted to "check up on you." I didn't have the heart to tell him you seemed totally unbothered by the breakup. So I told him you missed him, but you knew ending things was the right thing to do. He kept begging me for explanations. I guess he didn't understand what happened, and he thought I would.

Imogen: He shouldn't have done that.

Julie: Maybe. But I didn't mind. He's a nice guy.

Imogen: He's a blowhard.

Julie: Oh, you mean you didn't want to hear him compare himself to the Joker and talk about what an epic film Joker was, again?

Imogen: Somehow, no.

Julie: There wasn't any funny business. Just so you know.

Imogen: I know.

Julie: How? He was good-looking. He paid attention to me. He could have done the wrong thing.

Imogen: Because I know he wouldn't. And I know you'd never do that to me.

Julie: That is true. The last part. The first, probably. But I'd never do anything to hurt you. Not on purpose. Are you mad? Don't be mad. I was going to tell you, but you got weird and I didn't know how to broach it.

Imogen: I'm not mad.

Julie: So you're hiding something big?

Imogen: How do you figure?

Julie: You should be mad.

Imogen: He approached you, right?

Julie: Yeah, he was crazy in love with you. Just couldn't get over it.

Imogen: He didn't really know me.

Julie: I saw that pretty quickly. The way he described you, I always thought, no way he's talking about my sister, Imogen, the badass who lectures me about Fiona Apple?

Imogen: Am I that much of a broken record?

Julie: A broken Fiona Apple record, yes.

Imogen: Patrick said the same thing.

Julie: Aww, you listened to Fiona together? True love.

Imogen: Not Fiona yet, actually. But he listened on his own. And we listened to something he loved.

Sorta.

Julie: Does he have bad taste?

Imogen: Yes, but he's aware of it.

Julie: How bad?

Imogen: Dad rock.

Julie: Our dad? Or general dads?

Imogen: General.

Julie: Oof.

Imogen: Please. You listen to Yop 40.

Julie: You're just jealous the music you like isn't popular anymore.

Imogen: People remember Fiona Apple. People won't remember whoever you're jamming.

Julie: Everyone will remember Taylor Swift and we both know you secretly love her.

Imogen: I enjoy some of her work.

Julie: OMG, you're so full of it. I remember you rocking out to all sorts of Swiftie jams, but okay, sure. Why are you embarrassed you like something popular anyway? Wasn't Fiona Apple popular in her day?

Imogen: Are you calling me basic?

Julie: OMG, GRANDMA. No one says basic anymore. But what's wrong with liking things other people like?

Imogen: How can something everyone likes be good?

Julie: Because it's easy to like.

Imogen: Exactly. I want something hard to like. I want something with sharp edges.

Julie: Well, you do sound like Imogen. The girl Zack described? Honestly, I was wondering if he was two-timing you and he'd accidentally written to the wrong ex-girlfriend's sister. I talked to him for such a long time, trying to get to the bottom of it. How could he have such a wrong impression? Was he not paying attention? Or was I wrong somehow?

Imogen: I didn't share myself with him.

Julie: I figured. I mean, when he said you watched four movies about violent dudes on four nights in a row… no way. You hate violent movies.

Imogen: I do.

Julie: And he thought you liked them! And that you liked his conversations about film because you didn't interrupt. I wanted to tell him, OMG, you have Immy so wrong! If she's quiet, she's thinking hard. Maybe about something important, something she really wants to tell you. Or maybe that you're an idiot, and she has no idea how to break it to you.

Imogen: I'm not that mean.

Julie: Not usually.

Imogen: His lectures were the worst.

Julie: Men are like that a lot.

Imogen: What men?

Julie: OMG DON'T EVEN!

Imogen: I mean… what do you mean?

Julie: Isn't that how he was? He'd talk to you, but really, he was talking to himself. He never made sure you were listening. He took silence as consent. And I don't mean sexually, so don't go there. I haven't gone that far with any guys.

Imogen: I wasn't going to go there.

Julie: I'll take Bullshit for 1000, Alex.

Imogen: Really.

Julie: They do it sexually too. That's what I hear from friends. Even now. They still act like nothing is yes, or I agree, or of course, you're brilliant. They don't even get that "hmm" or "I guess" or "maybe" is no. They don't understand the world women live in.

Imogen: That's smart.

Julie: I'm not just a jock.

Imogen: Your boyfriend is sweet to you?

Julie: Well…

Imogen: Do I need to kill someone?

Julie: You have to go first, okay? Tell me what happened with Patrick. Is he like Zack?

Imogen: No. He listens. He thinks I'm smart. Fuck, am I like Zack?

Julie: Do you ramble for ages without a response?

Imogen: Sometimes. Not usually.

Julie: You're probably good.

Imogen: Probably?

Julie: You're pretty. Maybe that's the interest.

Imogen: Was that a compliment or an insult?

Julie: An honest assessment of the twenty-something male mind.

Imogen: I'm the one studying psychology.

Julie: You rubbed off on me.

Imogen: You listen? Really?

Julie: See! You noticed I tune you out. You're not like Zack the Blowhard.

Imogen: He didn't really bring up Joker?

Julie: Of course he did.

Imogen: So glad we broke up.

Julie: Was that all it was? He was a tool, and you needed an excuse to end it?

Imogen: More or less.

Julie: Why did you stay with him so long?

Imogen: It seemed right, on paper. He was handsome; he was cultural, and he was decent in bed.

Julie: Decent, wow? So worth the annoyance.

Imogen: It wasn't just him.

Back then, I was on my first round of meds. I didn't know better there, either. They killed my O, and I didn't want to do the work of finding it or switching meds. It was easier to tell myself it didn't matter, to do whatever he suggested.

I barely questioned it.

So many of the girls I knew were the same. They were sexually curious, sure, but they were also willing to follow a guy's lead.

It seemed… normal.

Imogen: It wasn't just him. I wasn't open that way back then. And I figured that was sex. It was fun, in some ways, but more for connection than satisfaction.

Only I didn't feel connected with him either. But really, that wasn't on him. At least, not just him. I wasn't really there.

Julie: But not with Patrick?

Imogen: It feels different. But I don't know if I'm capable.

Julie: You're such a drama queen.

Imogen: It's possible. Maybe it's not for me.

Julie: You like him. I can tell. And you're obviously enjoying the sex.

Imogen: There's more to relationships than sex.

Julie: It's a start though. It's more than you had with Zack.

Imogen: I liked Zack.

Julie: After two weeks?

Imogen: At first, I thought he was smart and cool and opinionated. It took a while for the luster to wear off.

Julie: Why didn't you end things then?

Imogen: I wanted to see if it got better, to see if I would like it more.

Julie: But you never did?

Imogen: Never.

Julie: What happened with Patrick? You brought up his deep, dark secret?

Imogen: Don't mock.

Julie: Okay. I won't. But you did talk about the thing you found?

Imogen: We did. It felt good, actually. Like I could be myself with him.

Julie: The opposite of Zack?

Imogen: I guess so. But it's new. There's still plenty he doesn't know.

Julie: Like your love of Taylor Swift?

Imogen: Only you get to know that. And it's only the one album.

Julie: Uh-huh. Uh-huh.

Imogen: What were you saying? About sex?

Julie: Confession for confession. I need more.

Imogen: The sex we had after was amazing. Intimate in this whole other way. It wasn't freaky or kinky or weird, but it was just as sexy.

Julie: Love is sexy?

Imogen: I don't know. Maybe.

Julie: Wow. You're so vanilla. Turned on by emotional intimacy.

Imogen: You sound like Jade.

Julie: Oh. Freak alert!

Imogen: Is everything okay there? You can talk to me.

Julie: I am. You'll tell me what happens with Patrick?

Imogen: Not every detail.

Julie: Can I meet him?

Imogen: I'm not going to introduce him to Mom and Dad.

Julie: Duh! They won't like you dating a tattoo artist. Did he go to college?

Imogen: No.

Julie: Oh yeah. They aren't going to like that one bit. That's hot.

Imogen: Ahem.

Julie: Please. Like you don't like him more because they'd hate it.

Imogen: No comment.

Julie: Called it. Can I come there? To his tattoo shop? I have time.

Imogen: You're not getting a tattoo.

Julie: Then your apartment? Or we can do lunch. Here. There. Whatever. It's only an hour drive on the weekends. Maybe we can get coffee on Sunday, before family dinner time.

Imogen: He'll want to come.

Julie: Why not invite him to Mom and Dad's 4th of July party?

Imogen: Are you kidding? You want me to introduce them to my tattoo artist white boyfriend at a party?

Julie: Be American. Celebrate your right to screw anyone you want.

Imogen: Absolutely not.

Julie: But next Sunday? The two of us?

Imogen: I'll think about it.

Julie: That means no.

Imogen: I will. I promise.

Julie: In the next two weeks.

Imogen: Bossy.

Julie: Learned from the best.

Imogen: Are you going to tell me now?

Julie: Yeah, but you're building it up too much. It's not a big thing. Just something I want to tell you.

Imogen: Okay. I won't make it a big deal. Unless you're doing something unsafe.

Julie: I am seeing someone.

Imogen: The prom guy?

Julie: No. A teammate.

She's not in a co-ed league.

Oh—

Shit.

Julie: A woman, yes.

Imogen: Does she treat you well?

Julie: You can have an OMG moment.

I am surprised. She's never mentioned a crush. She doesn't even call female celebrities pretty, not really.

Well, sometimes.

A lot of times even.

Imogen: When did you know?

Julie: I always knew. And I never knew too. I thought it was normal to have sexual thoughts about women. Part of growing up in a culture where women are over-sexualized.

She does listen to me.

Julie: Then we were drinking at a party after a game—no lectures, please—and we were laughing and we kissed and it just felt really good. Right.

Imogen: That's who you're seeing now?

Julie: Yeah. And she treats me very well. And, no, we aren't having sex, but we both got tested and oral sex on women is really safe anyway. I knew you'd lecture me otherwise. She's more experienced than I am. And she only likes women. I still like guys.

Imogen: Cool.

Julie: Cool? That's all.

Imogen: Do you want me to be shocked?

Julie: I was.

Imogen: What was it like, kissing her?

Julie: Fireworks everywhere. Like the ones at freakin' Disneyland. I know her so well. I know her as a friend. I love her as a friend. And then this… I guess it's like you said with the hot tattoo artist. There is something more intimate about it.

Imogen: There is.

Julie: She intimidates me. Or maybe I'm just not ready for sex yet, I don't know. I trust her. But I'm scared too.

Imogen: It's always scary at first.

Julie: For you, really? You're so brave.

Imogen: For me too.

Julie: You didn't act that way.

Imogen: I put on a strong face.

Julie: Who was the first guy you *ahem*?

Imogen: *What does *ahem* stand for?*

Julie: *Oral sex.*

Imogen: *Me on him?*

Julie: *And the other way. But that first.*

Imogen: *You remember the guy who took me to winter formal?*

Julie: *He was cute.*

Imogen: *Yeah. And he was kinda sweet, too. Maybe that's why I tried it because he didn't push. There was this vibe at school, like all the girls were doing it, like it was unnatural to not blow a guy you've been dating for a few months. I want to say it was some douchebag dude who started the rumor, but I think it was women. I don't know why I bought it. My nerdy friends weren't ready either. But a few teammates… they would play Never Have I Ever on the bus and shoot sad looks at the girls without experience.*

Julie: *That's fucked up.*

Imogen: *That's why I worry about you.*

Julie: *Did you like it?*

Imogen: *Sorta. Sorta not. It's weird. But it's nice with a guy you like, a guy who's patient with you.*

Julie: *Patrick?*

Imogen: *Yes.*

Julie: *Zack?*

Imogen: *Sometimes. There is something sexy about it. But when a guy pushes… that kind of ruins the whole thing.*

Julie: *Did he go down on you? Was he the first?*

Imogen: *He was.*

Julie: *The winter formal guy didn't offer?*

Imogen: *He did, but I was too nervous. Embarrassed, I guess. People said it was a way to stay in control, to keep your clothes on, and it is, in some ways, but it's not in others.*

Julie: *Maybe I should stick with women.*

Imogen: *Whoever treats you well.*

Julie: *Was that hard to say?*

Imogen: *Yes.*

Julie: *Sexist!*

Imogen: *I know. Women are as bad as men sometimes, but not there.*

Julie: How would you know?
Imogen: I know men.

My phone buzzes with another text.

Patrick.

Patrick: I've been listening to Fiona Apple all morning.
Imogen: This is dirty talk.
Patrick: Call me and we'll keep talking.

Chapter Thirty-Five

PATRICK

I mogen texts back right away.

Imogen: I'm on with my sister.

Patrick: And?

Imogen: I have homework.

Patrick: And?

Imogen: You'll enjoy waiting more than I will. Are you home?

Patrick: I have a few hours of work here. After that, I won't sit around waiting.

Imogen: Good. I'd rather catch you when you're in public.

She's good at this. Too good at this.

Imogen: Soon. I promise.

Soon is too far from now. Not because I need to see her, though I do. Not because I want to hear her groan in my ear, though I do.

Because soon leaves time for my thoughts to return, for me to ask myself how long I can keep this to myself.

I need to tell her eventually. But not today, not on the phone, not until I find a way to explain myself.

I can take a few days.

That's reasonable.

I try to clear my head with a sketch session. Then a workout at

251

the fancy gym in Marina Del Rey (they transferred Deidre's membership to me and she'd prepaid for years). A shower. Dinner.

Imogen sends a picture with a note.

Imogen: You're the one who has to wait this time.

Her legs stretched over the sheets, her panties around her ankles.

Sexy as fuck.

And with her, sex is easy. Is it so bad if I keep things sexual for a few days? If I call her and get her off and make sure she's satisfied?

I'm not going to win the Nobel Prize for generosity (It should be a category) but I am going to make her come.

And that counts for a lot.

Still, the next time my phone buzzes, with a new post from *Hearts and Thorns* my hands itch to read. My head screams *this is fucked up* and *take every one of her thoughts* at the same time.

So I do the last thing I want to do.

I ask for help.

————

I SWING BY THE FANCY ORGANIC STORE ON THE WAY TO LUNA'S place, buy the single-origin chocolate Oliver recommended, grab two overpriced iced coffee drinks from the cooler.

Luna opens the door with a smile. The second she looks at my face, she shakes her head. "Tricky, you look terrible."

"You give great compliments."

She laughs. "You're still beautiful. But you look strung out. Like you haven't slept or ate."

I hold up the bag.

"You didn't have to bribe me." She motions for me to come in and closes the door behind me.

"You don't want the chocolate?"

"That's not what I mean." She motions to the white leather

couch in the middle of the room. "You want anything else? Coffee, tea, alcohol? Mom opened a bottle of wine last night."

"I'm good." I sit on the expensive white leather.

She places the drinks on the coffee table and plops on the couch across from me. "Ollie is on his way."

I raise a brow.

"You need backup."

"Relationship advice from Oliver?"

"Which of you is in a long-term relationship?" she asks.

"We don't talk about this shit," I say.

"I'll send him outside if you want. He was already coming and I… if this is a real girl-talk emergency, I'll send him home. I promise."

But she doesn't want to cancel plans with her boyfriend for this conversation. Because he'll get jealous or because he'll feel neglected or because she wants to see him.

It would have annoyed me a few weeks ago.

Now, I get it.

"Sure." I open the bottle of cold brew. "Thanks for making the time."

"So formal," she says. "Is it that bad?"

"I don't know. Maybe."

"She looked a little shell-shocked at the party," Luna says. "Do you know what happened?"

"Dare said something about Deidre."

"Oh." Luna's eyes turn down. She knows I lost my sister—everyone knows—but in the same way I know her parents divorced. I don't know the details. I didn't see the mess. I didn't discuss it with her.

She kept her pain to herself.

Or, at least, she kept it from me.

"It's kind of a long story," I say.

"You're messed up over it?" she asks.

I run my hand through my hair so I don't grab my phone. I

want to read her entry. I want to understand everything I can. "I guess so."

"I'll tell Ollie I'll meet him at his place," she says.

"Doesn't he live with his dad and sister?"

"Not anymore." She grabs her phone and taps a text. "But I appreciate you looking out for my ability to get laid."

"You have sex here?" I ask.

"Oh? You never had sex in your parents' place?"

In high school, sure. Now? No. "Not when they're home."

"Mom is working late," she says.

"So you're alone a lot?"

"Yeah," she says. "Now that Divya isn't here. She was always my primary caretaker. But I'm going to meet her in London in August and we're going to tour Europe together."

"You *want* to travel with your mom?"

"Of course," Luna says. "But I hate traveling with Allison, so I get the hesitation."

"Why is it different with Divya?"

"Both my moms say I'm more like the other. I guess I'm like them in different ways," she says. "Divya and I are more in sync with rest and relaxation. She's better at it than me, actually. She loves the world, the beauty and wonder and thrill of it. You know?"

"Yeah."

"So." She smiles as her cell pings with a reply. Blushes as she reads. "Let's talk Patrick business." She sets her cell face down on the table next to mine. They're the same model. Imogen has the same model too.

It's a popular one. I usually don't notice.

But right now?

There's so much temptation and information on my phone. The thought of her grabbing mine, reading every entry of *Hearts and Thorns?*

I hate it.

Luna focuses her attention on me. "What happened?"

"You're going to think I'm an asshole."

"Probably." She opens her coffee. "But I'll refrain from commentary."

"I really like her," I say. "I don't want to fuck this up."

She softens. "I won't judge. I promise."

I raise a brow.

"Really. We all do fucked-up shit. I've seen you with her. I can tell you care about her."

"I do."

"That's what matters."

"Other things matter," I say.

"Yeah. But that matters a lot." She motions go on.

I start at the beginning. Finding Imogen's online diary, falling for that version of her, meeting her at the shop, accepting her invitation.

Realizing the women who thrilled my body and my mind were, in fact, the same woman.

I don't share the details—the sexual ones, or the ugly ones. I don't tell her what Imogen did, exactly what drove me to look for meaning after Deidre died, but she guesses anyway.

"It wasn't an accident, was it?" Luna asks.

"Depends how you define accident," I say.

"And you went looking to understand why someone would do that."

It's not a question, but I nod anyway. I cover for Imogen without thinking. "She writes about her struggle with depression, but it's never depressing. It's heavy sometimes, but it's funny too. She's got a wicked sense of humor."

"Like Ollie."

He did make a lot of dark jokes, back in the day. "He's still funny?"

"Sober? Yeah. Way more funny if you ask me. But you didn't. So, don't try to distract me by talking about my boyfriend."

"I want to do the right thing."

She leans back on the couch. "And that is?"

"I thought you could help me figure it out."

"Really, Tricky? She has a tattoo that says 'truth is my light' in Latin."

"She didn't tell me."

"So?"

She's right. I should tell her. That's what she would want. But I can't. "She'll run away."

"Maybe. But that's her choice, isn't it?"

"Easy to say."

"Yes. It's always easy to make the right choice for someone else. There's nothing at stake. But that doesn't change things."

"What would you do?"

"Honestly?"

"Yeah." I take another sip. Fail to find understanding in my coffee drink.

"If I stumbled on Oliver's online journal?"

"Yeah."

"Before we were really together or now?"

"Now."

"I'd read it, see what he says about me, if he's hiding anything, if he's drinking in secret."

"That was fast."

"I don't lie to myself," she says.

"Do you think most people would do the same?"

"I think we're curious and we're used to the idea of anything online being fair game."

"You're people smart for a nerd."

"I'm not a nerd," she says. "But thanks."

"Would it be wrong if you read Ollie's online journal?"

"Yeah."

"But you'd do it anyway?"

"I love him," she says. "But there's so much in that love. In that trust even. The desire for honesty and the nagging at the back of my head—what if he's not being honest? What if he's hiding something? Maybe I don't read him as well as I think I do. Maybe it's different for other people. Maybe I'm weak or maybe it's his alcoholism. He didn't share it with me for a while. And that was his right, but it still…"

"Made you wonder?"

"Everyone has something."

"And you had Daisy too," I say.

"It's not the same as your sister. I'd never say it is." She opens her bar of chocolate and offers me a piece.

I take it. "How is it different?"

"We had a happy ending. So I can barely imagine how you feel. Because I asked myself all the same questions. What did I miss? How did I influence her? Was it my fault?"

Daisy, her best friend, wasn't depressed or suicidal. Not exactly. She had an eating disorder. One she denied for a long time.

I only know the rough sketch. She is Oliver's sister, after all, and I've known him a long time. She's younger. And when she was at her worst, she was young. Fifteen, maybe sixteen. I was younger too, but still too old to gawk at a fifteen-year-old girl.

If I caught myself checking her out, I averted my eyes.

But I still noticed the changes in her. She was always uptight and shy—the type of girl who would rather read than go to a party—but she sank into herself. Started dressing in baggy black clothes, avoiding our bullshit as often as possible.

I barely knew her. She was just my friend's kid sister and I noticed. Luna was, is, her best friend.

"Your chocolate is melting." Luna motions to the brown goo spreading over my fingers. "It melts at body temperature."

I pop the piece in my mouth, suck the remnants from my fingers. It could be sexual, but with her here, it's just not. "Thinking."

"I figured."

"I don't blame you for looking," she says. "But I wouldn't blame Imogen for feeling betrayed either."

Yeah.

"And the longer you go without telling her, the worse it will be."

"I stopped reading."

"For how long?"

Am I that obvious?

"How would you feel?" Luna asks. "If it was your diary?"

"I don't keep a diary."

"Private sketches then."

There are sketches I don't share, but they're strange and abstract. No one can find the secrets in them. "I'd understand the curiosity."

"What if there was something that really was yours?"

"Like what?"

"A drawing of someone tied to your bed."

"Where do you get this?"

"Inked Hearts." Our parent shop. The guys who run Inked Hearts expanded by opening Inked Love. That's all way above my paygrade, but we see them often enough. "Rumors about one of the couples there."

"No way."

"Way. You know the tall brooding guy with the cute blonde?"

"The one brooding tattoo artist?"

She laughs. "Brendon. And the girl… she wears blue glasses."

That's vaguely familiar.

"That's where I hear, anyway. That Kaylee peeked in his sketchbook and found all these dirty drawings of her."

"Are you making this up?" I ask.

"Does it matter? It's an illustration of my point."

"They've been together a long time." I think. "If it is true, the evidence speaks for itself."

"But how would you feel?" she asks. "If that was the situation?"

"Relieved. To not have to keep a secret anymore."

"Maybe that's an answer," she says. "Maybe you need to let go of this secret and tell her."

That's a good argument.

It makes sense.

A lot of sense.

"You have to tell her eventually," she says. "And the longer you wait, the worse it will be."

"I know," I say.

"So… what are you going to do?"

Chapter Thirty-Six

PATRICK

L una doesn't force me to answer, but we both know the truth.

I can only stop reading Imogen's site for so long. I need her words, her honesty, her intimacy.

And I need to do right by her.

Which only leaves one option, the option that might ruin everything.

After I say goodbye, I walk home and avoid Imogen's entry all night.

I toss and turn, but I make it through the night without giving in to temptation.

All day, my fingers itch to open my phone, read the site, let her words pour over me.

All day, I resist.

I focus on the one thing that makes sense, the one way I absolutely know how to do right by her.

Sex.

Patrick: I want another round on the balcony.

Imogen: The same balcony?

Patrick: No. Different place, same idea. If you're game.

Imogen: Ready when you are.

Patrick: Thursday. I'll pick you up. Take you out.
Imogen: Take me where?
Patrick: It's a surprise.
Imogen: What's the dress code?
Patrick: Anything.
Imogen: Really? Sweats.
Patrick: Casual to dressy. Outside. Bring a sweater. And a swimsuit.
Imogen: I'm intrigued.
Patrick: Perfect.

————

THE GREAT THING ABOUT MY JOB, A LOT OF PEOPLE WANT TO convince me they're cool. With a few texts, I score invites to three different parties. A club in WeHo. A celebrity's place in the Hills. A music mogul's Malibu mansion. He's recently divorced and courting a reputation as an open-minded single dude.

Perfect.

Terrifying.

Exactly what Imogen wants.

She trusts me here. And I can give her what she needs here. Everything she needs.

All week, my nerves spin. I'm a confident guy, most of the time, but this is way past my comfort zone.

Thursday, I barely manage to finish lunch. I skip coffee. I do everything it takes to keep my head on straight.

Then I get to Imogen's place and I see the anticipation all over her face, and my nerves fall away.

I lead her to the car and help her into her seat.

She smiles as I play Fiona Apple. "Are you trying to seduce me?"

"Of course," I say.

"Do I get a clue?" She drops her purse between her legs. "To where we're going?"

"One." I pull out of the parking lot. "Malibu."

"That's not a clue. That's an answer."

"Technically." How can I increase her anticipation without pushing her too far? "Somewhere you fantasized about."

"Somewhere I told you I fantasized about?"

I nod.

She presses her palms together, thinking. "Hmm." She looks to me. "No."

"Maybe."

"Maybe." She nods. "Malibu. The beach?"

"We're not playing twenty questions."

"Answer one question."

"If you answer mine first."

"Okay." She smiles. "Shoot."

"What are you wearing under that?"

Chapter Thirty-Seven

IMOGEN

We flirt for the entire drive up Pacific Coast Highway. My boldness fades as we turn into a neighborhood. We're moving toward the ocean, but there isn't beach access here. Is there? And I didn't tell him about any fantasies of sex in the ocean. Or did I?

That's one side effect of growing up on swim team. My sexual feelings developed on the swim team. They attached to the guys on my team. In their swimsuits, gliding through the water, smooth and fast and gorgeous.

I've only tried sex in the water once. It was terrible—no lubrication and no friction either—but I still have all the fantasies my swim career bloomed.

We pass a row of mid-sized mansions. They're "only" worth five or ten million apiece. Four or five bedrooms, pools, beach views. Not the twenty million plus places further up the 1.

They remind me of the houses in Newport. A mix of modern glass, white and blue beach shack, mission style. They have the same feel. Expensive in an easygoing way.

We part at the end of the street, in front of a mission-style house with white walls and a clay red roof.

"Is this it?" The house is beautiful. And quiet. There are lights on upstairs, but that's the only sign of life.

"Other side of the street."

The side facing the ocean.

"Two doors down."

"It's dark."

"It's that kind of party," he says.

The place—one of the modern mansions with an Apple Store aesthetic—looks empty at a glance. But there are dim lights on upstairs. There's music coming from the house. There's a sign over the door and a bucket of roses on each side of the wood. "Is this an orgy?" Are orgies real?

"It's explicitly not an orgy."

"But…"

"It's for open-minded people."

"What does that mean?"

"People won't care if I fuck you in the pool," he says.

My cheeks flush. "Will there be other people…"

"Having sex?"

I nod.

"Upstairs. That's what my friend told me. The further you go, the weirder it gets."

"The pool isn't upstairs."

"It's past the main house."

"So other people will be out there?" I don't add *having sex*, but it lingers in the air anyway.

"Probably." He undoes his seat belt and turns to me. "Is it too much?"

My cheeks flush. My chest too. My brain wants to scream *yes, of course this is too much, are you crazy?* It doesn't even want to stop and excuse my use of the word crazy.

But my body?

It's completely and totally on board.

"Is it too much for you?" I ask.

266

"I don't know." He reaches over and undoes my seat belt. "But I want to try."

"Me too." I grab my purse.

Patrick nods, pushes out of his seat, helps me out of the car. "You have your jacket?"

"My what?" I ask.

He smiles. "Take mine." He takes his leather jacket and drapes it over my shoulders.

It feels good. Warm and heavy in that perfect, comfortable way. And it's his. It smells like him. It feels like him. "Won't you be cold?"

"I have a hoodie in the trunk."

"A hoodie? For your Sinful Serenade shirt?"

"Fuck yeah." He smiles.

He looks good. Jeans, a button-up shirt, boots. Smart casual. Is that what you wear to a not-orgy? I don't know.

But we're not here for other people.

We're only here for us.

And it's explicitly not an orgy. (Which is more damming than saying "it's totally an orgy").

But I don't care about that either.

I'm officially out of my mind.

Well, I've been officially out of my mind for a long time. But I'm on some new level. One reserved for people with another diagnosis.

Or maybe I'm finally acting normally, thinking with the brain below my waist. Everyone expects men to do it. Why not a book-smart science loving woman too?

"Ready?" I ask.

Patrick nods, wraps his arm around me, and leads me to the house.

Nothing about the place screams *sex club*. Maybe the quiet EDM. Otherwise, it looks sleeker and safer than every frat party I've ever attended.

A woman in a designer suit checks our name is on the list. It's all perfectly normal until she explains the guidelines. The main room is for mingling. Outside, things get a little more open, but mostly people are watching. Upstairs? Anything goes. The bar is here. Drinks are welcome anywhere, but no party drugs.

She doesn't want to ask us to leave, but she will.

She hands us a row of condoms, says, "safe is sexy," and nods goodbye.

Tricky leads me through the foyer, into the main room. People in cocktail gear and casual outfits flirt, dance, drink, talk, kiss.

It's surprisingly sweet, but there's still a charge in the air, a suggestion of more.

"You want a drink?" Patrick nods to the bar on the left, a long cart manned by a guy in jeans and a vest.

"Absolutely," I say.

He laughs. "You're nervous?"

"Very."

"Just one?" he asks.

"Probably smart." I want two, three, four. As many as it takes to calm the nerves in my stomach. But I want to feel this too. All of it.

Patrick orders, makes small talk with the bartender. While we wait, I try to imagine a version of myself who would invite a third party to join.

I almost see it, the two of us upstairs, in a silk bed. But the other person isn't participating, exactly. They're watching.

It's really fucking hot, but it's terrifying too.

The bartender refuses a tip. Everything is paid for, apparently. Or maybe that's normal at these kinds of parties.

I know people with money, but they're all friends' parents or friends of my parents. Their adult lives are a mystery to me.

"How do you know the host?" I take my drink and follow Patrick outside.

The backyard is huge, the size of my apartment. It's not as crowded as the inside of the party, but it's not private either.

Two people in jeans admire the succulent garden. A throuple sits around the patio table, sipping cocktails, watching the action.

Two women in swim bottoms make out on a plush couch. A woman in a loose coverup sits on a lounger, her hand under the bottom of her skirt. A man and woman strip out of their casual clothes and jump into the long pool.

It's gorgeous, straight out of my dreams, long and deep enough for swimming laps or diving far beneath the surface, with a shallow end the perfect height for touching discretely below the waist.

Not that the two seem interested in discretion.

For a few minutes, they swim, laugh, splash.

Then they start kissing.

Touching.

Fucking.

"You want to keep watching?" Patrick pulls me closer.

"I'm staring, aren't I?"

"Gawking, yeah, but I don't think they mind."

The woman glances in my direction, catches me staring, shoots me a come-hither look.

"You want to sit?" he asks.

"Sitting is good."

He leads me to a pair of lounge chairs in the corner and sits across from me.

We're as secluded as we can be out here.

In view but in our own world too.

It's perfect.

I'm in the backyard of a stranger's house, twenty feet from two people having sex in a pool, and I'm in the perfect place.

What happened to my normal life?

"Is that a good blank stare or a bad blank stare?" Patrick asks.

"Sorry."

"Don't apologize. You're cute when you stare."

"Cute?"

"Sexy." He brings his drink to his lips. "Are you watching?"

"Sorta."

"You want to keep watching?"

"We can't see much from here."

He smiles. "We can move closer."

"No. This is good. This is perfect. That's what I was thinking, how odd it is I'm in the perfect place at a party that's explicitly not an orgy."

He laughs. "We can leave at any point."

"Do you want to?"

"No."

"Me neither." I take a sip. Watch the couple writhe against the wall.

Again, Patrick laughs. "If you want to watch, watch."

"Sorry. I said… I'm ignoring you."

"You're doing what I invited you here to do."

"I'm just… I've never watched anyone have sex." This is a good way to start, actually. I can only see the R-rated version of things. It's not as overwhelming as the X-rated version.

"At a party?"

"No. Well, I don't think so. Make outs, sure. Under the clothes touching, even. But never sex."

"Did you ever?" he asks.

"Huh?"

"Touch under the clothes at a party?"

"Yes," I say.

"Do you think about it when you fuck yourself?"

"Sometimes."

"Anything else like that?" he asks.

"At a pool once. Everyone had cleared out of a party. It was me and a guy I knew from swim team and we started kissing and he took off my bikini top and it was thrilling, knowing I was at someone else's house half-naked."

"You want to wear the swimsuit?"

"I am." My cheeks flush. "Under this."

"Oh yeah?"

"It felt right."

"Show me."

I slide the leather jacket off my shoulders. Then I do away with my blouse.

His eyes go to my yellow bikini top. "Fuck. Imogen."

My cheeks flush.

"Come here."

I shake my head. "That isn't how this goes."

"How does it go?"

I take another sip of my gin and tonic, let the mix of sweet and bitter center me. Then I set the drink on the concrete, stand, position myself in front of Patrick.

He looks up at me like I'm heaven-sent.

I look back at him as I undo the knot of my bikini top.

The fabric falls at my feet.

His eyes go wide. He traces a line down my body, from the top of my head to my wedge sandals.

Then back up again.

The snug denim skirt wrapped around my hips.

The bare skin of my stomach, chest, shoulders.

"Fuck," he says it again. "Come here."

This time, I follow his instruction. I slide onto the lounge chair next to him, my bare thigh against the rough fabric of his jeans.

I want to do everything to him.

I want him to do everything to me.

It's as visceral as the first time. As intimate as the last time.

Sex and trust, all mixed up together in one delicious ball of need.

He pulls me into a kiss.

I wrap my hand around his thigh. I'm not patient. I don't tease him.

I rub him over his jeans.

He groans against my lips as he brings his hand to my breast and toys with my nipple. He works me with perfect strokes, the exact rhythm, the exact pressure, but there's no patience in his movements.

He wants this too, needs this too.

I undo the button of his jeans. The zipper.

His cock springs free of his boxers.

I wrap my hand around him and run my thumb over his tip. For one brief moment, I soak in the feel of him, the feel of touching him here.

So much like our tryst at the balcony but so different too. Safer. More dangerous.

Not because we're surrounded by strangers at a sex party in Malibu. Because I trust him elsewhere. Because I want him everywhere.

And here. I really want him here.

I pump him with a steady stroke.

He pulls back with a sigh and tugs at my skirt. "Off."

"Not yet." I shift my hips, so I can do away with my bikini bottom, but I keep my skirt on. "Like you said. On the phone."

I pump him again, then I drop to my knees and wrap my lips around him.

His hand goes to my hair immediately. "You're gonna make me come."

I take him deeper.

"Fuck." His eyes flutter closed. His fingers knot in my hair.

He fights himself. His desire to win, to make me come, to come inside me. I'm not sure.

I only know I love the feel of it.

I take him deeper.

Deeper.

Until his head falls back.

Until he surrenders.

I wrap my lips around my teeth, pull back, take him again. A little harder, a little faster.

Again.

Again.

His hips buck. His palm presses against the back of my head, guiding me farther.

Again and again.

Then he pulls me back onto his lap and flips me onto my back. "Baby, you're going to pay for that."

He climbs down my body, rolls my skirt up my thighs, and brings his mouth to me.

He's not patient either. He works me with hard, fast flicks of his tongue. He tests the speed until I tug at his hair. Then the pressure.

He's there quickly, giving me exactly what I need, working me with his warm, wet tongue.

I fall back; I let my eyes close. I let my body respond to his.

Fuck, he's good at this.

Really fucking good at this.

He toys with me again and again. He winds me tighter and tighter, so tight I'm sure I'm going to break.

Then I hear the splash of the pool. I remember where we are. I blink my eyes open and I survey the scene.

The woman from the pool is finished and she's watching us.

Her partner too.

I don't look back at her. I don't shrink away. I soak in the feeling of being watched.

And I surrender.

With the next flick of his tongue, I come, pulsing against his lips, groaning his name, tugging at the soft fabric of the lounge chair.

He works me through my orgasm, then he releases me, works his way up my body, brings his lips to my neck.

"Fuck me," I breathe.

"No," he copies my words. "Not yet." He brings our bodies closer, so he's almost against me—

But he's not.

He toys with my breasts as he sucks on my neck, moving closer and closer.

Until his tip brushes my sex.

One perfect, moment then he pulls back.

Again and again.

Until I'm aching and dizzy.

Then again and again.

"Please," I breathe. "Please."

He responds by teasing me again and again.

Until it's too much to take.

I shift to my side and push him to his. It's awkward, changing positions on the tiny chair, but there's something right about that.

Like I'll go into free fall if I move off the cushion. If I let go.

Or maybe I'm already in free fall.

I push Patrick onto his back, I shift on top of him, and I ride him again and again.

I come fast, pulsing around him, pulling him closer and deeper, pulling him over the edge with me.

He groans my name as he comes.

I work through his orgasm, soaking in every sweet moment. The bliss coursing through my veins, the sheer satisfaction of him pulsing inside me, the people around us, close enough to watch.

I'm out of my fucking mind.

And I love every second of it.

Chapter Thirty-Eight

PATRICK

I mogen collapses on the lounger, sweaty and sticky and spent. When she comes to, I help her into her clothes, onto her feet, back into the world around us.

She looks around the backyard, shy and eager at once. "Do you think anyone watched?"

"Yes." I'm sure they did. But I barely noticed anyone else. Even now, I barely see anyone else. Only the satisfaction in her dark eyes, the smile on her wine lips.

We don't finish our drinks.

We don't stay and mingle.

We walk around the side yard, out to the street, to my car.

Then she stops. "We didn't swim."

"We can." I motion to the house.

She shakes her head. "No." She motions to the ocean.

"I didn't bring a suit."

"I know." She takes my hand and leads me to the quiet beach.

She looks me in the eyes and she strips out of her clothes. Then she watches me do the same. There's desire in her eyes, but it's not just a physical desire.

It's mental, emotional.

The desire for more.

For the kind of raw intimacy she offers on her website.

That's the way to make this fair.

To share with her, show her where I hurt.

Not just Deidre. The other places too.

I can do that.

Even if it's more terrifying than anything.

———

THE NIGHT IS PERFECT. WE SHOWER TOGETHER, FALL ASLEEP IN my bed, sleep soundly.

A dream.

Until I wake up to the sound of Imogen's gasp.

She stares at her cell in horror. "My sister is here." She paces around the room. "We have find-my-phone and I promised she could meet you and she… took matters into her own hands."

"I'm good with sisters."

"You haven't met mine."

Chapter Thirty-Nine

PATRICK

"We're here," Imogen calls as she opens the door and invites her sister inside.

"Hello," a loud voice follows. Similar to Imogen's voice in some hard to explain way. The cadence sisters often share.

Deidre and Molly were the same.

I wasn't. I didn't fit into their world of sisterhood. There was something I never could understand, that they never believed I could understand.

When I was a kid, I hated it. Then, I understood. Now?

Well, I guess none of us really understood.

"Are you decent?" Imogen's sister calls with excitement.

"He is." Imogen looks up at me and sends a wave. "Sorry."

I wave back.

Imogen's sister drops the hands she has over her eyes. "Boo. No fun."

"Don't even," Imogen says.

"Hi, Patrick. I'm Julie." Julie waves. "Were you two having sex when I texted?"

"Sleeping," I say.

"Sleeping off sex?" she asks.

"Sorry. I haven't had a boyfriend in a long time." The word boyfriend rolls off her tongue casually, as if it's obvious, as if she's been using it for years.

My entire body flushes. I'm warm everywhere. I'm her boyfriend. It's such a simple label, but it feels so good.

Imogen notices, smiles, continues, "Julie has a lot of stored *I need to torture your boyfriend* energy."

"I love torture." I slip on my shoes and move down the stairs. "You hungry?" I ask them both.

"Starving," Julie says. "Do you have coffee?"

"Let's go out," Imogen says.

"No! Let's stay in your boyfriend's apartment," Julie says.

"So you can snoop?" Imogen asks.

Julie holds up crossed fingers. "Never."

"We don't have a lot to eat," I say.

"Please. If Immy spent the night, there's oatmeal," Julie says. "You're like a robot with your routine."

Imogen blushes. "Lots of people eat the same thing for breakfast every day."

"Let's suffer through some oatmeal," Julie says. "Then we can go out for coffee. Deal?"

"Seems fair," I say.

She laughs. "See, your boyfriend agrees."

"I like her oatmeal," I say.

"And the chai too?" Julie asks.

"Who wouldn't?" I ask.

"Really? The star anise? It's a little cliché, don't you think? The Viet girl adding star anise?" Julie asks.

"Fuck off," Imogen says.

"She's not embarrassed by her obviousness," Julie says. "She's embarrassed because Mom makes her chais with extra star anise too."

"Don't they own a coffee shop?" I ask.

"And bakery, yes. So when Mom wants something special, she wants tea, not coffee." Julie scans the counter until she finds the tin of chai. "At least you don't go out of your way to add Saigon Cinnamon."

"You're a flavor philistine," Imogen says.

"It's okay. I am too. I drink Bud Light." I shoot Imogen a wink.

She laughs. "You're improving."

"Oh, let me guess. The fancy tonic water." When Imogen pouts, Julie laughs. "Just like Mom."

"No. She uses Q," Imogen says.

"Oh, so you use Fever Tree. Please. She loves Fever Tree too. She's probably infusing a bottle of gin with star anise right now." Julie shakes her head. "Like mother, like daughter, you know?"

"Lots of people love the flavors their parents use in their cooking," Imogen says.

"Yeah, but you know that's not what I meant." Julie pulls out a chair and sits at the main table. "You're both tough as nails and good at keeping secrets."

"Isn't that a paradox?" I ask.

"Hmm. Maybe. If they're that good, I wouldn't know," Julie says. "Or maybe I'm really good at uncovering secrets."

"Okay, Sherlock," Imogen says.

Julie flips her off.

Imogen returns it.

Their expressions are playful, but there's something under them too.

Of course there is.

Imogen hasn't told her sister about her attempt. There's no way Julie didn't notice a change in her behavior, in her relationship with her mom.

Even I noticed how weird shit was with Deidre.

"Do you need help?" Julie asks.

"Keep Patrick company," Imogen asks.

"Permission to torture him? Score." Julie stands and offers a hand.

I shake. "Nice to make a formal introduction."

"One more word about the chai and you don't get one," Imogen says.

Julie mimes zipping her lips and turns to me. She studies me, carefully, assessing me as worthy or not-worthy of her sister.

"You're cuter than your pictures," she says.

"Oh my god, Jules, I will restrain you if you don't behave," Imogen says.

"Is that what she says to you too?" Julie winks.

Imogen turns to hide her blush. "I will deprive you of that chai."

"You won't. You're not capable. But I'll be nice. Ish," Julie says. "And it is nice to say someone is cuter in person."

Imogen motions *so-so*. "Don't listen to her. She's messing with you."

"Oh. I know." I motion for Julie to sit at the table.

She does.

"I'm a younger sibling too."

"So the game is on?" she asks.

"Absolutely."

She smiles.

"Are you as competitive as your sister?" I ask.

"No, no, no. We're not here to talk about me. We're here to talk about you," she says.

"Are you?" I ask.

She nods. "Way more."

"You look like her too," I say.

"But I'm cuter?" she asks.

"Our secret." I sit across from her.

"She's taller." Julie shakes her head. "It's not fair. But I guess it's fitting, the older sister being taller. It's weird when a younger sibling is taller. Don't you think?"

"Kinda," I say. "When you're a kid, it seems off."

"Has Imogen repeatedly reminded you I'm a naive seventeen-year-old?" she asks.

"Only once or twice," I say.

"I'll be a senior next year," she says. "We're four years apart. That's unusual."

"My sisters too," he says.

"Older or younger?" she asks.

At the counter, Imogen freezes.

Julie reads her sister too well—we're facing each other, but we're both in eye shot of Imogen. She notices and raises a brow.

"My sister died," I say. "Last year. Deidre. This was her place."

"Oh, shit. Imogen mentioned that and I totally spaced. I'm sorry." Julie sinks into her seat, deflated. It's not fun to tease the guy with the dead sister.

"Thanks." I hate this. The way the air changes when I mention her death. I don't blame Imogen for keeping her secrets to herself, keeping them from her sister.

I hate it, as a younger sibling—

But I get it.

"My older sister, Molly, she was about four years older than Deidre," I say. "She's in her thirties."

"Like a real adult?" Julie's voice stays tenuous. "Like old-old."

"She's a lawyer, yeah. Wears a suit to work every day," I say.

"Really? A suit? What color?" Julie asks.

"All sorts," I say. "She loves a power suit."

"No beige?" Julie asks.

"Never beige. She's always been bold. She's a lot like Imogen, actually. Tough in an untouchable way. Expressing it to the world in a dark pink or teal green suit," I say.

"I can see Immy in a dark pink suit," she says. "And you're Irish, right?"

I nod.

"Does she look like you?" Julie asks.

"No. She's got red hair."

"Red with pink? That's bold. I like it. Does she rock forest green?"

"Her power color," I say.

"Not black, like Immy?" she asks.

"Don't knock black. It's classic," I say. "And she has plenty of fuchsia too."

"You really are good with colors. Imogen is hopeless. She doesn't know the difference between seafoam and turquoise," she says.

"Pathetic, yeah." The mood is lighter, but not enough. I need to push off the subject of my family and onto hers. Or, at least, onto something easy. "Your sister said I'm her first boyfriend in a while. Who was the last?"

"Oh my god, she hasn't talked to you about Zack?" She sheds half the heaviness. "The film major who loved the sound of his own voice."

Imogen watches her sister shift into playful mode, then turns her attention to fixing oatmeal and tea.

"Not a fan?" I ask.

"He was hot. Really hot," she says.

"Hey," I tease.

"Not hotter than you are. Just different," she says. "Smart hot. Not that he was intelligent. Honestly, I think, deep down, he was an idiot, and it was worse, because he thought he was smart. There's nothing worse than an idiot who thinks they're smart, you know?"

"I know the type," I say.

"Right. You work with artists too. They can be divas," she says.

"Are you an artist?" I ask.

She laughs. "No. I just like art class. I'd never try to make it a career. Too unstable."

"It can be," I say.

"I think it's good you are, though. Imogen needs that. Someone with a creative spirit."

"But not Zack?" I ask.

"Omg, no. He rocked tweed blazers all summer and only drank IPAs. He was such a blowhard. I don't think she even liked him. I don't think she even liked *ahem* with him."

Imogen shakes her head but she doesn't interrupt us.

"I know, she'll say I couldn't tell, but sometimes chemistry is obvious," Julie says. "You two… whew. I'm not sure how much she actually likes you, but she definitely likes that."

Imogen clears her throat.

"And that's good for her. She's so high-strung. She needs someone who puts her in her body. And not in a pervy way, though I know she thinks I'm a sex-obsessed teenager," Julie says.

"Not at all?" I ask.

"She needs someone who helps her relax and feel," Julie says.

"I didn't realize this would be nonstop character assassination," Imogen says.

"I can say it nicely." Julie laughs. "Imogen is very studious. Thoughtful. She gets lost in her big, beautiful head." She looks to Imogen and raises a brow *better?*

"Barely." Imogen drops off our chai lattes. "Oatmeal is almost done."

"Thanks! I mean it that way, you know. I admire your intelligence," Julie says.

"Thank you," Imogen says.

"You're supposed to say something you admire about me now," Julie says.

"I admire your perseverance. Even though it's annoying." Imogen smiles and returns to the oatmeal.

"It's a compliment," I say.

"Oh yeah. Our job, as younger siblings." Julie takes a long sip and lets out an easy sigh.

I let the mix of cinnamon and ginger wash away the last bit of heaviness.

Julie does too. After another sip, she returns to her assessment. "Imogen is smart and gorgeous, as we covered. Always in her head. So she needs someone more… living in the physical world. And, no, I don't mean sex. I mean this." She motions to the tattoos on my forearms. "You're an artist, so you can understand where she goes, but your art is on people's skin, so you understand actual things. That's what she needs. In my head, it was always a doctor, a surgeon, or someone with a very matter-of-fact specialty. Not an internist, you know?"

"Someone who deals in the literal but understands the abstract," I say.

"Exactly. And better that you aren't a doctor. Because she'd never date a guy our parents' want for her. Maybe that's why she dated Zack for so long. Because he was studying film and Mom hated that. They won't like the tattoo artist thing. But they don't like anything. Don't take it personally."

"I won't," I say.

"Or maybe… I don't know. Mom is so weird lately. She caught me vaping and stole my pen and started using it!"

"Maybe she wants to make it look uncool," I say.

"Yeah, but she's out there huffing nicotine every twenty minutes now." Julie shakes her head. "And, honestly, I think I smelled pot on her a few times. Can you believe that?"

Imogen's posture changes, but she doesn't say anything, and Julie doesn't notice.

"Do you talk to her?" I ask.

She looks at me funny. "Talk to my mom?"

I nod.

"Have you ever talked to your mom and asked why she was being weird?" she asks.

"No," I admit. "But I'm not as smart or mature as you are."

"Nice try." Julie laughs. "But I'm not that easy to flatter."

"Oh, I can do way better with flattery," I say.

She laughs again. "Probably. But we're getting off track. This is Imogen's first relationship in a while, and I think, as her only sister, I have a right to approve or disapprove."

"I'm on trial?" I ask.

"Nothing that official," she says. "But I have to make sure you're a good guy."

"Ignore her," Imogen says.

Julie shakes her head. "I have a few questions. Three."

"Shoot," I say.

"How did you meet?" she asks.

"She PMed me on Instagram with a tattoo request," I say.

"And you took advantage?" she asks.

"No," I say. "I was all business at first. We worked on the design, she came to the shop for work. You've seen her tattoo?"

Julie nods.

"It's a sensitive place. Hard to cover. She kept holding her boobs until I offered to make her a top out of tape. And she just dropped her hands and said, 'thank god' and looked at me like… it's okay to stare."

"Really?" Julie asks her sister.

"It wasn't torrid," Imogen says. "It was like he was a doctor."

"And it was okay for him to see you naked?" Julie asks.

"She's right. It's all skin," I say.

"So you didn't check out her hot bod?" Julie asks.

"I'm human," I say.

Julie laughs. "Okay, then?"

"When we checked out, she said, 'you've already seen me topless,' and wrote her number on the receipt."

"Really? What game! Damn Immy, that's good," she says.

"Did it really sound that seductive?" Imogen turns to us.

"Yeah," I say. "But I might have heard what I wanted to hear."

"No way. Imogen is always direct," she says. "It's scared guys before. So many guys act like it's a dream come true, you know, for a woman to use them for sex. But when it's someone as smart and cool as my sister, it's a problem."

"They're intimidated by her." I nod.

"She's kind of intense," she says. "I don't think she realizes it."

"I think she does," I say.

Imogen blushes.

"She's the one who texted me," I say. "Just like that. Straight up-booty call. 'I need help with after-care. Can you come over?'"

Julie laughs. "Less direct than DTF."

"Yeah, but men like to be romanced a little too," I say. "How would you feel if someone you like texted DTF?"

"Am I horny?" Julie asks.

"Sure," I say.

"It does feel like a mass message. Do they want me? Or anybody who will show up at their apartment? Yeah, I guess you're right. It's best to be direct in a flirty way," Julie says.

"He crossed the 405 for me," Imogen says.

Julie stares at her blankly.

"You'll get it when you live in LA," Imogen says.

"Live in LA? Fat chance," Julie says. "It's traffic hell here. I know I should hate Orange County because it's so fake, but I love it."

"Nothing wrong with that," I say.

"I know. I talk such big talk about going to Stanford or Princeton but I really want to go to UCI," she says.

"You do?" Imogen asks.

"Yeah. I'm sorry. I know you want me to go far away," Julie says.

"No." Imogen turns to us. "I want you nearby, but that's self-ish. I don't want to push you to stay because I want you here. I want you to have all the space to grow and thrive."

"But not everyone is as brave as you," she says.

"I went somewhere hour away," Imogen says.

"You didn't know anyone," Julie says. "You moved out. You took this big leap and it was what you needed to thrive."

"I didn't thrive—"

"Can we talk about that?" Julie asks.

"Jules—"

"Is this just going to be more bullshit?" Julie asks.

"Can we talk later?" she asks.

"I'll give you guys the room," I say.

"Does he know what it is?" she asks. "Why things are so weird with you and Mom?"

Yes.

"No. It's not that simple," Imogen says. "There isn't one thing. There are a million things."

"She's not doing well," Julie says. "She's vaping!"

"Maybe she's with the times," Imogen says.

"No. She's drinking a lot. And she's dragging herself to work. Whatever it is, she's not happy."

"Is that why you want to stay?" Imogen asks. "For her?"

"No. I want to be near my family. I want a support network," Julie says. "Some of us need that."

"Jules—"

"Whatever. I didn't come here for this, but… I should go. I didn't want to ruin your morning. And I just… I'm sorry, Patrick. You seem like a good guy. I hope my sister is more honest with you than she is with me." Julie stands and grabs her stuff.

Imogen watches her leave.

I don't think. I run after Julie.

Chapter Forty

PATRICK

I find Julie sitting on the steps of the apartment complex.

"Hey." I sit next to her. "You want to stay here or take a walk?"

She looks up at me with surprise. "Did Immy put you up to this?"

"No."

She wipes a tear from her eyes. "Sorry. I really didn't want to crash your date."

"It's okay."

"It's not. It's really rude."

"I forgive you," I say. "And I'll forgive you more if you let me buy you a coffee."

"That seems backward. Shouldn't I buy you a coffee to apologize for interrupting?" she asks. "I mean, you two were totally going to do it before I showed up right?"

"We were sleeping," I say.

"Then for waking you up," she says.

"Okay. You are an Orange County girl. You must have money." I stand and offer my hand.

She lets me help her up. "Okay, Mr. I Live Off Abbott-Kinney. Do tattoo artists really make this much money?"

"No." If we're getting real, I might as well talk to her. "This was my sister's place. She left it to me."

"Oh. Shit. Right," she says. "And I'm complaining my sister doesn't talk to me."

"It's not a competition." I move down the stairs and motion for her to follow.

She does. "Old and wise?"

"Basically."

"Can you afford that?" she asks. "Whatever was left on the mortgage?"

"Her life insurance covered it."

"Oh."

"It's standard with loans these days." I lead her around the corner where Abbot-Kinney begins. It is a hipster street, but it starts slowly, with the yellow California casual lemonade and salad place. Then a coffee shop. "What do you normally drink?"

"My parents make this Vietnamese iced coffee," she says. "But like… a bougie version, with less sugar, and coconut milk. They made that for Imogen, you know. Because she's lactose intolerant. Mom says it was the key to their business hitting the next level."

"Really?" I ask.

"Yeah, I guess people think coconut is South Asian. I don't know? It was hip but authentic and they can do it keto. So it's win-win."

"You like sweet and creamy?" I ask.

She nods. "But not too much sugar. My coach got us to all skip sugar for the season. Well, mostly. After, it was just… ugh. I used to love eating Sour Patch Kids. Now, I get a wicked headache after. Is that what it feels like to get old?"

"Kinda, yeah." I stop at the coffee shop. "This place has a good cold brew."

"I like an iced latte. With oat milk. Don't tell Imogen." Julie shakes her head. "She hates oat milk."

"She's behind the times," I say.

"She hates that, too."

We move into line behind a group of girls in cover-ups. They take turns ordering drinks with various non-dairy milks.

They move away. We step forward. Julie orders an oat milk latte. I order the same.

After I pay (she doesn't fight me), she laughs. "That's such a guy-date move, ordering the same thing."

"How many guys have you dated?" I ask.

"Don't even. I looked at your Instagram. I saw all the different women who tagged you. The ones who weren't rocking their new ink in their pictures." She raises a brow. "There were a lot."

"How far back did you go?" I ask.

"Far enough. Past, uh… I guess before you sister died. Did that change things for you?"

"It did."

"Did you and Imogen talk about that?"

I nod. "It woke me up, made me realize how much of my life was bullshit."

"She's not like that," Julie says. "Sometimes, I think she's too much not like that. She can only have conversations where she's checked out or where she's intense and honest."

"You don't like it?"

"I do. But sometimes I want to talk about a hot celebrity without her lecturing me on safe sex. Or I want to talk about eyeliner or dresses. But I'm becoming more like her too… obviously."

I move to the side of the coffee shop.

Julie follows. "You know, 'cause I tried to show up here and have fun and instead I started asking why she's fake all the time now."

"All the time?"

"When it's about her. She's good at big sister mode. She was really cool about me casually dropping I have a girlfriend."

"First girlfriend?"

She nods.

"What's she like?"

"Smart. Pretty. Intimidating. Maybe I should ask you for tips there."

"I don't know if I have any."

"But Imogen is happy," she says. "At least, as happy as I've seen her."

"Your girlfriend isn't?"

"I don't know. I can't tell with her."

"Have you asked?"

"Ugh. Don't be such a grown-up."

"It's the best way to do things," I say.

She sticks out her tongue.

"What do you like about her?"

"She's confident. And she's sexy in this cool way. Too cool. I feel so inexperienced around her and it makes me lock up. I want to be with her but I'm worried I'll make a fool of myself."

"Tell her that."

"Really?" she asks.

"Trust me. It's flattering. And it's sexy."

"Being a clueless virgin?" she asks.

"Being honest and vulnerable."

"Ugh, you sound like Imogen," she says. "I wanted like… advice on eating pussy."

"You have a peach? I can show you."

"You cannot."

"I can," I say. "But your sister will kill me."

"I won't tell her."

"And I can only show you the basics. The woman you're with… she'll like what she likes. You have to explore. Find out."

Again, her nose scrunches.

"Trust me. It works."

"What if it doesn't? What if it's awkward?"

"Sex is awkward sometimes."

"Really? You think that… you?"

"I'm not that much of a slut."

She clears her throat.

"I'm not. A lot of those women… we dated, flirted, whatever. I didn't take them all home."

"Mm-hmm."

"One-night stands aren't good sex. Sex with someone new is always a little stiff."

"Stiff, really?"

I laugh. "Yeah. Stiff."

"What about when Imogen booty called you?"

"She made it comfortable, by being straight with me, but it was nothing compared to the second time. Or the third. It gets better, the more comfortable you get with someone."

"She does have a lot of game. I mean, she's cute, but kind of… quiet. I didn't expect that."

"Quiet is good. Thoughtful."

"Yeah, she is that."

The barista calls her name and drops off our drinks.

Julie pounces, sips, sighs. "This is good."

I take mine. "Should we walk?" When she nods, I lead her out of the coffee shop.

Julie surveys the sleepy street the way Imogen does, taking in everything around her carefully. "I was never nervous when I dated guys. I like guys too. I don't know why it's different."

"Did you really like them, the guys?"

"Kinda. But not the way I like her," she says.

"That's different."

"Yeah. I guess. I should talk to her, huh?"

I nod.

"You're too mature. It's annoying."

"Thanks."

"You're probably going to tell me something dumb with Imogen too. Like, wait for her to come around. The more you push, the more she'll run away. Trust is a two-way street."

"You said it well enough."

"I know." She glances at the bar where Imogen and I experimented. "But I miss her so much. The closeness we had before everything got so weird."

"How did it happen?" I ask.

"I don't know. I guess it started when she went to school. Maybe that's most of it. Maybe this is part of growing up. But it's more than that. She's different when she's home. She's not all the way there." Julie eyes the plates of stacked waffles and tofu scrambles. "That looks good."

"You want to stop?"

She shakes her head. "We used to share the secrets we kept from our parents. She stopped."

"That is part of growing up," I say.

"But what about the rest?"

The rest… I know. But I can still answer as a kid sibling. "If I tell you something, you have to promise to be cool about it."

"No way! What if you tell me you're cheating on my sister?"

"About me. My family."

"I'll try."

"Fair." I offer my hand.

She shakes.

"My sister died by suicide."

"Shit," she mutters.

"Before… she was weird. Evasive. Pulling away. It felt like something was off, but I didn't say anything. I hid from it."

"Is that what happened with Imogen?" Her eyes go wide. "Did she tell you?"

"She hasn't told me anything."

"But you know something?" she asks.

Yes.

"How do you know?" She looks at me. "Did someone tell you?"

I don't want to lie to her, but I can't be the one to tell her either. "Let me start over."

She frowns but nods *go ahead*.

"I didn't give my sister space to talk to me. I abandoned her. I think she felt that. But Molly, our older sister, she pushed. And she felt that too."

"Okay…"

"You need to tell her you're there… when she's ready, and let her come to you."

She pouts. "This all sounds very mature."

"It can be."

"I don't like it."

"I know."

"Are you sure you don't want to tell me everything?" she asks.

"I am."

"But she freaked out the other day over something she found. And it was about you. It must have been about your sister."

Shit.

"Is that what happened with her, too? I know more than she tells me. She was depressed. It was obvious. I don't know how she thinks I didn't see it. I've seen her medication. And Mom… she thinks I don't understand Vietnamese, but I do."

I say nothing.

"Did she try? Is that why things have been so weird?"

"Julie—"

"She did, didn't she?"

"She hasn't told me that."

"What if she did? Wouldn't that bother you?" she asks.

"Does it bother you?"

"Yes. It's scary. Why couldn't she tell me?"

"Do you really need me to answer that?"

"Right. Your sister is dead. Mine is here. I'm an immature asshole."

"You're scared. It's okay."

"What if she did?" Julie asks. "Would you stay with her?"

"Who would break up with someone over that?"

"Don't be naive."

That's true. The guy I used to be would have run from a

disclosure like that. "It would scare me, sure, but I would still love her."

"You love her?"

"I haven't said it yet."

"I won't tell her." She walks past the pink and green matcha shop and rolls her eyes. "How can people act like matcha is this trendy new superfood? It's been drunk in Japan for two thousand years. White people. No offense."

"None taken."

"Did she tell you what happened?"

"You trying to trick me?" I ask.

"Is it working?"

I shake my head.

"Will you talk to her, for me?"

"Yeah, but it's better if you talk to her."

"Stop being mature."

"Okay. Then tell me about your girlfriend."

"You're trying to distract me."

"Tell me anyway," I say.

She does.

We make it to the beach, then halfway to Santa Monica, before Julie decides to text Imogen to let her know we're okay.

"Do you want to do the honors? Or should I?" I ask.

"We both can." She pulls out her cell, reads the message, taps a text.

I do the same.

Imogen: Hey! No rush, but let me know if Julie is okay.

Patrick: She's good.

Imogen: Thanks. Oh. She's texting now.

Patrick: She decided to not torture you.

Imogen: Did she torture you too much?

Patrick: No. She's a good kid.

Imogen: She is.

Patrick: She's just worried about you.

Imogen: I know. I should talk to her. It's just… complicated. Are relationships supposed to be complicated this fast?

Patrick: I'm not an expert. But I don't mind it.

Imogen: Are you sure?

Patrick: Yeah. I can wait to learn more about what's in your big, beautiful brain.

Imogen: I can't believe she said that.

Patrick: She's right. You're a thinker. I get it. I love it, actually. And I can be patient with it.

More or less.

Maybe less.

I need to stick with where I'm good here.

Patrick: I'm glad to be here for her. Besides, we can make up for the lost day later this week.

Imogen: Oh?

Patrick: Yeah. When I call you Monday night.

Chapter Forty-One

IMOGEN

When I take Julie to breakfast, I expect her to demand an explanation. Instead, she says she's sorry for pushing and she's here when I need her. When I promise I'm okay, she believes me.

When I change the subject to her off-season fitness routine, she talks about sprinting on the sand, hitting the batting cages at Boomers, and running drills with her girlfriend.

For a few hours, I feel like an actual big sister. Like a good sister. Then, I hug her goodbye, and slip back into Patrick's place.

A million questions swirl in my mind. What the hell did he tell her? It must be more than a younger sibling to younger sibling explanation.

Nothing clears my head, not Patrick's goodbye hug or his promise to call Monday.

After an extra swim, a double-grilled cheese sandwich dinner, and a study session on the couch, I give up.

I open my laptop drop my thoughts in an entry.

Then I wake up and I do it again.

I drive to Orange County for dinner; I make small talk about my sister's softball schedule; I drive home, and I pour my thoughts out again.

The same, on Monday.

Up until my phone buzzes with Patrick's text, and I finally shift out of my head and into my body.

———

PATRICK: *I'M FREE FOR THE NEXT TWO HOURS. SEND ME A PIC when you're ready for my call.*

I'm not sure if I'm ready to talk about anything, period, but I'm ready to not talk.

I'm so, so ready to not talk.

Now, how to torture him the most?

I try a selfie, but I don't look cute in my study outfit—a baggy tee, a bralette, athletic shorts.

I ditch the tee.

Then the shorts.

There. Better. I try another picture. There's an intimacy to it, but there's not enough sizzle.

I grab my lipstick from my desk, apply a coat of Wine Not, and try again from my nose to my waist, the sheer pink bralette showing just enough to tease him.

There.

I hit send.

Again, my skin flushes. My sex clenches. My thoughts scatter.

It feels so good, being here, in my body, far, far away from ugly, complicated things.

My phone buzzes in my hand.

Patrick: Are you trying to kill me?

Imogen: Yes.

Patrick: Keep trying.

A dare. I love a dare.

My underwear isn't cute, but I have a sexy-enough pair of pale pink panties somewhere.

I find them in my drawer, change into them, cop a sexy pose —my thumb pulling the fabric down, over my hip.

There.

I send, flush, pant.

A perfect, beautiful pattern.

This time, he replies with a call.

I answer right away. "What are you wearing?"

"That's my line." There's an edge to his voice, like he's already panting with desire.

I love it. I need it. "You already know."

"I don't know the shoes."

"No shoes." I sit on my bed. "I'm going to put you on speaker."

"Already?"

"Already." I tap the button, stretch out over my bed, lay the phone next to my chest.

"What if I want some foreplay?"

"What do you call this?"

He laughs. "Conversational foreplay?"

"Really? 'Send me a pic when you're ready' is a request for conversation now?"

"I thought it would be your Fiona Apple shirt."

"Bullshit."

"Yeah." He laughs. "Are you good? After Saturday?"

"Good enough."

"You want to talk about it?"

"No. Is that okay?"

He hesitates. "Yeah. Of course."

"Really, Tricky, if you're feeling used"—it takes all my self-control to force the words from my brain, but I do—"we can stop."

"Talk?"

"No… I mean, I'm not up to talking, but we can plan a time for later."

"I like feeling used."

"Yeah?"

"But only by you."

My chest flushes.

"I love the thought of it." His voice shifts to something all seduction. "Being the guy you call when you want to come."

"You are."

"I know." He doesn't add *but there's more and I want to talk about the more too*.

Maybe it isn't there. Maybe I'm imagining it. "What are you wearing?" I push aside my thoughts.

"Jeans. A t-shirt."

"What color?"

"Teal."

"I've never seen you in teal."

"Next time," he says.

"Shoes?"

"No shoes."

"Are you home?" I ask.

"Yeah." He laughs. "Disappointed?"

"Kind of."

"Bad girl."

"But if you're home… I want to hear you too."

He lets out a heavy sigh. "I never have."

"Really?"

"Yeah."

"I'm popping your cherry this time?"

"Baby, you're going to make me incoherent."

"Good," I say.

"Before you do—"

I close my eyes, bracing for a horrible request to talk. Really, anything that isn't *come for me immediately*—

"I have a plan for this weekend. For us," he says. "Come over Friday night. Or Saturday if that's better."

"Sunday night?"

"Will you have the energy?" He doesn't add *after dinner with your family* but it's there.

"Friday," I say. "What's the plan?"

"Oh no. That's a secret."

"Do I get a hint?"

"Hmm… maybe. If you can convince me."

Another dare. Perfect. "What type of convincing do you want?"

"You can't come over here and fuck me."

"I can." I laugh. "And I would. But I have homework." It's mostly true.

"Hmm… what can you do from there? I wonder?"

Does he want a picture? Or a roleplay? I'm not sure. I'm not sure which entices me more.

But I know I love this—

I arrange my hair over my eyes, lift my phone over my head, and take another picture—as close to full body as I can get.

Woosh.

Send.

My entire body flushes. It feels more intimate, including my face in the shot.

"Fuck." His breath catches in his throat. "You're fucking perfect."

"Thank you." My blush deepens. "Take off your shirt."

"You done convincing me already?"

"That wasn't enough?"

"Not yet," he says.

The dare makes my entire body buzz. I want to send him more. I want to send him everything—all of me, in nothing, my hand between my legs, my pleasure all over my face.

That isn't smart.

But, right now, I don't care.

I point my phone at my collarbone, and I snap a photo.

My face.

My neck.

My chest.

Me, completely and totally exposed for him.

Woosh.

"Fuck."

Then I push my bra aside and take another.

I roll my finger over my nipple and take another.

A groan falls off my lips.

"Are you starting without me?" he asks.

"If that's what it takes."

"You'll like it."

"That's not a clue." I reach around my back, unhook my bra, snap another picture.

Woosh.

Blush.

Buzz.

It's a perfect, delicious rhythm.

"Imogen—"

"Tell me."

"Another chance to be watched."

"Where?"

"My place."

"Are you inviting someone?"

"No."

"A mirror?"

"More than a mirror."

A camera. He wants to record us.

I nearly come on the spot.

I lose my head completely. "Show me."

"Show you?"

"Lose the clothes and show me."

"Uh-uh. You're first."

A whine spills from my lips, but I don't object.

"Panties off."

I shove them to my ankles. Even though he doesn't ask for a picture, I take one.

He responds with a groan. "Baby——"

"Shirt."

He doesn't object. He shifts. Moves.

It takes a minute, but he does what I ask. He sends a photo of his shoulders, chest, stomach.

"Pants," I say.

"Uh-uh," he says. "Not until I hear you come."

Which is more selfish, accepting his offer or insisting on the photo first? I don't know. I don't care.

I know I need satisfaction.

My body responds for me.

My hand slips between my legs. "Where are we?"

"The party."

"Where?"

"Outside, but not off to the side. In front of everyone. The people in the pool, the people at the table, the people inside. We're in view of everyone."

"Yeah?"

"You're in that gorgeous bikini. Barefoot. Sopping wet. I'm in jeans and a t-shirt."

I close my eyes and let myself drift to the scene.

"You undo the strap of your bikini. And everyone watches with rapt attention, desperate to see your breasts. Then the bottoms too. And you're standing there, naked, and wet in front of everyone."

"And you stay dressed."

"At first. I pull you against me."

"Even though I'm soaking wet?"

"Yeah. My shirt and jeans get wet, but I don't care. I hold you close and show you off to the entire room. Then I whisper in your ear, 'I want everyone to see how pretty you are when you come,' and I slip my hand between your legs."

"My head falls back and you press your lips to my neck."

"And I work you slowly, so everyone can watch the pleasure spread all over your face."

I can see it in my head. It's the perfect fantasy—too revealing to attempt in real life, so enticing here.

"You come hard and fast, and everyone watches with rapt attention, like you're they're favorite movie."

"Then?" I'm close. So close. I rub myself with the strokes I need, again and again.

"I undo my jeans and arch your back and drive right into you. Everyone watches as I fuck you, right there on the concrete. You're on display to the entire fucking room."

There. With the next brush of my fingers, I come. The tension inside me unravels. Pleasure spills through my torso, down my legs, all the way to my fingers and toes.

I can practically feel his body against mine, his cock inside me, those eyes on us.

I want that—

But I want this more—the two of us sharing this intimate fantasy together.

"Your turn," I say.

"I like it this way."

"Please."

He lets out a heavy sigh.

"I can narrate. Whatever you want to imagine."

"No. I want this. The two of us on the phone, you begging to hear me come."

"Please, Tricky."

A zipper releases.

"A picture. Please. I want to see you, how much you want me, how badly I drive you out of your mind."

His breath catches.

"I want to touch myself to it later."

"Fuck."

"And I want your face in it. I want to see the desire in your eyes."

"Not sure I can capture my eyes."

"The mouth then. I love your mouth."

He lets out a heavy sigh, moves, and adjusts something.

My phone buzzes with an image.

Patrick, from his nose to his thighs, buck naked, his hand wrapped around his cock.

It's not the most likely angle or the best lighting, but I love it all the same. More because it's rushed and needy and desperate.

"Please," I say it again. "Fuck yourself. For me."

His breaths run together.

A moan falls from his lips.

Then something deeper, needier.

"Come for me." I blush, but I press on. "Please. I want to hear you."

He lets out a low, deep groan.

And he lets go. Those beautiful, perfect sounds run together. His movements speed.

And then here's there, groaning my name into the receiver, working through his orgasm.

There's something about hearing him, sharing this fantasy, a whole other kind of intimacy.

It feels really fucking good.

He catches his breath and mutters obscenities into the phone.

"Thank you," I say.

He laughs. "Thank you again?"

"It worked the first time."

"I like it."

"Is it sexy?" I ask.

"Yeah. It's Imogen."

"Then you're welcome. Or thank you. I'm not sure where that lands."

"Me either."

"Is it okay if I sign off?" I ask. "I do have a lot of homework."

"If I see you Friday night."

"Do we have to talk?"

"No," he says.

"You sure?"

He hesitates, but he still says, "yes."

Chapter Forty-Two

PATRICK

All week, my phone buzzes.

New entry from Hearts & Thorns.

The reminders rack up on my screen, in my emails, in my head.

I test my will, reading the snippets in my inbox.

I worry about her so much. It's not fair. She's almost grown and I'm not her mother.

Now, it's sexy too. I've been a bad, bad girl. More sexy because of the fucked-up implications.

Is there a reason to keep writing? For me, yes, but why would anyone keep reading when I spin the same thing again and again?

I resist.

It takes all my self-control, but I resist. Through boring shifts, after conversations with Luna, while I shoot the shit with Dare—his other best friend, the girl next door, is coming back from her study abroad for a few weeks, and he wants to show her a good time.

He's actually nervous.

Which is weird.

And kinda cute, in a weird way. It's a good focus for my attention. His crush. Even if he says it's not a crush. Even if he says it's because he admires her. She's smart. Not that I'd get that.

"Hey, I love smart chicks," I say.

"Chicks, seriously?" Luna asks.

I wink at her.

"Seriously, Moonlight, you're too easy," Dare says.

"Call me Moonlight again, I dare you."

"Oh, you dare me?"

"You think I can't take you?" she asks.

He gives her a quick once-over. "Yeah. What are you? five ten, one forty?"

"Excuse me!" She folds her arms.

"One fifty?" he taunts her.

"Seriously, Dare?" I shake my head. "Asking a woman's weight?"

"She's the one who wants to pick a fight." He turns to Luna. "I've got fifty pounds on you."

"I'm scrappy," she says. "And you're stupid."

"Yeah. But I could still crush you like a bug," he says.

"When did you get violent?" I ask.

"It's not violence. It's logic. Men can hurt women. That's why women are afraid of them," he says.

Luna shoots me a *where did he get this* look.

I shrug.

"Have you been listening to me?" she asks.

He laughs. "No. Valeria."

Luna shoots me another look *see.*

I nod. I see. Everyone sees.

"Hey! I'm not blind. And you two aren't subtle," Dare says.

"You like her," Luna says.

"She's my best friend," he says. "No offense, Tricky."

"She's cuter. I get it," I say.

He laughs like the suggestion is ridiculous. "Valeria?"

"Are you kidding? Haven't you seen her Instagram?" Luna asks. "She's a total babe."

"I don't go on Instagram," he says.

"Well, you should check. She looks hot." Luna pulls out her cell and finds his friend's profile. A picture of her, on the beach in Barcelona, in a string bikini.

His eyes go wide, but he shakes it off, signals the phone away. "She's like my sister. You're weird."

"Okay, and if your sister was hot, you'd be able to admit it," she says.

He looks to me for support.

"I don't know about that one. I can see Molly is conventionally attractive. And I know a lot of people have the hots for red-headed women. But I wouldn't call her hot," I say.

"No way! Molly is smoking hot! In those suits? I want her to boss me around," she says.

"Wait. You like girls?" Dare asks. "Since when? Can I watch?"

"I don't know if I *like* girls," she says. "But I find them attractive."

"You daydream about fucking his sister?" Dare asks.

"I don't daydream. I see the appeal," she says.

"You're bi?" he asks.

"A Kinsey 1," she says. "Fleeting thoughts." When neither of us object, she says, "How the hell do you two know the Kinsey scale?"

"Everyone knows the Kinsey scale," Dare says. "Get real."

"Right. And your girlfriend is a psych major," Luna says. "How is she, by the way?"

"Good," I say.

She shoots me another knowing look.

I return one that says *drop it*.

"You know, it's offensive you suggest we only know things because of the women in our lives," Dare says. "How would you like if we did the same?"

"Are you reading books on human sexuality of your own accord?" she asks.

"Do I suggest you only know about cars 'cause of Oliver?" he asks.

"I don't know anything about cars and neither does Oliver," she says.

"Drinking until you pass out then?" he asks.

She glares.

"Seriously, Dare?" I ask.

He shrugs *whatever*. "I'm just saying. I don't suggest you fucked your way into this job or your knowledge of spreadsheets."

"Did I say anything about sex?" she asks.

"The point stands," he says.

Luna looks to me for support.

"You would be pissed," I say. "You are pissed over less."

"Okay, fine," she concedes. "I apologize for insulting your intellectual curiosity."

"Are you buying that?" he asks.

I motion *so-so*. "You did learn that from Valeria."

"Of course," he says. "But I made an effort. I read a book."

"A book with words?" she asks.

"I know I'm a beautiful hunk of meat to you," he teases her. "I don't blame you for missing my intellect. It's hard to believe someone so beautiful could be so smart too. But you should get it, 'cause it's the same for you."

The flattery wins her over. "That's true."

"I think she feels bad," I say.

He copies my *so-so* motion. "I'll forgive you if you help with the barbecue."

"Are you sure she wants to hang with all of us?" Luna asks. "And not with you, alone?"

"I'm sure," he says.

"Really?" she asks.

"Yeah, she wants to sit by the pool, eat dinner at six, and hang out with people who won't talk about the differences between Barcelona and San Diego," he says. "Her words."

"Hang by the pool in a bikini?" she asks.

He shoots her a *don't* look.

It's serious for him. This is the longest I've seen him keep a straight face in ages.

"Then we're going to the beach after," he says. "She misses the Pacific."

"I forgot how much I like her," Luna says.

"Are you going to help or not?" he asks.

"Have I ever been a bad hostess?" she asks.

"It's not your party," he says.

"Have I ever neglected to make an Inked Love party amazing?"

"Yeah, Tricky's parties suck," he says. "And I want this to be special."

"You like her," she says.

"Yeah. She's my friend," he says. "What is complicated about this?"

"Sure. I'll help your *friend* have a great time." She turns to me. "What about you, Tricky? Are you bringing Imogen?"

"Is she invited?" I ask.

"Of course," he says. "We need to balance out your dumbness with another smart chick."

Again, Luna shoots him a glare.

Again, he chuckles *too easy*.

"Sure. Of course," I say. "I'll ask her Saturday."

"Ask her now," Dare says.

Luna laughs. "Aww, impatient. So much love."

Patrick: Hey. What are you doing the weekend after next?

Imogen: You, I hope.

Patrick: Cheesy.

Imogen: I know.

Patrick: I like it.

Imogen: Good.

Patrick: After that?

Imogen: You again?

Patrick: Dare is having a party for his BFF. She's home from Spain (study abroad) and she wants to hang with some cool Americans.

Imogen: Where will you find those?

Patrick: I know, it's tough, but we have you and Luna. We're making progress.

When she doesn't reply immediately, I sweeten the deal.

Patrick: There's a pool.

Imogen: You didn't lead with that?

Patrick: It's probably not up to your standards.

Imogen: A pool is a pool

Patrick: Come to my place early. We can drive together.

Imogen: No, I have a lesson the Saturday after next. I'll meet you there.

PATRICK: *I'll send the address. What's your BBQ poison?*

Imogen: Grilled chicken. And corn on the cob.

Patrick: Done.

Imogen: Is that all?

Patrick: I'm at work.

Imogen: Even so.

Patrick: Bad girl.

Imogen: I know.

Patrick: I have an appointment soon. But I'd love to break to a picture.

Imogen: Make it worth my while.

Patrick: My response will.

Imogen: Hardball, huh?

Patrick: Absolutely.

I can see her smile. I can see her falling into this teasing. It's easy. I want to stay here with her forever, too.

But the second I close our texts, reality crashes into me.

I need to read her entries.

I need to tell her.

"Oh my god, is he sexting here?" Luna asks. "Gross."

"Can I see?" Dare asks.

"Fuck no," I say.

"If it's just words—"

"Fuck. No."

"Aw, he's protective. Isn't that cute?" Dare asks.

"And if I say your 'best friend' is hot? You don't feel any need to protect her?" Luna asks.

"No," he insists.

"What if Tricky says it?" she asks.

"Are you kidding? He's in love," Dare says.

"A single guy? What if she comes back with a boyfriend? Won't that bother you?" she asks.

"No." He doesn't sell it.

She doesn't buy it, but she lets the subject drop anyway. Sorta. She asks how they can make the event memorable and they start talking mixed drinks and appetizers. Anything but ham. She never wants to see Iberian ham again.

My three o'clock arrives. My thoughts turn to work. For an hour and a half, I'm one with the ink, or some cheesy shit like that.

My picture message from Imogen keeps reality at bay—her, in a tiny black tank top, the strap falling off her shoulder.

All night, we flirt.

She comes over. We fuck on the couch, against the wall, over the kitchen counter. We're too excited to make it to the camera in the bedroom. Or maybe we both realize it's too much, demanding intimacy in every fucking arena.

She stays there, in that place that's all desire.

All night.

————

IN THE MORNING, I WAKE TO IMOGEN TYPING ON HER COMPUTER, frustration all over her face.

She shakes it off the second she sees me. She slips into something sunny (well, her version of it), fixes chai and oatmeal, chit-chats about the book she's reading.

"Are you okay?" I ask.

"Yeah," she lies.

We fade back into that space, but it's not the same.

I feel the distance when we chat, as we watch a movie, as we kiss.

Even when we fuck in my bed, lie together, revel in the aftershocks.

Then she leaves and it's even more obvious.

She's running away.

An hour later, an alert arrives in my email.

New entry from Hearts and Thorns.

I don't call her to talk. I don't confess. I do the one thing I shouldn't: I read everything.

Chapter Forty-Three

PATRICK

The summer days pass quickly. Appointments, chats with Luna and Dare, texts with Imogen, sessions in my apartment.

She doesn't ask me to open my heart, and I don't press her. I do the wrong thing, again and again. I take every part of her body, then I take her head and her heart too, drinking her thoughts with the thirst of a man in the desert.

They're for anyone, for strangers, but I know it's wrong. I admit it's wrong.

I do it anyway.

She slips into that rhythm just as easily. Sex and fun and easy conversation. The heavy things far beneath the surface.

With her. With Luna. With my sister and my parents and everyone else in my life.

She comes closer every time we touch. Then, when we finish and she cleans and dresses, she slips away again.

Chapter Forty-Four

IMOGEN

E ven with the usual Saturday traffic, the drive goes quickly. The day feels easy. I even find parking in under five minutes.

Mmm, saltwater, charcoal, chlorine, sunscreen. The scents of summer. The good things in life.

I don't need to check the address. I can hear Dare and Patrick teasing each other. I can feel the lightness between them.

I grab my supplies, buzz into the complex, meet the crew by the pool.

The apartment complex is a lot like mine. A dozen or so apartments surrounding a large courtyard. A small pool, half a dozen loungers, two patio tables and chairs, succulents, and palm trees.

The Inked Love crew at the party.

Luna in a black bikini top and high-waist shorts. Her boyfriend, Oliver, in a black v-neck and black jeans, seemingly unfazed by the eighty degree weather.

A cute blonde in a baby blue dress, reading on a lounger, next to a tallish guy with a troublemaking smile.

"Daisy and Holden," Patrick offers. He grabs my mini-cooler and places it next to a massive red cooler.

"Tonic water and coleslaw," I say. "I didn't think to bring gin. Should I grab some?"

"I have gin," Dare calls from his spot at the grill.

"Good gin?" Patrick asks.

"Yeah, Val brought it," he says. "Gin tonic is big in Spain."

"Isn't it gin and tonic?" Patrick asks.

"Not in Spain." Dare shoots Patrick a look that says *duh*.

Patrick laughs. "I'm not sophisticated?"

"Guess not," Dare says.

"You look cute." Luna bounces away from her boyfriend and pulls me into a tight hug.

"You're making me jealous," Oliver says.

"You should be jealous of her style. You only wear black," Luna says.

"Not that kind of jealous," he says.

"I don't know, Moonlight," Dare says. "I heard something about a Kinsey 1. Now, you know us men are too stupid to understand what that means."

"Call me Moonlight again and I'm pushing you into the pool," she says.

"It's your name," he says.

"No. My name is Luna Anushka Locke," she says. "And it might mean Moonlight, but only people I like can call me that."

"Even then." Oliver makes a *you're dead* motion.

"Just kinda redundant, naming you Luna Moonlight, you know," Dare says.

"I think that counts." She jumps into a fighting stance.

"I can take you." But Dare still pulls his cell from his pocket and discards his muscle tank.

And he's actually… hot. Like really hot. It's hard to see past the *omg look at me starting shit, playing dumb* attitude, but without all those clothes covering his muscles—

Damn.

He looks good in those blue board shorts. A little more built than Patrick, with slightly darker skin, and a massive dragon curling around his torso.

He doesn't notice me staring. He moves to the pool and stands at the edge. "Let's go."

"You're ruining the fun." Luna shakes her head.

"Am I?" he asks.

She nods. Then, when he drops his guard, and looks at the water, she charges.

They both tumble into the pool with a splash and emerge with a laugh.

"That doesn't make you jealous?" Patrick asks Oliver.

"Dare? Are you kidding?" Oliver lets out a low, throaty laugh. "Yeah, right."

"'Cause he's into Val?" Patrick asks.

"'Cause he's Dare," Oliver says.

"He's conventionally attractive," I say.

Patrick laughs. The people on the lounger too.

Oliver shrugs, unbothered. "And my dad is hot. I'm not jealous Luna notices."

"Gross," the blonde, Daisy, says.

"His sister," Patrick explains.

"So her dad too?" I ask.

"He is hot though," Patrick says. "It's pretty much science."

"How can a subjective attraction be science?" Daisy asks.

Patrick looks to me.

"There are metrics of attraction consistent in different cultures," I say. "Facial symmetry, mostly. And waist/hip ratio for women."

"She's a scientist." Patrick beams with pride.

"Oh, so that's why she's with you? It's an experiment?" Oliver teases.

"An experiment to see how much fun we can have together, yeah," Patrick says.

His friend looks to me.

I shrug. That is the truth, basically. "A lot so far."

"What are the notes? Even though he finishes in three minutes, we have a good time?" Oliver chuckles.

Daisy rolls her eyes.

Her boyfriend too. "Really, Ollie, that's weak. A minuteman joke? Kinda unspecific."

"I haven't started timing things yet," I say. "But I could. There are global averages. I think, average is around five minutes, for uh, the act itself. But I'm not a sex researcher. Psychology and economics."

"So you like dumb guys then?" Oliver asks.

Daisy and Holden laugh.

"Not exactly. I like guys who don't try to prove they're smarter than I am. And that's hard to find in college," I say.

"UCLA, right? Like Luna?" Daisy asks.

I nod.

"It's the same at Berkeley. A lot of guys are cool. But there are so many blowhards who want to lecture you on philosophy. They think they're experts after a single class." She shakes her head and her wavy blond locks fall over her face.

"She likes them cute and dumb." Her boyfriend Holden sits next to her and pulls her into his lap. "Right?"

She nods.

He pulls her closer.

She blushes, shy, but she still leans into the gesture.

Their kiss isn't full-on PDA, but there's heat in it.

Oliver sticks his tongue out. "Gross."

"Why are you watching them?" Patrick asks.

Oliver just shakes his head *I will not watch my sister make out* and he turns to me. "So it's the same with you and Tricky?"

"Why do you think any of the women here showed?" Patrick asks. "For our brilliant minds?" He flexes a bicep.

"That's Dare's move," Oliver says.

"It still works," Patrick says.

"Eh. He's got better biceps," Oliver says.

"That's the first nice thing you've ever said about him," Patrick says.

"I say lots of nice things. I'm the nicest guy in the world." Oliver laughs.

Patrick shakes his head and turns to me. "Are you following this bullshit at all?"

"It sounds healthy, that Oliver isn't jealous of his girlfriend's guy friends," I say.

Oliver actually smiles. "Healthy. That's a new label."

Patrick chuckles. "Yeah, I think that's the first time anyone has called him well-adjusted."

Right. He had a drinking problem. Has a drinking problem.

Luna climbs out of the pool, shifts out of her shorts, sits on her boyfriend's lap even though she's soaking wet. "Hey."

"Hey, yourself," he says.

"You looked lonely," she says.

"Felt lonely." He pulls her into a kiss.

And, bam, they're making out.

Holden rolls his eyes. He and Daisy are no longer making out, but they're sitting together in an extremely cute, loving way.

Patrick shakes his head. "This is revenge. For… well, you know." He winks at me.

For the time he called while he was at work. Was she there? Did she hear? My cheeks flush.

"You do look hot," he says.

My cheeks flush. "Thanks."

He pulls me into another hug and whispers in my ear, "You good otherwise?"

"Really good," I whisper back. "Nice morning, easy lesson, party with my favorite tattoo artist."

"That's my designation?" he asks.

"My favorite sexual partner?"

He laughs. "I'll take that." He pulls me into a soft, slow kiss.

It feels good. Too good. I'm already dizzy.

"You hungry?" he asks.

"Not yet," I say.

"Thirsty?"

I nod.

"Dare," he calls to his friend, who's still lounging in the pool. "You want to get the gin? Help your friend finish changing?" There's intent in his voice. He's suggesting something. I guess that Dare likes his friend.

"She doesn't need help," he says. "Get real."

"The gin then?" Patrick asks. "I don't want to walk in on her."

But that's not a concern. The door in front of us opens, and a woman steps out in a white string bikini, a beach towel draped over her arm.

Dare's eyes nearly pop out of his head.

I can't blame him. She's a total knockout. Curvy, gorgeous, chic.

"Hey." She waves to us. "Good turnout."

"Can you grab the gin?" Tricky asks.

"Sure." She turns and steps through the door.

"Did you like staring coming or going better?" Patrick asks Dare.

"Fuck off." Dare pushes out of the pool and rushes to his apartment.

"He does like her," I say.

"Yeah, he always has, but now that she's…" He glances at Luna, makes sure she's making out with her boyfriend, not listening. "She's really hot."

"She wasn't before?" I ask.

"Not in the conventional ways," he says. "And it's not just the curves or the haircut. It's the way she carries herself too."

"Are they old friends?" I ask.

He nods.

"So he always saw her as a girl, a kid, and now she's obviously a woman?" I ask.

"Exactly. But he's in denial. He's so fucked. He's going back to Spain with her for a few weeks." Patrick shakes his head. "He thinks he'll crash on her couch, no problem."

"She's still in Spain?" I ask.

"For the summer. Internship, I guess," he says.

"So he's gonna fuck himself three times a day and do what with the other twenty-three hours and forty-five minutes?" Oliver asks.

"When did you stop making out?" Patrick asks.

Oliver pulls his girlfriend closer. "She heard you."

"Are you a fucking bat?" Patrick asks.

"No. I'm Daredevil," she says.

"So you can hear his board shorts getting tight?" Oliver asks.

Patrick laughs. "You set yourself up for that one."

"You think your lame sex jokes bother me?" Luna asks. "I can be even more perverted than either of you."

Oliver and Patrick trade a look that says *no way*.

Luna shakes her head. "But you are going to scare off Patrick's new girlfriend. At least ease her into your perversions."

"I thought you were the super freak?" Patrick asks.

"I don't brag about it twenty-four seven," she says.

"And yet, you interrupted us mocking Dare to mention your kinky thoughts," Patrick says.

Ollie laughs and whispers in her ear.

She whispers back.

And, bam, they're making out.

Patrick chuckles. "They are insatiable."

"It's sweet," I say.

He moves closer, pulls me into another tight hug. "We can be insatiable too."

I respond by pressing my lips to his. It feels so good to kiss him like this. Desire courses through my veins.

But the physical need gives way to the emotional. I want to

drag him to his apartment and fuck him senseless and talk to him all night.

I want to tell him this.

I want to hear him say *I understand.*

I want it so badly, and every second I spend with my body near his, I feel it more intensely.

Only I feel my fear more intensely too. There's too much at risk. I can't lose this.

He pulls back with a sigh. "You keep doing that and I'll fuck you right here."

"You think I won't?" I ask.

He nods.

I blush. He's right. In front of strangers is one thing. In front of his friends?

That's terrifying.

His friends interrupt before I can respond. Dare and the Spain-bound Val emerge with a bottle of gin and a handful of limes (her) and a bag of ice and a stack of cups (him).

She introduces herself, offers to fix me a gin and tonic, asks me a billion and one questions about my flavor preferences.

We shift into an easy conversation about travel and school and guys.

Patrick and Dare sit on a lounger, shooting the shit as they watch us talk. I keep feeling his eyes on me.

I'm not sure Val feels Dare's eyes on her, but every time I glance in the guy's direction, I see him staring.

I fall into the party spirit. Gin and tonic and conversation. A silly game of truth or dare, mostly filled with jokes about Dare needing to dare a woman to touch him, questions about past crushes, and dives into the pool.

Grilled chicken and corn on the cob and salt and pepper potato chips.

A walk to the beach and sunset and kissing on the sand.

Everything is perfect and easy until we get back to the apartment complex, and I grab my phone to check my texts from Julie.

But it's not my phone.

It's Patrick's.

And it's there, right on the lock screen: *New Comment on Hearts and Thorns.*

Chapter Forty-Five

IMOGEN

For a minute, I stare at the cell, dumbstruck.

Maybe this is a mistake.

Maybe it's my phone.

Maybe I changed my notifications setting by accident.

The devices look the same from the outside, but my thumb doesn't work as an unlock.

My passcode fails.

The lock screen picture of me gives everything away.

Patrick took this picture, in his apartment, when he said I looked adorable in his shirt. One of the times, anyway.

It was on his phone.

He never sent it to me.

And I'd never set an image of myself as my background. My background is always some body of water.

Without thinking, I punch his birthday into the phone.

No good.

Month and day only.

Woosh. It unlocks.

And it's there, right in his browser.

My site.

He's reading.

How long has he been reading?

How long has he known without telling me?

I never used our names, but everything else is obvious.

Did he see my site on my computer? My phone? Did I accidentally cross-post to Instagram? Leave some other clue?

I don't know.

It doesn't matter.

He knows.

He knows everything, and he hasn't said anything.

I drop his phone on Dare's couch. I find mine.

Same password, same lock screen, same home screen.

One text from Julie, requesting an update on my *activities*.

The normal emails. Updates on class, sales, notifications on my site.

Which of my followers is he?

Has he ever left a comment?

What did he say under the guise of anonymity?

I slip my cell in my purse, and I rush out of the apartment.

The party has wound down, only Dare and his friend Val, Luna keeping Patrick company.

He lights up when he sees me. Then he notices my expression, and he dims.

Guilt spreads all over his face.

He knows I know.

How does he know?

Has he really been waiting to tell me all this time?

"Excuse me," I mutter as I rush to the door. "I have to get home."

"Imogen—" He turns to me but he doesn't chase after me. He watches me go.

He says something to his friend.

She says something back.

And then he stays.

He lets me go.

He lets me get in my car and drive away.

Chapter Forty-Six

PATRICK

The drive home is a blur. I shower, change my clothes, fix something to eat.

All of it, a blur.

She doesn't text.

She doesn't call.

She doesn't update her site.

All night, I toss and turn. Apologies form on my tongue. *I'm sorry, Imogen.* But they dissolve the second I reach for my phone.

I'm sorry isn't enough.

And it's not right either. Because I'll never be sorry I stumbled on her site, dove into her words, fell in love with her through her posts.

How can I apologize for that?

Chapter Forty-Seven

PATRICK

My cell buzzes against my sheets.

I reach for it reflexively.

A million words form in my throat and dissolve on my tongue, all in the time it takes to answer the call.

"Hello," I say.

"Tricky?"

It's not her. It's Luna. Why the fuck is Luna calling me?

"I'm out front. Open up," she says.

"How did you get my address?" I ask.

"It's in your file," she says. "Buzz me in first."

"Go away."

"Try again."

I give her the code. I end the call. I check for any contact from Imogen.

There's something.

An entry on her site.

The notification is there, in my email, on my home screen.

Blazed into my brain.

I get up, move through my morning routine, meet Luna at the front door.

She's standing in the sun, the same vivacious, easy to tease, impossibly hip friend (she's rocking a floral sundress and white kicks). "Since I owe you one." She holds out a takeout tray of coffee.

She's the same as always.

I'm the one who's different.

I let her in.

She steps inside, sets the coffee on the table, takes in the place with wide eyes. "Wow, Tricky, this is nice."

"It was Deidre's."

"I figured."

"The books?"

"Yeah."

"'Cause I don't read?" I ask.

"Don't act offended." She slips into a chair and turns to face me. "I've never seen you read, so I found the stocked shelf strange, then I saw the books teenage girls love, and I… guessed."

"I've read most of them."

"I'm sorry," she says.

"It's okay. You're right—"

"About Deidre. Dare told me what happened last night. That it wasn't an accidental overdose. I… I'm really sorry."

"Dare knows?"

She looks at me funny. "Yeah, he said you used to cry about it when you got drunk."

I did?

"He was worried, but he didn't really know how to handle it. I told him he was an idiot and he should have asked me."

"Did 'you're an idiot' not convince him to trust you with his feelings?"

"I guess not." She smiles. "Are you okay?"

"What do you think?"

"Did you sleep?"

"Not really," I say.

"Eat?"

I shake my head and take the coffee. "This is all I need."

"I can make something."

"You're going to cook in my apartment?"

"It's what I'd do for Daisy. Well, what I'd do for Daisy before things got complicated with her and food. So, uh, where's the pancake mix and where are the chocolate chips?"

"Why would I have either of those?"

"Boys are no fun. Seriously. Okay, let's see." She moves into the kitchen and scans the cabinets. Then the fridge. "I can make this work."

"I'm not hungry," I say.

"Too bad. Sit. I'll cook. Then we talk."

"All right." I do.

She pulls out a container of eggs, finds oil, warms a pan.

I stare at the *New Entry* email.

I don't know what to say. This isn't a safe space anymore. It isn't mine anymore. But what right do I have to complain? I knew the...

I stare at the link until Luna drops off the food.

She sits across from me, sips her coffee, stares.

"Thanks." I pick up my fork, bring a sliver of scrambled eggs to my lips. "Really."

"You're welcome." She waits.

I eat.

"Is that her?" She motions to my cell.

"Yeah."

"She called?"

"No. Her site."

She frowns. "You didn't tell her?"

"No."

"You shouldn't read."

"What's it matter now?" I ask.

"Did she end things?" she asks.

"She will."

"How do you figure?"

"How could she not?" I ask.

"Well, you could do this crazy thing… most men are unfamiliar with the concept. It's called an apology."

"Luna, I don't—"

"Okay. I won't be snarky. But, seriously, Tricky, you're crazy about her. Are you really going to let her go?"

"I can't."

"Can't what?"

"Apologize for reading her site. It would be admitting it was wrong. And it wasn't. I needed that. I needed her."

Luna's eyes narrow.

"What?"

"That's bullshit."

I don't object.

"And, worse, you know it's bullshit."

"No. It's hard to explain. I know I should have stopped reading. I know I should have told her. But apologizing for that feels like admitting I should never have read her site, never fallen in love with her words, and I can't do that."

"Did you really fall in love with her words?"

"Yeah."

"Have you told her that?" she asks.

"No."

She lets out a low sigh. "Seriously, Tricky? You didn't tell her that?"

"It was last night," I say.

"So?"

"She left. She wanted space. I gave it to her."

She leans back in her seat, mollified. "That's perceptive."

"Don't sound so surprised."

"Tell her that." She takes a long sip of her coffee. "Tell her how much she means to you. Trust me, that goes a long way."

But not all the way.

It's not always enough.

———

Luna stays for a few episodes of trashy reality TV. She invites me to come to Oliver's family lunch, but she doesn't press when I say no. She hugs me goodbye with a, "Seriously, fix this, she's amazing."

In the quiet afternoon air, I feel my sister's absence more. The ache that goes to my bones. The desperate need to understand.

I do what I always do. I look through Deidre's stuff. I turn over old photos.

I open Imogen's site.

It's still there, and it's still offering all this unfiltered understanding.

A gift I took.

A gift I didn't repay.

That's what I need to do.

I need to thank her.

And I need to show her I understand too.

Chapter Forty-Eight

IMOGEN

Patrick texts *I'm sorry. Can we talk when you're ready?*

I reply *I'm not ready yet*, then I turn off my cell, close my *Hearts and Thorns* email, bury myself in swimming and schoolwork.

All week, I stay busy.

All week, I keep my mind occupied.

Until I'm in my car, parked outside my parents' place.

The second I turn off the engine, my thoughts hit me.

All the things I want to say to Patrick, to Julie, to Mom.

How the hell do I do this?

It's easier, throwing my thoughts into the universe. Even knowing the universe is there, knowing he's reading.

Is he reading?

Or did he stop?

I don't know.

I want to turn on my phone. I want to check. I want to read every single comment, asking myself if any of them are his. And what does that mean?

How long has he been reading?

Instead, I get out of my car, I gather my purse, I walk into the house.

I see Mom on the deck, staring at the ocean, vaping.

Mom vaping.

It's absurd.

She looks so sad and hurt, and I don't know what to say.

For once, I don't do what she did to me. I don't turn away and pretend I don't see. I move through the living room. I join her on the deck.

I stand next to her at the railing, letting the ocean breeze mingle with the strange bubblegum scent.

"It's your sister's." She exhales a cloud of vapor.

"So you're trying to convince her it's not cool?"

She laughs.

The sound hits me somewhere deep. It's been such a long time. Since before the incident. She laughs sometimes, now, but never like this. The full-throated, musical laugh.

The one she shares with me and me alone.

Because I'm her oldest. Because I understand things my sister doesn't. Because we share things our father doesn't.

Because she loves me and trusts me.

And I love her and trust her.

We never say any of that, but it's there, under the easy laughs.

"It's working." She laughs again. "No more vaping."

"Maybe she hides it better."

"No. She still smokes with her girlfriend. I smell the pot everywhere."

Her girlfriend? Julie told her?

Mom shakes her head. "You think I don't know anything because I'm older. But I was your age once. I was in love once."

"You don't love dad?"

"It's different. Softer. Safer."

"You do?" I ask.

"Of course. We're partners. But there isn't the passion I felt when I was your age."

Do she and Dad still seem in love? Sometimes. Other times, they're business partners first. But that is safer. And I…

Well, I never thought of her that way, as a woman who would choose between passion and stability.

As a woman who decided to marry my father.

"You're upset," she says. "School?"

I shake my head.

"Another white boy?"

"What's that matter?" I ask.

"Wealthy parents?"

"Mom!"

She laughs. "You have wealthy parents. Why does he need them?"

"He does… I think. I don't know. I haven't met his parents."

"You love him?"

"Yes."

She hesitates. "Does he know?" It's there, in her voice. Not *does he know you love him?* It's *does he know what happened last year?*

I nod.

Her face softens. Her entire body softens. "You told him?"

"It's complicated."

She understands immediately. "I'm sorry, Imogen." She looks to the sand. "I thought it was better to look away from these things. I thought looking gave them power. I was scared. Too scared to face it. But that's my job. I'm your mother. I'm supposed to be ready to face anything."

A tear rolls down my cheek.

"It's my fault you're this way."

I shake my head.

"No. Not there. Here." She taps her forehead. "I had the same problems. I never talked about them. I thought… I was like my mother, so you were like me."

"Did Julie talk to you?"

"Yes."

"Does she know?"

"I don't know," she says. "I didn't tell her. But she saw something in you. Maybe she feels it too. Or maybe she takes after your father. He's different. That's why I loved him, why I love him now. He breathes joy. It always looked impossible to me, like a fish breathing water. But you're a fish, Imogen. You breathe water. So maybe you can do it."

"I have no idea what that means."

She laughs. "You're the best parts of me. And the worst too. But we're in a different place now. We're Americans. And what's more American than therapy and medication?"

"Mom!"

"What? You know it's true. You're a future shrink."

"Behavioral economist."

"Economics is for business." She shakes her head. "Psychology is for people. For watching people. For you."

It is?

"When you were little, you watched everyone and everything. I worried you were like me there too, resigned to the sidelines. But you're like your father, drinking knowledge the way he drinks joy. And you use it to move toward better things."

"I'm not going to be a shrink," I say.

"But you can, if you want. I understand now. Julie… she talked me into it. Therapy. It's good. It helps."

"She did?"

She nods. "I understand better what happened, how I reacted. Why it happened. I tried the same way, once, when I was a girl. Before I met your father. I thought it was my lack of options. It was. But it always is. It's always the same; that seems like the best option."

"What happened?"

"You want to talk about this now?" she asks.

"Now."

"Okay. But we need tea for this. Put on the chai."

I do.

And we talk until Julie and Dad return from the batting

cages. They see us, eyes puffy from tears, cheeks red from laughter, and they trade a look I haven't seen in ages.

Mom and Imogen are up to it again.

We would watch her Chinese soaps, the ones dubbed in Vietnamese, up until she decided we needed to be "normal" and switched to Shonda shows.

But the conversations—

They're an old habit too.

One that was always ours. That Dad and Julie never understood.

For the first time in a long time, I steer the conversation at dinner. I talk about my classes and my ideas for our vacation and my plans for next year.

I walk the beach with Julie. I tell her what happened with Patrick.

All of it.

She pulls out her phone. "I figured it out after we talked. I guess I'd seen it for a while. I knew, but I didn't know. You know?"

I do.

"Then I found your site and I… I don't know. I guess I see why he kept reading. You're a really good writer."

My cheeks flush. From the flattery. And the knowledge my sister reads my site. Every sexual thing. Every ugly thing. Every beautiful thing.

"You haven't checked in all week?"

I shake my head.

"So you didn't see this?"

"See what?"

She shows me a comment on my latest post.

Fair is Fair.

From OneTrickPony

With a link to another journal site.

His.

And it's already filled with entries.

———

"You've been reading this?" I ask.

She nods.

"Stop."

"It's public."

"Stop reading his," I say. "It's for me."

She smiles.

"What?"

"You love him."

"Shut up."

"So, you forgive him?" she asks.

"I don't know yet."

"I think you do."

Chapter Forty-Nine

"Start at the Beginning."
By One Trick Pony
Sunday July 31st, 3 P.M.

Dear Diary,
She doesn't start this way, but D did. M too.
I know, I know, what kind of monster reads both his sisters' diaries? And his girlfriend's diary?

A curious one.

I have an excuse for hers. Really. I don't want to spin excuses. But I have reasons.

I needed to understand.

After D died, I needed to understand. I would have done anything to understand. And her site—D was a subscriber—dropped in my lap.

Who could have turned away?

She's a great writer too. Witty and smart and brave as hell.

She offered me her heart, and I drank with greedy sips.

Those are reasons.

And this is the story I tell myself, the story I've told myself again and again.

It feels true.

But I know there's more.

Somewhere.

———

"Start at the Beginning. Again."
Posted by One Trick Pony
Tuesday August 2nd, 8 P.M.

DEAR DIARY,

THIS IS HARD. HOW DOES SHE GO FOR HUNDREDS OF WORDS? Thousands?

There is something about the feeling of putting words on paper.

It releases them.

But there's more to say. A lot more.

I don't spin words the way she does. I don't spin much.

Maybe I can post a drawing. Maybe that will make some kind of sense.

But how would it look?

A lost boy, running back and forth, alternating between trying to hide from his pain and trying to understand it.

Running to the guy he used to be?

The shallow dude who loved to keep it casual.

I didn't think about anything besides drawing, drinking, and fucking.

That isn't completely true. I had moments, especially with my sisters, but I hid from them.

I was scared of them.

And, after D died, I couldn't hide anymore. Not with my usual methods—work and women.

I needed more. Enough alcohol to forget.

It worked for a while. Then it didn't.

I went deeper into my head.

I felt the pretense.

There's a reason so many pop songs are about partying. It's so you don't stop to ask yourself, "What the hell am I doing here? Why am I doing this?"

I was no longer the guy who rocked along to the incomprehensible Top 40 songs.

I heard the lyrics.

I heard my sisters arguing about which of the songs at a party were more pointless.

I'd heard that before. In person, in text, in my head. But it had never hurt before. It always made me smile. Oh, D and M at it again.

It became, D can never tell me this again.

She's gone.

She's gone, and she'd hate the guy I've become.

She's gone, and she hurt all that time, and she didn't know how to tell me.

And, yeah, some of that is on her. But a lot of it is on me too.

How could she tell a guy who ran from any hint of depth that she was depressed? Suicidal?

Who could?

I didn't see that.

For a long time, I didn't see that. I'm not even sure when I saw it.

Only that I never would have seen it without her.

I would never have understood without her.

Is it still an excuse? I don't know.

She was a life raft, and I was drowning.

What else could I have done?

I wanted, so badly, to understand why my sister took her life, and there she was, an open book. I fell in love with the honesty. The understanding. The openness.

I got addicted to the feeling of taking.

I didn't need my life raft anymore. I wasn't thriving, but I was treading water. I was surviving.

I understood.

Not enough. But enough to go out on my own and look for understanding.

I didn't see it. I told myself I didn't know enough. And, yeah, I kept reading, and I kept learning.

But it was more than an intellectual or emotional curiosity.

I fell in love with her.

Here.

And then there.

I didn't know at first. At least, I didn't think I knew. But maybe I always did. Maybe some part of me knew I captured some part of her.

Maybe that's why I answered her call.

Okay, that's BS. It's because she's fine as fuck.

Okay, that's BS too. She is fine as fuck. But I wasn't accepting booty calls at that point. It was the way she looked at me, the way she asked, point-blank for what she wanted.

I told myself this was my insight into her head, and it was.

But she was always honest with me.

I was always the one who shied away.

No more.

I'm trying to pour my heart out.

But it's really fucking hard. How the hell does she do this every week? Twice a week?

Every day sometimes.

———

"A Mistake"
One Trick Pony
Friday August 4th, 11 P.M.

DEAR DIARY,

She's braver than I am. She always will be. But I can try to do the right thing. I can try to share. I love her. That isn't going to change.

I didn't want to face it either.

I didn't want to look at where I hurt.

How could I open myself up to this? To someone who tried? Who might try again?

I wanted, so badly, to be strong enough I didn't care. I told myself I didn't care.

And in some ways, that was true.

I didn't care in the sense it was a deal breaker.

But I cared… I cared in every bone in my body.

Because some part of me thought *hey, I can do it right this time.*

I won't mess it up this time.

And as long as I have access to every one of her thoughts, as long as she can't hide the truth?

Well… I can do that.

But that was always bullshit.

Because she can still hide.

Even if she's honest here—and she is, more than anyone I've ever met—she can hide from herself.

I loved that she didn't, that she strove for full disclosure. I still love it.

But nothing is forever.

This might not be forever.

I told myself I deserved to see into her head. I earned it.

Because D hid.

But that's bullshit.

Yeah, my sister didn't share with me. But she didn't owe me that. And, even if she did, there's no spying karma.

Once I knew who she was—

It was wrong to keep reading.

And, yes, I did it because I needed it, because I craved it, because I loved it.

Because I loved her.

But that doesn't make it okay.

I didn't want to apologize because I can't apologize for falling in love with her here.

I can't apologize for craving her words.

But that isn't where I went wrong.

I knew I needed to tell her.

I knew she was pulling away, and I knew I needed to do the hard thing and talk to her in person.

I knew honesty and vulnerability were a two-way street. It wasn't fair to pull back at the first sign of resistance.

It was bullshit, like my friend said, and worse, because I knew it was bullshit.

I still wrestle with it. I know it's not right, but I still think *don't I deserve to know?*

Don't I deserve this insight, after everything?

I want it, every one of her thoughts.

I'm terrified.

I can't lose her too.

And I know control isn't love. But it didn't feel like control. It felt like some kind of hack. Maybe it was. But, whatever happens, I have to let go too.

I have to find the bravery she has.

How the fuck do I do that?

Chapter Fifty

IMOGEN

I spend the night in my old room. I read over my old journals, the paper ones I locked in my desk, the ones I kept on Word Docs, the entry on Hearts and Thorns.

And then everything he's left for me.

Finally, after my third read through, I turn on my phone.

And I reply to his text.

Imogen: I can come over tonight.

Patrick: Is 10 too late? I have work.

Imogen: 10 works.

Patrick: You sure? We can wait until tomorrow.

Imogen: Do you want to wait?

Patrick: No.

Imogen: What time do you get to Inked Love?

Patrick: Two. Are you in Orange County?

Imogen: How'd you know?

Patrick: Your sister texted me.

Imogen: She did not.

Patrick: Yeah. She said she did this with your ex, only it was him texting her, so she wanted to get ahead of it. Just in case.

Imogen: I'm going to kill her.

Patrick: Don't. I'll miss you too much when they throw you in jail.

351

Imogen: Okay. For you.
Patrick: I appreciate that.
Imogen: What did she say?
Patrick: I'm an idiot and I hurt you.
Imogen: That's true.
Patrick: I'm sorry.
Imogen: I know. I am too. This got… complicated.
Patrick: The best things always do.

Julie interrupts with a request to take a walk. We talk about her mostly, then I say goodbye, and I head home.

Only I don't go to my place.

I go to him.

────────

My hands shake as I reach for the door. I don't know what to say, where to start. Only that I need to see him. I really need to see him.

The bell rings.

Attention turns to me.

Luna, at the front desk, chatting with Dare.

Patrick.

He freezes the moment he sees me.

The entire room goes silent.

"Let's take ten." Patrick cleans up his client. Washes up. Comes to me.

"Hey." There are too many words on the top of my tongue.

"Hey." He moves closer. "I'm sorry."

"Yeah?"

"Yeah." Closer. "I found you after Deidre died and I needed you. I needed that understanding, so badly. I wasn't ready to let go."

"How long did you know?" he asks.

"I didn't put it together until you decided to end things. I should have told you then, but I—Well, I told myself we would have had more time to have fun if Dare hadn't opened his big mouth—" He looks to his friend, who is totally listening.

Dare waves.

"We're not listening." Luna barely tries to sell it.

"Do you want to go outside?" he asks.

I shake my head.

He moves to me until he's right there, his hand inches from mine. "I told myself it was because we deserved more time to have fun. And that was true. I wanted more time with you, figuring out what you liked, listening to you talk about movies."

I wanted that too.

"But it was more, too. I didn't want to risk losing you here. Or there."

"You loved my site that much?"

"More," he says. "But I should have told you anyway. I'm sorry."

I nod.

"I reasoned with myself every way from Sunday. And all of it was true—it's a public site, you didn't tell me this big thing, you were willing to share with strangers—but it wasn't honest. I knew it would feel like a betrayal and I did it anyway."

"I should have told you."

"No," he says. "That was yours to tell. On your time." He moves closer. "I'm sorry, Imogen. I fell in love with your words. That's no excuse, but… I hope you can understand how hard it was to let go."

"My words?"

"With you. Here. And there. I meant what I wrote."

My cheeks flush.

"You read it?"

"Every word."

"How did it feel?" he asks.

"Strange."

"For me too." He brings his hand to my cheek. "I meant it. I love you."

"I love you too."

"You do?" He brightens.

I nod.

"If you can't trust me. If you don't want to give this another shot—"

"Shut up and kiss me."

Epilogue

PATRICK

On my computer screen, Dare frowns, dead serious.

He's been dead serious for ten minutes now. And I sympathize, I do. But I promised Imogen we'd use the webcam in a different way, and this isn't the kind of waiting I enjoy.

"It's not that bad," I say.

He shakes his head *you couldn't be more wrong.* "She saw me naked."

"Was there shrinkage?"

"If I wanted to hear stupid shit, I'd call Holden."

"Was there?"

"Worse."

"Worse?"

He nods. "I was…" He looks around the room, double-checking the coast is clear. "At half-mast."

"So?"

"So? My best friend saw me preparing to fuck myself. And I have to look her in the eye in"—he checks the time on the screen —"twenty minutes."

"You're just friends?"

He scoffs.

"Really?"

"Well…"

Exactly.

He shakes his head, declaring his previous thought ridiculous. "Of course we're just friends. I mean, really, Val? Yeah, she's gorgeous now, but she's…"

"Like a sister?"

"Does is sound that weak when I say it?"

"Yeah," I say.

"Yeah, I want to fuck her. But it's weird. Wrong."

"Why?"

"'Cause she's Val."

"And…?"

He looks at me like I'm dense.

I guess I am. I've never had a close girl comma friend. And a lot of my not-so-close girl comma friends ended up girl-no-comma friends.

But there's always Luna.

I mean, yeah, Luna is a babe.

But gross.

"Is it the same with Luna?" I ask.

Again, he looks at me like I'm dense.

"You flirt with her, but it doesn't mean anything."

"Exactly. 'Cause we both know it doesn't mean anything. And she has a boyfriend."

"Doesn't Val?"

"They broke up."

Oh.

"So you see the problem?"

No.

"Tricky, I swear." He shakes his head, again. "How can you not see it?"

"Break it down for me with tiny words."

"She's my best friend."

"Right."

"I can't fuck that up."

"Then don't."

"What if I already did?" The sound of the door calls his attention.

But it's not on his end. It's me. I motion for him to hold on. "Imogen is here."

"I'm cock-blocking you?"

"Yeah, but I like to make her wait," I say.

"I heard that," she calls from downstairs. She drops her key on the kitchen table and slides out of her shoes.

I know it's kind of crazy to give her a key this early—shit, wild, not crazy—but with our schedules so different, it works.

I like knowing she's here when I'm at work.

I like coming home to the smell of chai.

I like knowing she can use my bed for any untoward purpose she wants—

And she does.

She sends me the photographic evidence too.

She tortures me as well as I torture her.

"Imogen is smart, right?" Dare asks from the video-call. "I mean, not smart enough to find a better guy—"

She moves up the stairs.

He fails to hold on to his lightness. "I'll ask her."

Really? "You want to tell her you…"

"Yeah," he says.

She spots the call and whispers *sorry, I'll wait*.

I motion come here. "No, Dare wants to talk to you."

"Really? How sweet." She moves to the desk and leans forward, so her cleavage spills from her shirt.

He tries to look away.

I don't.

"Hey, Dare." She catches the, uh, oversight, but she doesn't correct it. She winks at me and slides into my lap. "How's Spain?"

"Hot," he says.

"Does Barcelona really look like San Diego?" she asks.

He makes an ugh sound. Like Valeria, he's already sick of the topic. "Some parts, yeah. The harbor. How's Tricky?"

"You didn't ask him?" she asks.

"In bed," he says. "He playing his A-game?"

She laughs. "Yeah. We have plans after this, actually."

"He mentioned that," Dare says.

I pull her closer.

Again, she laughs, but this time she tries to shift her focus to Dare. "Is this a friendly hello or…?"

"You're a girl," he says.

"A woman, yes, but I don't speak for all of us," she says.

"Still. You study psychology. And you're smart," he says.

"I try," she says.

He looks away from the camera as his cheeks flush. "I have a situation."

"What kind?" she asks.

"Val, she… she walked in on me."

"With another woman?"

"With myself."

"Oh." Imogen blushes too. "When was that?"

"Last night. She apologized and ran to her bedroom. She got up before I did, snuck out of the place. We haven't talked since."

"She was embarrassed?" Imogen asks.

"I think so, but I was a little… distracted." His blush deepens. "I didn't catch everything."

"You're travel partners. It happens."

"But she…" He clears his throat. "I think she heard me."

"Your sounds?" She keeps a straight face.

"Her name," he says. "I said it."

"You were thinking about her?" she asks.

"To rid myself of the impulse. 'Cause we're friends and I'd never put that in jeopardy," he says. "Never."

"You like her?" she asks.

"It doesn't matter," he says. "It can't happen."

"Tell her that," she says.

"Won't that sound like bullshit? 'I know you caught me stroking the sausage thinking of you but pretend it never happened.'"

"Oh my god." She collects herself.

A door opens. On his end this time.

"Fuck," he says.

"Just be honest with her," she says. "Even if it's hard. Especially if it's hard. You're good friends. You can make it through anything if you're honest."

"Yeah. Maybe. Have fun with Tricky." He closes the laptop and the call ends.

She lets out a soft sigh. "You think he'll be okay?"

"Not if he keeps lying to himself," I say.

"I guess you'd know."

"Hey." I wrap my hand around her thigh. "You're sweet to talk to him."

"I'm not sure I helped," she says.

"Probably helped more than I did," I say.

"I guess the results will show the overall level of our help."

"What do you think will happen?"

"I don't know them that well."

"Even so," I say.

"Europe in the summer? It's romantic. If there's any inkling…"

"Nonstop sex?"

"Basically." She groans as I slip my hand up her thigh. "Tricky."

"Yeah, baby?" I press my lips to her neck.

"This isn't the position."

"It could be." I motion to the camera. "We're set up for a video call."

"But there isn't a view of the action," she says.

"Bad girl," I say.

She arches into me. "You'd rather capture this angle?"

359

"Yeah."

"Our faces?"

I nod into her neck.

Her eyes flutter closed. "Okay."

"You sure?"

"Yes." She arches into me again. "Are we recording?"

"Not yet." I keep my hand on her thigh. "Are you ready?"

"Less talking. More this—" She wraps her fingers around my wrist and slides my hand up her thigh.

I nod into her neck and turn the camera on.

She stares at her reflection as I press the record button.

Her cheeks flush.

Mine do too.

This is only for us, sure, but it's a lot more than we've ever shared.

The two of us, together, our faces clearly visible.

It's more intimate this way.

More revealing.

Infinitely more terrifying.

Yes, I want to take the full body video too. Hell, I want the close-up of me driving into her again and again.

But I want this more.

I want her more than I've ever wanted anything.

We're still new, but I already know.

I need her.

A part of me will always need a part of her.

And even if I lose her one day—

I'll always love her.

She'll always be here, with me, in my head and my heart.

But, hey, this is no time to think. There's plenty of time to think later. And, really, getting lost in thought is her thing—

Even if there are a billion considerations—

But right now, I'm not worried where she'll apply to grad school (I'm sure she'll have plenty of choices on where to attend —she's smart as hell) or what that means for us—

Because I know I want to be with her.

And that's bigger than anything.

And this—

This is the perfect way to show her.

I slip my hand between her legs and rub her over her panties.

Her head falls back, rests in the crook of my neck. She groans as I toy with her.

I draw slow circles over her, pressing the soft cotton against her tender skin. Again and again, driving her out of her mind.

So close to what she needs—

But not quite.

Again.

Again.

Again.

Until she's panting and clawing at my thighs.

Then, in one smooth motion, I push her panties aside and bring my fingers to her clit.

She comes quickly, groaning my name, tugging at my jeans.

"More?" I whisper in her ear.

"Fuck me." There's no pretense in her voice. No tease. No patience. Only pure, raw, need.

She shifts off me, pushes her panties to her ankles, does away with her yellow sundress.

Her bra.

She turns away from the camera, so she's facing me, so she's staring right into my eyes.

Those gorgeous dark eyes on fire with need.

She's still the most beautiful woman I've ever seen.

And the sexiest.

I bring my hands to her hips and pull her into my lap.

She pulls my shirt over my head.

Then it's the button of my jeans.

The zipper.

She brings her lips to mine as she wraps her hand around me.

My eyes close. My tongue slips into her mouth.

She pumps me with steady strokes, then she brings her hands to my shoulders and shifts onto me.

A quick, perfect tease.

Then I sink into her one inch at a time.

She feels so fucking good. She always does.

I pull back to catch my breath. I look up at her, soak in the sight of the woman I love in my lap, the two of us tangled in every possible way.

Then I close my eyes, I kiss her, and I guide her over me.

We move together in perfect rhythm, her body taking mine, her lips locked with mine, until she's close.

Then I shift, to give her exactly what she needs to come.

My thumb against her clit, my lips around her nipple.

The pressure, the speed.

There.

She rakes her nails against my skin, claiming me here, claiming me everywhere.

When she's finished, she takes a second to catch her breath, then she drives onto me again and again.

She pulls me right over the edge.

I groan against her chest, holding tight to her hips, rocking through the perfect feeling of pulsing inside her.

We collapse together, sweaty and spent.

Slowly, I untangle our bodies, right our clothes, carry her to the bed, help her clean.

We lie there, easy and tired and comfortable.

Exactly where we're supposed to be.

When she catches her breath, she rolls onto her side and brings her hand to my chest. "Hey."

"Hey yourself."

"You want to do another one?" She traces the hearts and thorns tattoo on my chest. The one I got for her. Because she'll always be here, always be a part of me.

"Already?"

"When you're ready." Her eyes flit to my crotch. "Oh. You are ready."

Is it that obvious? "I can be."

"You are." She brings her hand to the waistband of my jeans. "I am."

She looks to the computer screen, sees our reflection. A very specific reflection—from my chest to my knees, her hand at my pants. "Well." She undoes the button. "As long as we're in frame…"

Author's Note

I restarted this book three times.

I restart books all the time. Sometimes the first attempt just isn't it, so I have to try again. That's part of the process of intuitive writing.

But I'd never restarted a book twice, much less three times.

I kept asking myself *what the hell is wrong with me?* Sure, it had been a long, long time since I'd been in the world of Inked Love (I started *The Roomie Rulebook* BEFORE the pandemic hit), but could that really be it? Could it really be the six books I'd written in between, in a different world, with a totally different style?

It sounds obvious that way. And that was part of it, yes. But there was another part. This was supposed to be *my* book. The one I wrote primarily because it interested me. So, of course, I had to write it for myself. I had to write something I could never write normally. Maybe a Cyrano de Bergerac trope! (Cyrano continues to defy my attempts). But that wasn't the story. I wasn't following the characters where they wanted to go.

Once I let go of the idea this book had to be extra special, I was free to follow the characters on their journey.

And, in my not-so-humble opinion, the book turned out extra special anyway. It's still *my* book. It's still what I wanted to write--a heroine discovering her sexual side after libido killing side-effects; an online journal; a heroine dealing with a suicide attempt--but it's not *for* me. It's for readers.

I know my readers, the ones who've been with me for a long time, the ones who *get me* will love this one. Not just the readers who are already fans of Sinful Serenade and Inked Hearts. The readers with the potential to become fans, who just haven't found the books yet.

Other people needed this book too. After all, how often do we see depression in romance novels? Libido-killing side effects of depression? Maybe, sometimes, in "angstwhore" books or other books labeled as emotionally intense and not-at-all humorous. But in funny books? Fun books?

I could feel it when I started to send the book to betas. There was something special about *The Hookup Experiment*. Or maybe it was that it wasn't really special.

After all, Imogen's situation isn't special. Not the sexual part of it, anyway. (So many of my beta readers said they loved hearing about her side effects, because they'd been through it, on their end or their partners'). And not the depression either. (Statistics suggest 15% of people will deal with depression in their lifetime).

And there was something else too. The book was me. A version of myself I'd lost in the stress of the last few years.

Don't get me wrong. I love all my books. (Have I mentioned how much I love *Dirty Desires* recently? Secret journal!!!). But I don't love them the same way, for the same reasons. And the Inked books... those are me. They just fit.

Then the pandemic hit. There were other things going on too--I'd been struggling with finding my center for awhile--but that really knocked me off balance. I still remember writing one of the scenes in *The Roomie Rulebook*, one that took place in a grocery store, crying because I missed "normal" life and I had no idea if I'd ever get it back. Then I lost my mom, and the stress and confinement of the pandemic sent *my* mental health and my marriage to bad places, and I just couldn't access the thing I love most about these books:

Fun.

It was so far out of place in my life. Even when the world returned to normal (ish), I didn't feel normal. My chronic pain issues were through the roof. My relationship with my main partner-in-fun was in shambles. I was in the habit of hanging out with friends who brought out my judgmental side or my intellectual side or my responsible side.

What happened to fun?

I fit better in a more heightened world, one with brooding billionaires and villains and balcony sex (okay, the balcony sex is a constant). But I stayed too long. The inertia of that world kept me in moodiness. It wasn't until I finally picked up Inked Love, finally got into the series, that I realized what I was missing.

Life imitates art then art imitations life then life imitates art again.

I guess what I'm saying is:

I needed this book. I needed a lot of other help too, but I needed this book.

Thank you, for reading, for being a part of this journey with me.

I hope you needed this book too.

If you didn't need it but you *wanted* it or you *loved it*--

I'm good with that.

Love,
Crystal

Acknowledgments

My first thanks goes to my husband, for his support when I'm lost in bookland and for generally being the sun in my sky. Sweetheart, you're better than all the broken bad boys in the world.

The second goes to my father, for insisting I go to the best film school in the country, everything else be damned. I wouldn't love movies, writing, or storytelling half as much if not for all our afternoon trips to the bookstore and weekends at the movies. You've always been supportive of my goals, and that means the world to me.

A big shout out to all my beta readers. And also to my ARC readers for helping spread the word to everyone else in the world.

To all my writer friends who talk me down from the ledge, hold my hand, and tell me when my ideas are terrible and when they're brilliant, thank you.

Thanks so much to my editor Marla, and to Melody Jeffries for the cover design.

As always, my biggest thanks goes to my readers. Thank you for picking up *The Hookup Experiment*.

Printed in Great Britain
by Amazon